EPIDEMIC
OF THE
LIVING DEAD

Novels by John Russo

EPIDEMIC OF THE LIVING DEAD

THE HUNGRY DEAD

UNDEAD

Published by Kensington Publishing Corporation

EPIDEMIC OF THE LIVING DEAD

John Russo

KENSINGTON BOOKS
www.kensingtonbooks.com

KENSINGTON BOOKS are published by

Kensington Publishing Corp.
119 West 40th Street
New York, NY 10018   SEP 1 4 2018

Copyright © 2018 by John Russo

All Kensington titles, imprints, and distributed lines are available at special quantity discounts for bulk purchases for sales promotion, premiums, fund-raising, educational, or institutional use.

Special book excerpts or customized printings can also be created to fit specific needs. For details, write or phone the office of the Kensington Sales Manager: Kensington Publishing Corp., 119 West 40th Street, New York, NY 10018. Attn. Sales Department. Phone: 1-800-221-2647.

Kensington and the K logo Reg. U.S. Pat. & TM Off.

eISBN-13: 1-4967-1667-5
eISBN-10: 1-4967-1667-1
First Kensington Electronic Edition: September 2018

ISBN-13: 978-1-4967-1666-8
ISBN-10: 1-4967-1666-3
First Kensington Trade Paperback Printing: September 2018

10 9 8 7 6 5 4 3 2 1

Printed in the United States of America

PROLOGUE

On the morning of his daughter's eighteenth birthday, Bill Curtis stepped off the elevator on the fifth floor of the Chapel Grove Medical Research Institute. He was only fifty years old, but tired, discouraged, and used up from the stress and anxiety of the past several years. In a fluorescent hallway devoid of any human presence, he pressed a waist-high metal wall plate, causing a steel door to swing open, granting him entrance to a lockdown ward, then he turned to watch the doors swing shut so none of the patients could sneak out. His daughter was not ambulatory, not allowed to walk around unsupervised, ever. She would be brought to him in chains for his visit.

At the security station he showed an armed guard the birthday present he had brought for Jodie, a tiny gold locket on a delicate gold chain. The guard opened the locket to ascertain that there were just photos inside, no capsules or powders that might be poisonous.

"The chain is too fragile to strangle anybody," Bill pointed out.

The guard said, "You still have to leave it with me, sir. I'll see that she gets it after you've gone."

"I wish it had come in a little jewelry box so I could've wrapped it with a ribbon and bow," Bill said.

"A short red ribbon or a piece of red yarn would've been permissible," the guard said. He eyed Bill sympathetically. "You know the drill. Go ahead and have a seat in the alcove."

"Thank you," Bill said, because he was being excused from normal procedure, which was for all visitors to be escorted by a guard who then stood over them till they were done visiting. But he was more trusted than others, not just because of the gold badge clipped to his belt, but also because everybody knew he had saved a lot of lives here in Chapel Grove during the town's first attack of the undead.

He pivoted and walked down a short hallway, then sat on a gray steel chair in front of a window of thick shatterproof glass with a little black speaker mounted chin high. Jodie would talk to him from the other side, if she felt like doing so. They would not be able to touch. He wished that someday she might want to press the palm of her hand against his, separated only by the one-inch thickness of the glass, as some patients or even prison inmates would do.

He waited only a few minutes before Jodie was escorted by an armed guard in a tan uniform to her seat on the opposite side of the glass barrier. She was wearing a faded gray sweatshirt and baggy maroon workout pants. Her wrists were handcuffed and her ankles were shackled, the chain between the shackles just long enough to allow her to walk rather than hobble.

After she sat, the guard stood back, careful not to get close enough for her to lunge and bite or try to loop the short, thick handcuff chain around his neck. Watching her warily from behind, he gave Bill a thumbs-up to assure him that she had been fed her meds: a powerful tranquilizer, plus a dose of the life-giving fluid that she so unnaturally craved.

Bill had to struggle to hold back tears every time he saw her like this. His wife never came to visit, because she could not bear it. Yet she still cared deeply about Jodie, every bit as much as he did. He hated to be here but he came once a week, not just because of his sense of duty but because his love for her persisted in spite of what she had become.

He used to wonder how some parents could love their homicidal sons and daughters and forgive them or refuse to believe in their guilt. But now he and Lauren *were* those parents. They had poured their hearts and souls into the raising of their daughter, and they had delighted in Jodie's maturing toward womanhood after suffering life-threatening childhood allergies that had led to several brushes with death. She had appeared to be doing well for a while, and they had entertained hopes of becoming a happy little family. That was before an enigmatic, insidious mutation of the plague had taken over Jodie's body and soul.

"Hello, honey," he managed to say, keeping his eyes focused on her face and her startlingly blue eyes, always so bright and innocent looking.

From the other side of the glass, she smiled sweetly and said, "Hello, Daddy. Thank you for coming to see me."

Her pale golden hair and unblemished countenance seemed almost angelic, but he reminded himself that her innate beauty was as deceptive as her soft, beguiling voice. He knew she was probably playing him, on the vague chance that he might eventually be the tool that could persuade her doctors to release her into his custody.

He said, "I brought you a necklace. For your birthday. They'll give it to you later."

"Fuck you and your necklace," she whispered, still smiling as sweetly as before, even as she had allowed her horribly nasty side to come out. She licked her pink tongue over her lips, and he knew how satisfied she was that she had hurt him deeply with mere words.

He swallowed hard, unable to speak because he did not want to say anything that might further damage any vestige of her remaining humanity. He was not a believer in prayer, so he could not pray; all he could do was wish that somehow, someday, the plague and its insidious new manifestation inside his daughter might be fully understood and cured. Whatever had made Jodie this way, he desperately hoped that science, not religion, could eventually exorcise it. But much of the time his faith in the scientific effort being put forth here at the institute wavered and seemed almost futile, and he tortured himself with angst-filled visions of what might have been, in his life and the lives of his wife and daughter, were it not for the evil that, unknown to him, was already festering eighteen years ago while Jodie was still innocently growing inside Lauren's womb.

CHAPTER 1

Eighteen Years Earlier

For Bill and Lauren Curtis, as for many others in the second decade of the twenty-first century, the joy of budding parenthood was tempered by their dread of the plague. Again and again, it had struck in dozens of communities all across the United States, turning decent people into mindless cravers of live human flesh. There were no vaccines, no cures. No one knew where it would strike next. It would flare up and be put down with guns, bombs and torches, then lie dormant till it struck somewhere else, with random, maddening frequency. Bill was a dedicated police officer, sworn to protect his friends and neighbors. But he knew that they might suddenly turn on him. Or he on them.

Lauren had tried to talk him into moving to Pittsburgh, forty miles away. But they both knew that the big cities were no safer than the small towns. So they stayed in Chapel Grove, Pennsylvania, where they had both grown up. The birth rate had shot up in recent years, as will happen when people are so scared that they will grasp at any affirmation of life.

Bill glanced lovingly at Lauren. She was washing breakfast dishes, and her swollen womb made her stand a foot back from the sink. She was into her seventh month now, and wanted badly to have a baby, even though she was scared to bring it into a plague-ridden world. Her first two pregnancies had ended in miscarriages. This time, she almost didn't dare to be hopeful. Her ultrasound test had revealed that she was going to have a baby girl. She wanted desperately to make it through a full nine months. She was afraid to jinx herself by decorating the spare room before the infant was born healthy and coming home.

Bill was proud of her for sticking to a healthful diet throughout her pregnancy. A petite ash blonde, she not only ate the right foods but also performed daily exercises recommended by her obstetrician. A passion for fitness was one of the things she and Bill had in common. She did her routine in the spare room, which, if all went well, would soon be transformed into a nursery, and he did his at the police gym where he could use state-of-the-art machines. At six-one and one-eighty, he was lanky but athletic looking, with light brown hair, a craggy face, alert brown eyes, and a dimpled chin. When he and Lauren were dressed for a night out, people often beamed at them and said they were a handsome couple.

Bill knew life hadn't been easy on his wife while he was in the army. He had survived two tours in Iraq and one in Afghanistan, and she had lived in fear of getting a dreaded MIA or KIA letter from the Defense Department. He still carried a small piece of shrapnel in his right thigh from an IED explosion, too close to the femoral artery to be removed by a scalpel. After he was wounded, he was offered an opportunity to become a training officer, but instead he came back home and enrolled in the police academy. In five years on the job, he had done well to rise from patrolman to lieutenant, yet Lauren kept wishing he'd quit and do something else.

As he was wolfing down his eggs and toast, in a hurry to get to the police station in time, his cell phone rang and it was his boss, Captain Pete Danko. "Don't sign in. Meet me at the Chapel Grove Medical Research Institute."

"What's up?"

"Some hypodermic needles have been stolen."

"Is that a big deal?" Bill asked.

"Don't ask questions, just get there."

Annoyed at not being filled in more, Bill grimaced as he plunked his cell phone on the kitchen table, and Lauren shot him a worried look. "Not a murder or a bad accident," he told her consolingly. "Only a petty theft. I've got to meet up with Pete."

"That man pushes you around too much," she said. "I wish you could find another job."

"Well, I don't like working with him, but if something bad happens, I want to be where I'm needed."

"That's what scares me, Bill. You'd risk your life for other people, and I don't want to be a widow or a single mother."

"This town is safer than most towns," he said, and swallowed the dregs of his coffee, which had gone cold.

She sighed and said, "Text me later so I'll know you're okay."

"Sure," he said. "Don't worry."

He kissed her good-bye, then headed for the institute on a two-lane blacktop shimmering in the morning sun. The woods and green fields all around looked so peaceful and pleasant in the orange light of dawn, it was hard to believe that the plague was a constant threat. In the face of it, people still had to go on with their daily lives. In about an hour, Lauren would head for the Quik-Mart on the other side of town, where she worked for her father, along with Pete Danko's wife, Wanda. The extra money helped Bill and Lauren pay bills and set aside money for a bigger and nicer house for the baby to grow up in, and Wanda's extra money helped the Dankos pay for their son's college tuition. It was a terrible thing in Bill's eyes that the normal goals and aspirations of ordinary families were now tinged with dread.

He arrived at the Medical Research Institute just as Pete did, and they slid into side-by-side parking slots. He got out of his three-year-old Malibu and Pete got out of his shiny new Mercedes. Pete was fifteen years Bill's senior, and in the army had been a major while Bill had been a sergeant; now he was the police captain, and Bill was his lieutenant. Pete had never shed his military bearing. His buzz cut was shaved to the bone around his ears, and his black suit, black shoes, and solid black tie might as well have been a uniform. He shot Bill a disparaging look for coming here in denim jeans, tan blazer, and open-necked yellow shirt, none of it against regulations, but not the way Pete thought his "inferior officer" should dress. As they walked toward the glass double doors of the gray concrete institutional building, he said sternly, "I'll do the talking. I know the director."

They signed in and were directed to Dr. Marissa Traeger's office by an armed security guard. She sat behind a gray steel desk, and they took seats on steel folding chairs facing her. She had a rectangular face, a prominent nose, and brownish-gray shoulder-length hair. When she laid her wire-rimmed eyeglasses on her desk blotter, Bill saw that her brow was furrowed and there were dark, puffy bags under her eyes. She said, "Gentlemen, I'll come straight to the point. We're facing a bad situation. A dozen hypodermic needles were stolen from us, and I have good reason to believe they're contaminated with the pathogen that causes the plague."

"How sure are you of that?" Bill asked.

"Let *me* do the talking," Pete said.

Dr. Traeger blinked at the severity of Pete's demeanor, but went on to answer Bill's question. "The needles were sent to us by a rural police department in West Virginia, after they were discovered on a dusty evidence shelf. They were collected during an outbreak ten years ago, so we knew they couldn't teach us anything we didn't already know. I consigned them to a hazmat disposal facility, but this morning I was told they never arrived. I confronted the orderly who made the run and made him think he wouldn't be prosecuted if he told me the truth. He broke down and admitted that he had dashed into a convenience store for cigarettes and left the Jeep unlocked for five minutes, and when he came back out the hazmat container was gone. If the needles are shared by drug addicts, we could be facing an epidemic."

"Why would you have thought this orderly was trustworthy?" Pete asked accusingly.

"He qualified for a secret clearance. And he's been here three years and never failed any of his urine tests."

Pete said, "Rounding up addicts and quarantining them, or even just rousting them without a warrant, would be against the law and might cause people to panic."

"I realize that," Dr. Traeger agreed. "I'm hoping you can recover the needles if you act quickly."

"Was your man parked in a high-crime area?" Pete asked her.

"He swears he parked on a nice side street downtown," she said. "But that's no excuse to leave the vehicle unattended, especially without locking it up."

"Where is he right now?"

"I made him wait in the basement, figuring you'd want to interrogate him. For God's sake, track down the missing needles and get them back, and don't let this incident leak out."

Bill shuddered inwardly, trying to take in what he had been hit with. He had left home on a bright and peaceful June morning, as near to "normal" as one could get these days. Now it was a day imbued with a weary malignant dread. He had reassured Lauren that he was only going to investigate a petty robbery. But instead it had turned into something that could wreak utter devastation if he and Pete couldn't stop it in time.

Pete turned to him and gave him orders. "Head for police headquarters, and I'll meet you there in a while. Sign out a squad car for us to use. If I can get something useful out of the orderly, I'll fill you in when we meet up."

Bill thought he should have been allowed to be present while the orderly was being questioned. Maybe Pete didn't want any witnesses. He had been an interrogation officer in Iraq when harsh, illegal things were done to prisoners, and he sometimes boasted of his successes, with sly hints that he had used his own "unique talents." Whether or not Pete had actually engaged in any illegal practices, Bill really didn't know. But he resented being treated more as an underling than a colleague. And he felt that he was capable of handling cases of much greater importance than the petty burglaries, car thefts, and domestic assaults that usually went down in Chapel Grove.

CHAPTER 2

Three months out of his third rehab, Ron Haley was back as lead guitarist for a mediocre heavy metal band called the Hateful Dead. They were onstage doing sound checks for a matinee performance at a defunct Catholic church that had been gutted and turned into a rock palace. Ron remembered when he used to come here as a child, while it was still a church. Now it was one of the "occasions of sin" that the church preached against.

Even as he did his guitar licks, he knew he couldn't remain drug-free if he didn't quit the band. He wanted badly to scratch himself because he was wearing itchy, sticky ghoul makeup. Like other costumed bands such as KISS and GWAR, they had their own shtick, which was to impersonate flesh-eating zombies. They sported greenish-gray dead-looking skin and ghastly wounds molded in latex and streaked with gobs of artificial blood, and they screamed obscene lyrics at an ear-splitting volume, while four pierced and tattooed babes in string bikinis cavorted amid fake tombstones, grinning skulls, and severed body parts.

Ron was wearing earplugs because his hearing was two-thirds gone and he didn't want to lose the rest of it. He darted his eyes left and right, half-expecting Bill Curtis to stomp in with Pete Danko, Curtis's boss, who always had a stick up his ass. Bill had cut Ron a break because they had been buddies in high school, but if Danko had handled the bust, no question "zero tolerance" would have been Ron's fate. In the fifteen years since they graduated, Bill had built a straight life for himself while Ron had gone pretty far crooked, and Ron knew that Bill still might send him to the slammer if he didn't stay clean. "Check into a treatment facility and keep me in the loop," Bill had warned him. "You do the right thing, I'll drop the charges against you to possession without intent to sell, and it won't carry jail time."

When Ron got out of rehab a week and a half ago, he called Bill at the police station. "I'm finally getting my act together," he promised. "I'm clean and I'm gonna stay that way."

"Glad to hear it," Bill said sternly, "because next time I won't bail you out."

Ron said, "I wasn't always a degenerate musician, remember, Bill? I played in the band and you were on the football team, and I used to be in the Honor Society, same as you."

Ron ruefully recalled that before he got hooked up with the Hateful Dead, he had a strong social conscience and a belief that life was meaningful. He got a degree in music education and cherished a mild but attainable ambition to become a teacher and band director at Chapel Grove High School. He hoped to revive that dream by quitting the band after tonight's gig and asking his girlfriend, Daisy, to marry him. She was one of the Hateful Dead dancing girls, and the only one who wasn't a druggie. Ron hated to see her prancing around damn near naked just because the band and their fans demanded the titillation. He felt bad that he used to take her tip money from her for drugs. He had completed his third rehab, and he was three months clean, and he knew that the numeral "3" was a mystical number in the New Testament. He told himself that maybe hope, like death, came in threes. He wanted to live past thirty-three, his next birthday, the same age Jesus was when he died.

Maybe if he married Daisy he'd go back to church, if he could somehow believe in it again. The Hateful Dead used to be his religion, but now, while he was clean, they seemed like a bunch of sick, toxic jerks. They couldn't be much more brain-dead if they were embalmed. By acting like zombies, they were aping the plague, shaking their fists at it and pretending that life was meaningless. Death was taking over. The only creatures who would survive, for a while at least, were the undead. Ron wondered who the undead ones would devour when all the disease-free human beings were gone. What would the ghouls do when there was nothing more for them to eat?

In the years prior to the plague outbreaks, Ron had worried much about issues like global warming, a concern that now seemed to take second or third place to the plague, even among environmental activists. This didn't seem rational, but it showed how people could forsake the things they had formerly believed in once they were wallowing in fear. How would the plague matter so much if the earth were burnt to a crisp? Ron believed the scientists who warned that the temperature of the oceans was rapidly elevating to the point where they could no longer hold enough oxygen for fish to survive, and when oceanic life was eliminated from the food chain, human beings would die off too. But now we didn't need global warming to destroy us. We were doing it to ourselves. The earth would become a dead planet all right, a planet of the undead. But only for a little while—till even the living dead would die of starvation without any live people to eat.

CHAPTER 3

As Dr. Traeger got on an elevator to descend to the basement of the Chapel Grove Medical Research Institute with Pete Danko, she was sure he would try to keep the lid on the situation, but if he sensed his own career in jeopardy he'd rather see her head roll than his own. He was a misogynist and a bully, in her eyes, but as necessary as a guard dog when it came to keeping the institute and its secrets safe and secure.

Stepping off the elevator, he said, "When all this blows over, I'll come back for another tour of the top floors. It's my duty to stay up-to-date on everything that goes on up there."

He was referring to the laboratories where the undead were caged, treated, and studied. Experiments on them while they were still "living" had been illegal for the past five years, but the institute was still doing them, under the clandestine auspices of the Homeland Security Department.

"Those needles getting loose could be our undoing," Danko said. "If the shit hits the fan, I won't be able to protect you from our superiors, much less the public, the right-to-lifers and the Congress. Since the fuck-up happened on your watch, you'll have to take the fall."

"I'm well aware of that," said Dr. Traeger. "That's why I'm

hoping to keep damage control local, at least for now, with your help. But what about Lieutenant Curtis? Can you control him?"

"That's why I'm keeping him close. If anything blows up in our face I can blame it on him. He knows that you do medical research here and your main mission is finding a cure for the plague, so he'll be as zealous as I am about finding the missing needles. He has to do whatever I tell him, without question. Or else I can get rid of him—with extreme prejudice, as the old CIA used to say."

Dr. Traeger hated that she had to rely greatly upon Pete Danko's ruthlessness. Privately she considered him a misogynist and a secret sociopath. He had been covertly inserted into his job as police chief, but in actuality he was an agent-in-place for HSD and was thus privy to what the Chapel Grove Medical Research Institute was all about. He knew enough to crucify her if push came to shove.

"What's our young culprit's name?" he asked as they walked down a long concrete-block wall.

"Jamie Dugan," Dr. Traeger replied. "I feel sorry for him."

"Don't," Danko said. "He fucked up and now he's going to pay for it."

"It's still a pity," said Dr. Traeger.

"Don't waste your pity on him," said Danko. "We're in a war against the plague, and if we weaken we're doomed. So don't go all weepy on me just because you're a woman."

Dr. Traeger snapped, "Don't give me your sexist crap. How many *men* could do the kinds of things I do here?"

He didn't answer her. Instead, he confronted a uniformed guard stationed by a steel door and gruffly asked, "Is our prisoner restrained?"

"Not yet, sir," the guard said as he unlocked the steel door and led them into a windowless, heavily padded, soundproofed room. "Hands behind your back," he barked, and put handcuffs on young, bland-looking Jamie Dugan, who began shaking and perspiring even before the cuffs were clamped on his wrists. The guard pushed him down onto a steel chair that was bolted to the floor, then wrapped and locked a chain around his chest and shackled his ankles to two steel rings at the base of the chair.

Dr. Traeger blanched and looked away as Jamie's eyes darted nervously from Danko to her, silently pleading, making her feel deeply sad and guilty. He had worked at the institute for several years and she had always been cordial toward him, and now she wished she could show him mercy. But she knew she couldn't show weakness in front of Danko.

Danko turned to the guard and asked, "Do you smoke?"

"Not in here," the guard said. "Not allowed."

"Well, it's allowed now because I said so. Light one up."

The guard pulled a filter tip from a half-flattened pack that was in his pants pocket, and lit it with a BIC plastic lighter.

"Burn his left forearm," Danko ordered.

The guard did it, and Jamie sucked in his breath with a soft whimper that doubtless would have been a scream if he had not controlled himself. Dr. Traeger tried not to be squeamish, but she flinched when she smelled hair and flesh burning. She told herself that, as distasteful as this extreme measure was, it nevertheless had to be implemented because Pete Danko needed to find out if Jamie was hiding any additional information that might lead to the retrieval of the missing needles.

"I already told you the truth!" Jamie yelled, tears flowing down his cheeks.

Danko said, "Keep going with the cigarette burns."

Jamie's screams got louder and more pitiful while multiple burns were administered one right after another on various parts of his body. Meanwhile Danko just stood there, looking on expectantly, as if his victim might blurt out something valuable due to the continuing torture, without even being asked any follow-up questions.

It was a long and agonizing process for Dr. Traeger as well as for the prisoner. She had to watch blisters being raised all over Jamie's arms, legs, and face, making him cry and scream worse than ever. Still, he didn't give in, and she wished he would so the torture would end. She became convinced that Danko would learn nothing more of any value. She felt sorry for Jamie. She had always thought of him as a polite and pleasant young fellow. She was stunned when he finally started whining through his tears, confessing to much more than he had told before.

"My wife was gonna divorce me because of my gambling. We were gonna have to file bankruptcy. I sold the needles and some of her jewelry to a street dealer they call Fishhead."

"*Fishhead?*" Danko scoffed. "Surely you can make up a better name than *that*, Jamie!"

"It's the God's truth! Please let me go," Jamie pleaded.

"Burn his left nipple," Danko told the guard.

The blistering, burning flesh brought forth the loudest screams that Dr. Traeger had ever heard. She wanted to put her hands over her ears but she didn't want to earn Danko's scorn.

"Do the right nipple," he told the guard.

"No . . . please!" Jamie cried out. "Logan Cronan! That's his real name! I swear!"

"Anything else you want to tell us?" Danko asked.

"That's all I know," Jamie whimpered.

"Burn the right one," Danko said once again.

The guard did it, and Dr. Traeger thought she would faint from the agony and sound of Jamie's screams. But no further disclosures came out of the young man's mouth.

Danko drew his pistol and said, "Stand back."

Dr. Traeger was already backed against one of the padded walls, wishing she could melt into the padding. The guard stepped back as far as he could in the eight-by-ten-foot room. Then Danko shot Jamie in the head, the report only slightly deadened by the soundproofing.

The young man sagged in his shackles, blood pouring down his cheeks and neck.

Dr. Traeger was appalled. She absolutely couldn't take it anymore. "Do you really think all this was necessary?" she blurted in a hoarse gasp.

"I had to be sure he was being truthful," Danko said nonchalantly. "Get rid of him. Feed him to some of your special patients. They need to eat, don't they? He's perfect for their carnivorous diet."

"His wife will report him missing. I'll be one of the first people she tries to call, even before she calls the police."

"Stonewall her. I'll do the same. That's why I'm the police chief."

Although they were both cogs in the big wheel of the Homeland Security Department and the United States government, Dr. Traeger considered herself to be more highly principled than Pete Danko. He seemed to enjoy killing and creating carnage. Nothing else could explain why he hadn't ordered the guard to strangle Jamie, instead of making such a horrible mess. He had probably gotten addicted to gory messes when he was in the Middle East war zones. He acted as though his ability to torture and kill unflinchingly made him a superior being. Dr. Traeger had little doubt that in the army he must have tortured many of his captives and had probably shot some of them dead. She believed that he liked that sort of thing even more when she was obliged to witness it, so he could watch her fidget and flinch and work hard to hold back her tears.

She was deeply disturbed by what she had just witnessed, but she knew she had to push it out of her mind. Her experiments at the institute must continue. The fate of the human race depended upon it. Devastating outbreaks of the plague were still happening. Religious people thought it was punishment from God, Christ, Allah, or Buddha, while moderates and atheists believed that it was an unfathomably incurable disease that might eventually be cured with a vaccination of some type, as with smallpox or polio. As a dedicated scientist in the vanguard of the intense effort against the plague, Dr. Traeger was heartened by the fact that AIDS had once seemed just as unfathomable, just as impossible to defeat, yet it had yielded to dedicated people of her calling.

Unfortunately, the true nature of her experiments had to be concealed, and she had to depend on Pete Danko in the event of any threatening occurrence. She relied on him like an abused woman relies on a husband who beats her, at bottom knowing that his very cruelty is what makes him an efficient protector. She wished that her work was done, so she could free herself from him, but for now there was no choice. If she asked her superiors to replace him and he found out about it, he'd turn on her like a snake. In his effort to take her down, he might even destroy all that she had accomplished.

Her mission was to find a cure for the plague, and she had to be relentless about it. But her methods would be considered crimes if they were made public. She considered herself an unsung hero. She knew she was never going to be as famous as Louis Pasteur, who discover the cure for smallpox, or Jonas Salk, who invented the vaccine that cured polio, because she could never openly reap any accolades. She was tormented by her knowledge that the most devastating disease known to man might be conquered by a woman, not a man, and the world would never know.

CHAPTER 4

Sissy Space-Out followed Nerdy Ferdy as he climbed rusty fire-escape stairs on the outside of a building with cracked stucco. She reached the landing as Ferdy knocked on the flimsy warped door of a second-story apartment above a dollar store. Sissy, nine months pregnant, stood there breathing hard and bouncing from one foot to another, her arms folded over a bulging belly encased in green spandex. She didn't want to make the dope run. After all, she hadn't used any since she became pregnant to Hal Rotini, one of the Hateful Dead band members. She hoped that if she helped make the score, Hal might treat her nicer, might even consider marrying her and accepting fatherhood—a vague, hopeful wish that she knew was probably doomed to failure.

Ferdy yelled, "Open up! You in there, Fishhead?"

Sissy said, "He could be lyin' in there OD'd."

She heard a groan. Then more groans.

Ferdy pounded on the door again.

Another groan came from inside, scaring Sissy badly.

Ferdy yelled at the door, "Fishhead? It's Ferdy and Sissy, man! Let us in! You all right, dude?"

Sissy said, "I don't wanna find him dead and have to deal with the cops. Why can't we just cut out?"

"Because Hal would be pissed. Come on, Fishhead, open the damned door!"

Sissy murmured, "You guys call me Sissy Space-Out. You think I'm dumb."

"We don't think you're dumb, we think you're spaced out, and you *are*. So shut up. I'm bustin' in."

"You ain't no muscle man, Ferdy. You'll bust your shoulder."

He rammed his thin upper body into the door, then doubled over, holding his shoulder and moaning, "Ow . . . ow . . . *ow!*"

Angry now, he reared back and kicked at the door with his engineer boots. It took him three or four kicks, but finally the door gave way, banging against the interior wall, and he hung onto the jamb to stop himself from falling.

Sissy could see past him now, and her mouth gaped open when she saw Fishhead sprawled flat on his back, glassy-eyed, on the floor. He had a necktie cinched around his left arm, and a needle was lying on the floor. The apartment would have been dark except for three lit candles on the kitchen table. Ferdy and Sissy had to step over an overturned garbage can as they squeezed in. She put her hand over her nose. "*Peeyew!* It stinks in here! *He* stinks! Is that why they call him Fishhead?"

Ferdy didn't answer her. He jumped back because Fishhead had a gun and was trying feebly to raise it to his own head. But Ferdy snatched it away.

Weakly, Fishhead mumbled, "Gimme . . . back . . . my gun."

Fishhead's chubby face was ghostly white and flecks of foamy saliva were on his lips. But the thing that shocked Sissy the most was a spidery pattern of thin black veins that radiated from the fresh needle mark on his left arm. She said, "*Eeeuw!* What is that ugly black webby thing?"

"God . . . I don't know," said Ferdy. "What—what's *wrong* with you, Fishhead?"

"Go away, Ferdy . . . let me die . . . gonna croak anyway. I loaded myself with crank . . . figgered I'd use the gun . . . to make sure."

"Don't talk like that, Fish. Me and Sissy Space-Out are gonna help you. Call the emergency room, Sissy."

But her attention was suddenly elsewhere. "Oh my God!" she

blurted. "Look at all this friggin' money!" She was standing by the kitchen table, which was piled with bundled-up bills and oodles of white dope in plastic bags.

Fishhead mumbled, "Money don't mean nothin' no more. We're all gonna turn into zombies."

Ferdy said, "I'll take the money and stuff and hide it, Fishhead. I'll only give the band their share."

With greater energy than before, Fishhead said, "You gotta kill 'em. They're all gonna turn into zombies."

"What the hell you talkin' about, Fish? You're delirious. We're gonna call the hospital and cut out." He reached in his pocket for his cell phone.

"No! Don't call *nobody!*" Fishhead pleaded. "Just shoot me in the head."

"You're talkin' crazy, Fish! Here . . . let me help you sit up. We gotta get you walkin'. Put you in the bathtub and run cold water over you. Sissy, go get bags of ice."

"What's wrong with him?" Sissy babbled. "Did he OD?"

"I don't know. Call the freakin' hospital, Sissy!"

Fishhead yelled, "No! You gotta listen to me, Ferdy! The needles—they're contaminated! And we're *infected!*"

"Who's infected? Not me!"

"Not you—'cause you wasn't there when we used the infected needles. You and Sissy are safe. She ain't been usin' 'cause she's pregnant."

"Well then, who the fuck're you talkin' about, Fish?"

"Me and the band! *All* of us except you and Sissy! The zombie plague's gonna start all over again, and it'll be *our* fault!"

Fishhead started to go into convulsions, clutching his heart and letting out a tremendous groan. Ferdy said, "Omigod!" Sissy watched, scared and repulsed, as Fishhead's convulsions and screams built to a furious crescendo and he started struggling to get to his feet. Then, with a violent shudder, he collapsed and died, staring wide-eyed up at the ceiling, his heavy body now perfectly still.

Sissy backed away. She ranted in terror, "We're gonna die! We're gonna die! We're gonna die!"

Ferdy hugged her and petted her, her bulging womb pressed against his stomach. "Calm down, Sissy. My head's all screwed up. I need time to think. Fish said you and me are safe from whatever killed him. Good thing we didn't use them damn needles."

Fishhead's eyes started to blink. Then his left arm twitched.

Ferdy pulled away from Sissy, his eyes wide, his face contorted in fear. She shrank back as he dropped Fishhead's gun on the kitchen table and stared at the bags of dope and stacks of money. "Get some plastic grocery bags from under the sink," he told Sissy. "I ain't leavin' any stuff for the cops to find."

"Cops?" she said. "We're not gonna call *them*, are we?"

"Somebody else will. Prob'ly in a couple days when Fishhead's body starts to smell."

"He stinks already," Sissy said.

Meantime Fishhead was twitching even more. Then he sat up and started struggling to his feet. Sissy was too stunned to move. Fishhead lunged at Ferdy, spun him around, and tried to bite into his face. Ferdy squirmed, then kicked Fishhead in the groin. Sissy screamed, frozen in her tracks. Ferdy clawed for the gun he had laid on the table. Fishhead snagged him by his belt, then bit into his arm. Ferdy managed to grab the gun, whirled, and fired. The bullet hit Fishhead in the shoulder, and he reeled back—but immediately came at Ferdy again.

Bleeding from the bite in his arm, Ferdy stepped back and fired the gun again, blowing Fishhead's brains against the kitchen wall. Fishhead crashed to the floor, undead no longer.

Ferdy fell back against the table, holding the smoking gun and staring at his bleeding arm.

True enough, he hadn't used the infected needles—Sissy was pretty sure of that. But now he was *bitten!* "Ferdy, what're we gonna do?" she wailed. "Don't try to move. I'll try to find you a Band-Aid."

In utter despair over what he was going to turn into, he said, "A Band-Aid ain't gonna fuckin' help."

CHAPTER 5

At the police station, Pete Danko got in the squad car that Bill Curtis had checked out and said with a thin smirk, "I didn't let Traeger's young flunky off the hook till he admitted he sold the needles to a dope dealer, street name Fishhead, real name Logan Cronan. I got Cronan's address out of him, but I also ran it by the DMV. Ran his sheet, too—breaking and entering, possession with intent, assaults, usually on women, and violations of restraining orders. He's not the brightest bulb in the chandelier, just a nasty small-time punk. We've got to get our mitts on him. Don't turn on your siren or he might skip."

"I never intended to," Bill said.

"You trying to be snotty?" Danko said.

Changing the subject, Bill said, "I wish we could alert the public to what's going on."

"No way!" Pete snapped.

"Everybody's in danger and they don't know it," Bill persisted. "Even our own wives. The Quik-Mart is on its lonesome out on the highway."

"Don't you dare phone over there," Pete said. "Its isolation should comfort you. The odds are way against any contact with an infected addict from town."

"We don't have to spell it out for them," Bill said. "Can't we just tell them something's in the works and they should be especially watchful?"

"No, we can't play favorites. If this shit blows up on us, we'll have hell to pay if it's found out we warned people close to us but not the general public."

"Maybe the general public is who *should* be warned."

"Can it, I told you! We're not gonna cause a panic and regret it later."

Bill dropped the subject, but remained disgruntled. After a while he asked, "Do you think Traeger's errand boy was being straight?"

"Oh, yes," Pete said. "He was very cooperative. You just have to know how to talk to these wimps. He was scared of me at first, but I schmoozed him and he opened up."

"What's his punishment going to be?"

"Dr. Traeger will suspend him without pay till we see how this whole deal shakes out. If we can put a lid on it, no harm, no foul. The young man didn't intentionally do anything wrong, he just made a bad judgment call."

Logan Cronan, aka Fishhead, lived in the most run-down part of town, Bill knew, just from the address Pete gave him. He had made lots of busts around here. He parked the squad car without turning on any flashing lights. He and Pete looked around, then climbed rusty black stairs that led up to a narrow landing and a wooden door with faded and peeling paint. The jamb was splintered and the door came open when he shoved at it.

"Shit!" Pete swore as he and Bill barged in.

Bill didn't see what Pete was swearing about at first because he wasn't looking downward. He almost tripped over a pair of shoes, then saw that the shoes were worn by a big fat dead body with a hairy belly.

"Fishhead, I presume," Pete quipped as Bill caught hold of the kitchen sink to stop himself from sliding into a puddle of blood.

They both drew their Glocks, figuring that whoever shot Fishhead could still be inside the apartment. Covering each other, moving quickly but on high alert, they looked under the smelly unmade bed and in each of the two dank closets in the bedroom and whipped open the grimy shower curtain in the bathroom. It didn't take long to clear the place. It was devoid of human occupancy except for the drug dealer's dead body. The corpse had a bullet hole in its temple and a weird spiderweb pattern emanating from an injection site in its left arm, which still had a necktie around it.

Pete pronounced, "All clear."

Then they heard a squeaky sound from somewhere, and it took Bill a breath or two to figure it out. He opened the door of the cabinet under the sink, and found a skinny little guy with a runny nose hiding there. Bill flashed on a true-crime book he had read in the army that said Charlie Manson was hiding that same way, under a sink, when he was finally captured. You wouldn't think any grown man could fit, yet there this other guy was, his body scrunched around the drain pipes. He was emaciated enough to pull it off, probably from trying to live on nothing but crack and meth, and that's why his nose was leaking and gave him away.

Bill hauled him out of his hidey-hole, handcuffed him, and slammed him down onto a ratty kitchen chair with a cracked vinyl seat. He blanched as he looked down at Mr. Logan Cronan, aka Fishhead, lying on the smeary, dirt-caked linoleum floor with a bullet hole in his head.

"I didn't kill him," the captive junky whined. "But I know who did. I figured I could come here and swipe his stash, but it's already cleaned out."

"Tell us what you know, and make it snappy," Pete said. "We'll see if we believe you."

"I didn't *do* it!" the junkie said.

"You got ID on you?"

"In my back pocket. The left one."

"Get it, Bill," Pete said.

Bill didn't want to do the distasteful task. The junkie smelled to high heaven. Grungy body odor, grime, and sweat. Bill held his breath and fished out a flimsy, half-rotted billfold that contained the junkie's driver's license. In the photo ID, he looked cleaner, less wild-eyed, and less scrawny, so it was likely taken before his addictions took total control of his life. The scruffy mustache and goatee weren't as wild as his beard was now. His name was Jack Shaheen, brown hair and brown eyes, age twenty-nine, five-ten and one thirty-seven, home address Scranton, PA.

Pete's eyes scanned the license, and then he said, "Start talking, Jack. Don't leave anything out. Make us believe you."

"You know who the Hateful Dead is?" Shaheen asked.

"The Grateful Dead?" Pete said.

"No, he means the Hateful Dead," Bill interjected. "A fucked-up heavy metal band. I went to high school with the lead guitarist, Ron Haley. He's trying to clean himself up."

"I'm one of their roadies," Shaheen bragged. He grinned smugly, then said, "See that cooler under the table?"

Bill glanced down and saw a red and white Coleman cooler like the ones used to transport organs for transplants. It was labeled *Medical Waste—Hazardous Material.* He dragged the cooler out, held his breath in expectation, and opened it. But it was empty. He exhaled and so did Pete, exhalations of grim disappointment.

"That's where the needles were," Shaheen said. "But somebody got to them before I did. Got everything else, too. Unless Nerdy Ferdy done it hisself. But he's not about to piss off the band. He'd suck their dicks if they asked him. One of the Hateful Dead band members, Hal Rotini, sent Nerdy Ferdy and Sissy Space-Out to make a score from Fishhead. We was all waitin' for what they'd bring back. While they was gone, some of the guys was shootin' up with the stuff left over from their last buy and usin' some of the needles that Fishhead laid on 'em for a sweetener."

Bill was hit hard by the revelation that the band was already shooting up with the infected needles. He stared at Pete, who was also stunned to silence.

"I sneaked outta there," the junkie went on. "But like I said, some lucky stiff got here before me and done me outta a big score."

Pete shouted, "Where the fuck are they—these Hateful Dead motherfuckers?"

In a whining tone, Shaheen said, "The Rock 'n' Shock out on Lovedale Road. They're givin' a free afternoon concert to kick off their new CD tour. Lotsa fans was already linin' up, smokin' dope, boozin' and raisin' hell, when I split the fuck outta there."

"You're coming with us," Pete said. "We don't have time right now to take you down to the station and book you."

"Book me for *what!?*" Shaheen cried.

"Breaking and entering, attempted burglary and Murder One."

"But I didn't *kill* the fat fuck!"

"We don't know that," said Pete. "All we have is *your* word, Jackie boy, and your word's not worth a damn to us."

Bill dragged the snot-dripping handcuffed junkie out the door and put him in the back seat of the squad car. Pete carried the hazmat container down to the street and locked it in the trunk. Bill figured he didn't want it to be found by anybody else because it could be tracked back to the Chapel Grove Medical Research Institute. He squealed tires pulling out, and Pete told him to hotfoot it but don't turn on the flashers or the siren.

Bill asked Pete, "Do you want me to tell the desk sergeant that Fishhead's place needs to be secured as a crime scene?"

"No," Pete said. "Hold back on that till we see how everything's going to shake down."

But Bill couldn't see how they were going to be able to proceed for long on the hush-hush. Just about anybody who came around might see that Fishhead's apartment door was busted, then creep in and find his dead body. Maybe that's what Pete wanted to happen. If somebody else reported it, he and Pete might never have any explaining to do.

But Bill was even more worried about his wife and the baby she was carrying, now that he knew for sure that the needles had fallen into the hands of a dead drug dealer. It was almost for sure now that people were going to shoot up with them. And he and Pete might not be able to prevent an outbreak of the plague.

CHAPTER 6

Dr. Traeger paced in her office, worried that Pete Danko, ruthless as he was, wouldn't be able to stop the worst from happening. He knew about the black spiderweb patterns, and that would help him find and single out anyone who had already been infected. He would promptly dispatch them, even if he had to do so over and above the objections of his lieutenant. And if he must, he would kill Bill Curtis, staging it as a friendly-fire accident or else claiming that Bill had been bitten and needed to be shot.

In her tenure as research director here at the institute, Dr. Traeger had discovered some critical factors about the way the infection behaved, whether caused by direct injection into the bloodstream or by a bite. It could take people from a few minutes to several hours to become ill, then die and "come back." The period of incubation depended upon their metabolism and the status of their immune systems. Furthermore, those who got the disease by injection developed the telltale spiderweb pattern, while those who were bitten did not.

The fact that some people could hold the infection at bay for longer than others was a hopeful sign for Dr. Traeger. She thought that if this latent period could somehow be prolonged by means of some kind of medicine yet to be discovered, it might furnish the key to a cure. And if all citizens could be inoculated, even if they weren't totally immune and still got the disease, it would provide enforcers like Pete Danko a longer grace period to ferret them out and kill them.

She understood herself well enough to realize that her fervor to end the plague forever was fueled by an outbreak that had almost claimed her, forty-odd years ago when she was only five years old, hiding under the cellar stairs while her mom got torn apart. In utter fear, she had to stifle her cries and whimpers as flecks of blood and pieces of flesh struck her face. She was rescued and the ghouls got shot by police, but it was too late to save her mom, so the rescuers shot her in the head. After that, her father having been killed in an auto accident before she was born, she now was an orphan.

Badly traumatized, she was placed in foster care and put through years of psychotherapy. In school, the other children chanted, *"Ghoulie Girl, Ghoulie Girl! Gonna getcha, Ghoulie Girl!"* She was virtually ostracized, a loner with few friends. But she was also unusually bright and ambitious, and she earned a raft of scholarships that carried her through high school, college, and medical school. Her record of depression, clinical anxiety, and panic attacks was expunged when she reached adulthood, otherwise she would have been ineligible for the directorship of the Chapel Grove Medical Research Institute. Now in her mid-forties, she was driven by her mother's terrible death to discover the mysterious causes of the epidemic of the living dead.

She couldn't push her worries about the stolen needles out of her mind. If they couldn't be recovered, and if they caused an outbreak of the plague, her experiments would be shut down, and she'd be living in shame, even if she were *allowed* to live.

So badly shaken that she could scarcely concentrate on her duties and responsibilities, she had to turn on the TV in her office and watch a newscast that was vitally important to her, should she somehow be able to avoid total disaster. An execution was going forward in Texas. Carl Landry, a convicted serial killer who had spent seventeen years on death row, was finally going to die by lethal injection. The governor had denied last-minute clemency. Crowds outside the penitentiary were carrying signs and chanting slogans. News coverage went on and on, till finally a female newscaster announced, "The infamous Carl Landry has been pronounced dead and a hearse bearing his remains has departed to an unknown destination."

Dr. Traeger knew what that destination actually was. And she knew that the serial killer was not really dead. Not yet.

Up until five years ago, during open outbreaks of the plague, specimens of the undead were routinely collected "live"—and were subjected to tests that might lead to a cure. But five years ago, the ACLU and the right-to-lifers, who had long been banded together to get those kinds of experiments banned, succeeded in getting a law passed in Congress that gave them what they wanted. The Supreme Court upheld the law and its basic premise that plague victims were not criminals but were sufferers from a bizarre disease that was not yet fully understood, and as such they still retained their basic human rights under the Constitution. Therefore they could not be wantonly used as lab animals.

As long as the Supreme Court continued to uphold this unfortunate law, Dr. Traeger feared she would be stymied. To her, the stupidity was on a par with the ban on stem cell research, which prevented research that could have cured many ordinary diseases less horrible than the plague but still needing to be eradicated.

Just when she had almost lost hope and was considering moving to a foreign country, the Homeland Security Department enlisted her to help set up and take part in a clandestine program that would rely on the fact that the Great State of Texas was executing more convicted murderers than any other state in the union. It was a daring strategy that involved a degree of pragmatism that bureaucrats didn't usually harbor, so Dr. Traeger was immediately heartened by it. With her advice and support, HSD secretly began colluding with the Texas prison system to provide condemned persons to the Chapel Grove Medical Research Institute for experimental purposes.

She would have thought such a setup to be immoral under normal circumstances, but since the death row inmates were already doomed, how could it be wrong to use them for the benefit of all mankind? Thus she was able to stifle her pangs of conscience when she must cause them either to *become* undead or be *fed* to the undead. After all, she did not personally select these specimens, they were selected by the criminal justice system. They were like organ donors but in a more generous way. But the bleeding hearts, of which there were many in this country, would be horrified if they found out. It was the great secret that she was feverishly trying to hide. If possible, she never wanted to admit to her superiors that any needles had gone missing, or at least not until the lid was on tight. The calamity was not her fault, and maybe they would eventually see it that way.

She would make excellent use of Mr. Landry. She would take blood samples, do CAT scans and EKGs, and make microscope slides from slivers of his organs. Then she would make him undead by injecting him with the blood of those who had "matriculated" before him. And after all experiments of any value were completed on him, she would reward him with the lethal injection that was denied him at the prison. Wryly, she thought of herself as a facilitator of the Texas justice system, just like the right-wing lawmakers, the redneck juries, the vindictive judges, and the sanctimonious two-term governor of that "Great State."

CHAPTER 7

A Hateful Dead roadie they called Road Kill was cooking heroin in a spoon over a lit candle while his babe, Charlene, looked on with a greedy gleam in her eyes. Three other band members showed up: drummer Hal Rotini and guitarists Clay Smith and Banger Bidwell, plus their luscious bombshells, Becky and Rhoda. The women were still in the skimpy bikinis that they wore onstage, and the guys were still in their zombie makeup. They pulled rubber tubing from pockets and purses and started tying the tubing around their arms.

Hal Rotini, a dark, swarthy, greasy-haired guy with a hook nose and a lecherous grin, said, "Back off, babes. I go first this time."

Rhoda said, "What about us girls? Ladies before gentlemen."

Rotini said, "Fuck you. Fuck both of you, in fact."

"You already did that," Becky said with a snort and a giggle.

Road Kill sucked dark brown syrupy heroin into a hypodermic he picked up from the workbench next to the candle and the pile of stash. "We're runnin' low," he said. "Why ain't Nerdy Ferdy and Sissy Space-Out back from their run?"

"They better get here soon or I'll kick their asses," Rotini said.

Clay said, "I need a fix real bad, man. I'm startin' to spaz. I almost didn't make it through the sound check."

Hal said, "Me too. My monkey is starvin'. And I ain't talkin' bananas."

They all burst into dope giggles as Hal took the syringe from Road Kill and punched the needle into a vein in his right arm.

Road Kill sucked more of the heroin syrup into a couple more syringes and passed them around till everybody had a chance to dose up, except Rhoda, who was going to be last and could hardly wait. She was licking her lips in anticipation.

Ferdy was sneaking down the basement stairs with Fishhead's gun in his hand. And Sissy was close behind him, scared and trembling. They crept softly toward the light from the naked light bulb above the workbench.

Just as Rhoda was shooting up, Ferdy and Sissy burst in on them.

"What the fuck!" Rotini cried out.

Seeing the gun, Banger Bidwell came up with a wisecrack. "Don't squirt me, Ferdy!"

And Road Kill said, "That damn well *better* be a water pistol or I'm takin' it offa you and shovin' it up your ass!"

"You're bringin' me down, man," Clay Smith griped.

"You're such a nerd!" Betty jeered.

"Nerd, nerd, nerd, Nerdy Ferdy," Rhoda sang in a twangy, squeaky voice.

Ferdy pointed his gun at Hal Rotini and said, "You won't be makin' fun of me much longer, dude."

Hal said, "What the hell you talkin' about, shit-for-brains?"

"The *shit* is in *your brain*, Hal! You're gonna turn into a *zombie.*"

Sissy said, "He's right! It happened to Fishhead! I was there—Ferdy had to shoot him. It was *awful!*"

"Fishhead bit me on the arm," Ferdy said. "I'm done for. I'm not gonna live long. And soon as I croak, I'm comin' back—if I don't stop myself."

Road Kill scoffed, "You're on some kinda fucked-up acid, man! You better go somewhere and chill out."

Ferdy said, "I'm tellin' you, the needles Fishhead gave us are bad news. They musta had zombie blood in them! It killed Fishhead, then it brought him back!"

"You're sayin' he bit you?" Clay murmured quizzically.

"Right here on my arm." Ferdy held the arm out so they all could see the wound with its missing chunk of raw, bloody flesh.

"Eeeeuw!" Rhoda gasped.

"Holy shit!" said Road Kill.

Ferdy said, "You know how we used to crack up watchin' that stupid old movie *Reefer Madness*? Well, this is for *real*. It's *zombie* madness—and we're in the starring role."

Road Kill said, "You are really stoned, man! Shut the fuck up and leave us alone. You're bringin' us down hard."

Ferdy said, "I don't wanna become one of those *things*, man! Maybe you do but I don't."

"I was scared he was gonna turn while we were drivin' over here!" Sissy cried.

"I'm turnin' now!" Ferdy said. "I can feel it!"

He put the gun to his own head.

The druggies just stared at him.

He pulled the trigger. BLAM! Blood gushed from his head front and back, and he fell to the concrete with a little whimper as he took his last breath.

Sissy cried, "No!" She knelt, picked up the gun, and put the muzzle against her temple.

"You ain't got the nerve," Hal Rotini said, sneering at her.

"Marry me," she said, "or I'll kill myself. Even if we *don't* turn into zombies."

"You can't prove I'm the daddy," he said, "long as I don't give no saliva swab."

"You're the father!" Sissy screamed at him.

"Don't be stupid," Banger Bidwell said. "You and Ferdy are gonna bring the band a lotta negative publicity."

Rhoda said, "There's no such thing. We need all we can get."

Nervous and shaky, Road Kill said, "You think we really did shoot up with zombie blood?"

Clay said, "There ain't never been no zombies in Chapel Grove. Except us. And *we're* fake."

Banger Bidwell said, "Let's just enjoy this good shit. There ain't nothin' wrong with it. I'm feelin' purty good right now."

Suddenly Hal screamed, clutched his chest, fell down to the floor, and went into convulsions. A spiderweb pattern erupted on his arm. Rhoda ran to him, knelt, and tried to touch him, but in a violent spasm he raked his nails across her cheek, clawing a bloody path. She jumped up and her hand went to her face and came away dripping blood.

The others just stood there watching Hal writhe and scream. He clawed at his fake zombie makeup, peeling it away in shreds, revealing the *real* dead skin underneath.

Then Clay clutched his heart and fell down, writhing and twitching just like Hal. He clawed at his latex scars and artificial blood.

Becky bent over Clay, crying, "Help me! We gotta give him mouth-to-mouth!"

But then she was hit with convulsions too, knocking her to her knees.

One by one, the rest of them fell—the whole bunch of them— all screaming and writhing in awful pain. Spiderweb patterns erupted on their arms, at the injection sites. The ones with fake zombie makeup clawed it off. Their convulsions subsided, and then stopped. They were all dead.

Road Kill was the first to revive. His eyes twitched, and he sat up, now zombified. He had been an ugly oaf while he was still alive, but he became even worse looking as one of the living dead.

The other band members and their groupies started to come back to life too.

In utter panic, Sissy Space-Out backed away from them and ran up the basement stairs.

Salivating and hissing hungrily, her undead friends came after her.

CHAPTER 8

As Bill sped onto the two-lane blacktop that led to the Rock 'n' Shock, Jackie the Junkie started running at the mouth again. He seemed especially hung up about the chick he called Sissy Space-Out, and Bill got the feeling that he might have a crush on her. "Hal Rotini knocked her up and everybody knows it," he babbled, "but Hal won't admit it. He says she's just one more air-headed groupie that was glad to put out for him, and he ain't about to pay no child support. He's the band's drummer, and she's gonna pop his kid out any day now. You wanna talk to Sissy—she can make a little sense now, 'cause she stopped usin' when she found out she was gonna have a kid. The other dude who might give ya the straight poop, 'cause he just got rehabbed, is Ron Haley—and his girlfriend, Daisy, who ain't usin'. She's one of the band's dancers, sexy as hell, a real looker. He's the lead guitarist, but he already told the band he's gonna quit after this road trip and he and Daisy are sick of the drug scene and they're gonna get married."

Bill Curtis was glad to hear that Ron Haley was still straight. Maybe he'd make something of himself yet. Bill had no quarrel with the type of music Ron played; he could even admit that Ron was a gifted guitarist. But he deplored the band's heavy use of drugs and the blatantly erotic antics of their scantily clad dancers.

He used to just take it in stride when he came here to check on Ron or arrest drunken, doped-up brawlers. But now that he was going to have a daughter of his own, he found himself devoutly wishing that she wouldn't ever lose her self-respect and nakedly disport herself in front of an unruly, sex-starved crowd.

When he pulled into the gravel parking lot of the Rock 'n' Shock, Bill was relieved to see that everything looked as quote-unquote normal as a buildup for a heavy-metal performance could possibly be. The lot was packed with cars, SUVs, vans, pickup trucks, and motorcycles, plus a few outlandishly expensive rides like Hummers, Corvettes, and Mercedes Benzes. Bill remembered when the rock joint used to be a church up until a few years ago when it got sold and the altar and pews were taken out.

There wasn't a Rock 'n' Shock sign on the defunct church, just a big garish neon one on a tall steel pole near the road. Bill couldn't drive up close to the front entrance because of the psyched-up crowd in front of the double doors, a huge, writhing phalanx of milling people, pushing and prodding, anxious to get in. Most of them had tattoos, body piercings, and dyed and butchered hair, often so many tats on their arms and legs that at a distance it looked like they were wearing long-sleeved sweaters and decorated skin-tight leggings.

They didn't make a buzz over the arrival of the squad car. It didn't cut any ice with anybody and nobody bothered to stare at it. Bill parked it at the far end of the lot, on an apron of weeds and grass that flanked the edges of the gravel. He and Pete got out and he pressed the lock button twice to lock all the doors, leaving the druggie, Jackie Shaheen, handcuffed in the back seat.

"Don't worry," Shaheen blathered. "I ain't goin' nowhere, I wanna be hidin' in here with the windows wound up if the shit hits the fan."

"What kind of shit?" Pete demanded.

"I dunno, just yakkin'," Shaheen said.

Pete and Bill slammed the doors on him and took a look around, then started walking. Just then a ripple went through the crowd, and their fussing and shouting reached a new level.

Bill saw that the front doors had come open. Cheers went up. The crowd pressed forward more than before, getting even tighter against one another, which Bill wouldn't have thought possible. Some of the people up front were pushing the ones behind, yelling at them to make way for somebody wanting to come out of the Rock 'n' Shock. The people up front saw who it was ahead of everybody else, and they started a chant:

"Rotini! Rotini! *Rotini!* ROTINI!"

Thinking they were going to get autographs and photo ops, a bunch of Rotini's fans started waving Hateful Dead hats, T-shirts, and eight-by-tens at him and snapping pictures with their cell phones. No question that they idolized him. An especially lewd and brazen young woman pulled her halter up, baring her huge breasts, and held out a Magic Marker for Rotini to sign his name on them. He folded his arms around her and she started grinding her crotch into him, and people yelled and applauded, urging her on.

Suddenly Rotini bit into her neck—and pulled away, growling and hissing, with a chunk of her bloody flesh dangling from his lips!

People clapped, shrieked, and whistled, and some kept using their cell phones to capture the exciting moment on high-def video.

Bill almost pulled his weapon. But from the way the crowd was whooping it up, he thought it must be yet another Hateful Dead stunt—the kind of thing they did onstage with special-effects makeup and hidden tubes pumping artificial blood.

But then other band members and their groupies shambled out, looking hungry and dead, and started attacking their rabid fans. It was clear to Bill now that people were being knocked down and bitten by the Hateful Dead! Their screams were loud and agonizing. What they had thought was going to be an orgy of fun and music had quickly turned to one of dread and terror. Some were already undead. And some were bitten but hadn't turned yet.

Bill glanced frantically at Pete. They were both so stunned, they were slow to react. Although they had dreaded the Plague of the Living Dead for so many years while it struck elsewhere, and they had tried to always be alert for any signs of it in their midst, it was still an overwhelming shock for them to realize, by being thrust suddenly into the middle of it, that the plague had finally arrived in Chapel Grove.

Bill spun and ran for the squad car, and Pete followed hot on his heels. They both knew that their sidearms weren't going to be of much use in such a horrific melee, so they were going for the riot guns they had in the trunk. Bill dug in his pants pocket for the remote and clicked the trunk open as he ran. Glancing back, he saw that more and more people were being choked, clawed, and bitten. In trying to escape through the panicked crowd, some were being trampled, ripped apart, and devoured. Some of them tried to help the ones being mauled or chomped on, and others simply fled to save their own lives.

Bill managed to make it back to the squad car and grabbed a riot gun—a pump-action shotgun loaded with fifteen powerful shells. Soaked with sweat and breathing heavily, he covered Pete for a few hasty minutes without moving toward the heavy action, while Pete used his cell phone to call headquarters for backup, knowing he'd have to overcome disbelief and denial on the part of officers who weren't seeing what he and Pete were seeing. But belief would probably come much more quickly than in the past, because nowadays everybody knew that these kinds of outbreaks were real. They had happened often and in many places by now, but still they were feared much more than they were understood.

Bill hoped backup would come soon. He didn't know how many of the undead had to be dealt with, but he knew their numbers were growing, thanks to the bitten ones who were able to die and come back. He felt the same mix of adrenaline and fear that he had felt going into combat in Fallujah, only maybe worse than that now, because he wasn't facing armed human beings whom he could sort of understand, but human facsimiles who had turned into something that seemed almost supernatural, and unfathomable in normal human terms. He and Pete were two against many, and with only two weapons apiece. If they chose to wait for the promised backup, many innocent people would die or be torn apart. And the ones who died were likely to come back in a hideously mutated form.

Luckily, the crowd was coming down from hundreds to a few dozen, thanks to those who had fled. Some had made it to their vehicles and managed to get the hell out of there, and others who got to their vehicles were hemmed in. Cars, pickups, and SUVs rammed one another over and over, going frontward and backward, screeching their tires and banging into one another, unable to make any headway at all. Some folks locked themselves in their cars and didn't take part in the collision derby, just sat there sobbing and screaming, utterly terrified.

Newly created zombies were already shambling around, drooling and hissing, trying to grope their way out of the parking lot. Bill Curtis understood, with a shudder, that they must be heading wherever blind instinct was telling them to go, in search of live human flesh. And at that moment he realized that his wife, Lauren, and Pete Danko's wife, Wanda, might be in real and imminent danger at the Quik-Mart, only about a half mile from the Rock 'n' Shock. Some of the zombies might already have wandered that far down the road. It made Bill remember, with a rush of guilt, that he had promised to text his wife to let her know he was okay. He hadn't done that, partly because he didn't want to hit her with a lie of omission after Pete had told him not to warn her or anybody else of anything before they had a chance to put a stop to the catastrophe. Now it might be too late. Cradling his riot gun, he reached for his cell phone, but two of the undead shambled from between two smashed cars and started toward him. Pete saw them and signaled that he would take the one on the left and Bill should take the one on the right—who happened to be the teenage girl who had bared her breasts so willingly for Hal Rotini, only to be bitten by him. The other one was a scruffy young man, naked except for ragged denim cutoffs and sockless sneakers, his bare torso covered with grotesque Hateful Dead tattoos. Neither Bill nor Pete wanted to waste shotgun shells on the ghouls, so they used their Glocks to blast them in their heads. They reeled backward, staggered a step or two, then fell.

By this time, about a dozen of the misbegotten creatures were mindlessly feasting on victims crawling on the gravel, writhing and screaming even as they were being devoured. Bill tried to spot anybody who had not been bitten yet and possibly could be saved. One young lady scrambled underneath a parked car, but three zombies were clawing at her, trying to grab hold of her and pull her out from under. Bill ran up and shot all three, then helped the girl to her feet. The car was unlocked and he pushed her in and locked it. He didn't know why she hadn't done that herself. Maybe it wasn't her own car, or maybe she thought she'd be safer beneath it, since it had been known ever since the very first outbreak of the plague that the undead were capable of smashing their way through car windows.

Bill and Pete worked together to kill the feasting zombies that remained in the lot. They also took care of ghoul-bitten people who would have turned into zombies had they not been dispatched with bullets to their brains.

The two cops were nearly out of ammunition when at last their backup showed up. A SWAT team vehicle and three squad cars churned up gravel, and reinforcements leaped out. "We killed all we could!" Pete yelled. "But a lot of them got away! You'll need to fan out and go after them!"

"Anybody inside this joint?" the SWAT captain asked.

"Don't have any way of knowing," said Pete.

"We'll have a look," said the captain. "We'll send search-and-destroy teams up and down the highway as well, and we'll have choppers in the air, reconnoitering in a mile-wide sweep of the countryside."

Unbeknownst to the police, Ron Haley and his girlfriend, Daisy, had been fighting for their lives inside the Rock 'n' Shock. Ron had been plunking coins into a soft-drink machine and punching buttons to get soft drinks for him and Daisy when they had heard what sounded like muffled gunshots—from down in the basement. There was always crazy shit going on around the Hateful Dead, so Ron shrugged, screwed a cap off a Coke, and handed it to Daisy.

Then they had heard another shot. So they started toward the basement.

Sissy Space-Out came running up the stairs screaming and brandishing a gun.

"What the hell!" Ron cried. "Who did you shoot?" It went through his head that maybe Sissy had killed Hal Rotini for not wanting to marry her or at least accept paternity.

"They're turning into *zombies!*" Sissy screamed.

Just then Road Kill came after her, up from the basement, baring his big yellow half-broken teeth.

Right behind him were the other newly created "drug zombies"—Becky, Rhoda, Clay, Banger Bidwell, and Hal Rotini.

Sissy wheeled around with the gun and blasted Road Kill in the shoulder. But he kept on coming till she shot him in the head. He went down, and Hal stumbled over him and fell.

Banger shuffled past them in the narrow hallway and reached for Sissy, and then she squeezed the trigger of the revolver—and got only a click!

She threw the gun at Banger and it struck him in the chest and bounced off. She turned and ran—and so did Ron and Daisy. With five zombies shambling after them, they scrammed down the hall, then split in opposite directions. Sissy locked herself in the ladies' room. Ron and Daisy burst into the lounge that adjoined the stage. That's when zombified Hal Rotini and zombified Becky, Rhoda, and Clay kept on going, out into the parking lot, and began to wreak havoc on the Hateful Dead fans.

For a moment, Ron Haley thought he and Daisy might be safe in the lounge if he could barricade the place. "Hide behind the bar!" Ron shouted at her, then wheeled around and went to close the doors—but zombified Banger barged right in on him.

Ron stepped backward and tripped over a mop bucket. In the nick of time, he picked up the bucket, swung it as hard as he could, and knocked Banger to the parquet floor. But Banger grabbed his ankle and pulled him down too. With Banger almost on top of him and trying to bite his face, he rolled up against a buffer machine. He felt the cord under him, the part of it that was snaking across the floor. He clawed at the cord till he managed to seize a section of it and wrap it around Banger's neck. He didn't know if a zombie could be strangled, but he desperately tried, pulling the cord as tight as he could. Banger, in his slow, dumb, zombified way, tried to claw the cord loose. Gnashing his teeth, he tried to bite Ron's face—and came really close.

Ron shoved and rolled out from under Banger and scrambled to his feet.

He glanced back to make sure Daisy was still hiding behind the bar. He didn't see her, so he thought that she probably was.

Banger Bidwell pulled himself up by grabbing on to the buffing machine—and when he did, his fingers inadvertently brushed the switch and turned it on. The buffer pulled Banger off his feet with a thud and started running wild, whirling in wild circles, dragging Banger by the part of the cord that was still wrapped around his neck.

Finally the buffer bounced through a tight spot between a concrete planter and a cigarette machine, taking Banger along with it and slamming Banger's head into the planter with a loud jolt, cracking his skull open and spilling a part of his brain.

Sickened, Ron gagged and backed away. He ran behind the bar and hugged Daisy and tried to think how he could make both of them safer.

By this time, out in the parking lot Bill Curtis and Pete Danko had fought their own battle with the ghouls, and the SWAT team had arrived and was implementing cleanup. That's when three people slinked out of the distant and dark doorway of the Rock 'n' Shock and exposed themselves in the bright sunlight. They all had their hands up—two women and one man—and the man cried out, "Don't shoot!"

"Have you been bitten?" Pete demanded.

"No, none of us!" the man yelled.

"They don't look too dangerous," Bill said.

"Please . . . don't shoot. I'm p-pregnant," one of the women stammered.

She was wearing spandex and jeans, while the other one wore only a bikini.

"Come on over here!" Pete called out. "Don't try anything funny."

As they took a few steps with their hands over their heads, Bill became pretty sure they must be unscathed and harmless. But he realized, from newsroom footage, that with the recently dead it might be hard to tell. After they were undead for a long enough time, they were often bloody and rotted, hideously transformed and easily recognized as transformed creatures who needed to be feared—or shot and then burned.

As the three of them came closer, Bill recognized one of them as Ron Haley, his former classmate who had become a druggie. Ron smiled sheepishly and said, "I been keepin' myself straight, Bill. If I wasn't I'd have turned into one of them *things*."

"You *know* this guy?" Pete said accusingly.

"From high school."

"Man, you keep some weird company! You sure you belong on my police force?"

Right then, as the young pregnant woman tried to sidestep past a "dead" zombie lying on the ground, he rolled over and grabbed her by her leg.

"*Hal! No!*" she cried.

But he pulled her down onto the gravel and took a bite out of her calf. Blood dripped from his lips as he chewed on a ragged piece of the girl's skin. Bill shot him in his head. "Are you Sissy?" he shouted.

She got to her feet, bleeding profusely from her right calf, and tearfully told him that he had just killed the father of her child.

"I had to do it," Bill said.

The SWAT captain came up to Pete. "You wanna be the one to shoot her, or should I do it myself?"

Pete said, "No, I'll do it. I'll wait till she turns."

Sissy screamed, "Please don't *shoot* me! I'm going into labor!"

Bill said, "We should try to let her deliver."

Pete stared at him and said, "You've lost your fuckin' mind."

"You fuckin' crazy?" the SWAT captain said.

Bill really didn't want to shoot a pregnant girl or watch some-one else do it, maybe because he and his wife were trying so hard to have a child of their own. But he didn't think Pete would have any qualms about it, so he tried to convince the SWAT captain. "Get her to a hospital," he pleaded. "It's the humane thing to do. Maybe we can salvage something positive from this tragedy. You can do what you have to do after she gives birth."

The SWAT captain seemed to be wavering, on the verge of agreeing. But Pete was implacable. He was raising his pistol to-ward Sissy's head when he was interrupted by the ringing of his cell phone. He listened, then said, "My wife! Ghouls are break-ing into the Quik-Mart!"

Bill felt a rush of terror and foreboding. If Wanda was in ex-treme danger, so were his wife and his father-in-law.

The SWAT captain yelled, "*Go!* I'll get this pregnant one to the hospital!"

A ghoul blocked Bill's way, stepping out from behind an SUV parked next to the squad car. It was Jackie Shaheen, the drug ad-dict. Bill realized he should have locked him in the car. Now Sha-heen was bitten and transformed, but still wearing handcuffs, a sick leer on his twisted, ghoulish face.

Pete shot Shaheen in the forehead, and Bill gasped as he yanked open the driver's-side door to the squad car. They jumped in, peeled out fast, and raced to the Quik-Mart. Half a mile down the road they pulled up in front of it and Bill slammed on the brakes. The glass front of the place was smashed in and shadowy figures could be glimpsed moving around inside. The two cops ran up and shot two of them in the head and they went down hard, blocking the way so that Bill and Pete had to step on them to get past. In an aisle full of canned goods rolling around on the floor, two zombies were hunched over Lauren's dad, tear-ing him to bloody pieces. Lauren came at them crying and screaming, beating them on their heads and shoulders with a broken broomstick.

Wanda, Pete's wife, was a few steps away, frozen in panic and dread—because the ghoul facing *her* was her own teenage son, Jerry! She was helplessly pleading with him as she backed away, but he kept coming at her, his arms reaching out as if he would hug her—but of course he wanted to bite into her cheek or neck. She backed away even more, and in that moment Bill shot the two ghouls who were devouring Lauren's dad. She fell into his arms in a tight, tear-ridden embrace, and as her pregnant belly pressed against him he experienced a pang of wonder as to why they really would want to bring new life into this hideous world. It crossed his mind in the heat of the moment that maybe he should be the one to dispatch Jerry, just to preserve Pete from that particular horror.

But Pete didn't hesitate. He shot his own son in the head.

After Jerry went down, Pete pointed his pistol at Wanda. Welcoming her death, she sank to her knees and pleaded with him, "Go on, Pete, shoot me like you did our son. I don't want to turn into one of those *things!*"

Bill tore himself loose from Lauren's embrace, peered closely into Wanda's eyes, then quickly scrutinized her arms, legs, and the rest of her clothed body, as much as he could see. Finally he yelled, "No! Don't shoot her, Pete! She hasn't been *bitten!*"

"Thank God!" Pete said, taking his sobbing wife into his arms even as she struggled to pull back from him, saying, "I want to die, Pete . . . I want to be in heaven . . . with Jerry. . . ."

Over Wanda's shoulder, Pete gave Bill an odd stare, trying to silently convey something to him. But what? A nod of permission to do what his wife was asking him to do? Or maybe he was silently trying to make sure Bill would grasp the necessity of keeping quiet, for the time being, about the stolen hypodermic needles and the part they may have played in this, the most recent ghoul ram in the United States.

CHAPTER 9

Dr. Traeger's heart pounded and her breath came in ragged gasps as she watched the aftermath of the outbreak unfolding on television. She was sorely afraid that if she didn't go to prison, she might simply be made to disappear. Perhaps she would spend the rest of her days in a secret Homeland Security sanitarium. Or else she might be made to inhale gas from a stove or be hanged from the rafters in her own home, a faked suicide that no one would question. If she had any doubts about that possibility, she had only to recall what Pete Danko had done to Jamie Dugan in the soundproof room in the basement of the institute.

She watched the TV in her office with the sound muted by closed captioning because she was on hold for a Skype conference with Homeland Security officials who feared that everything she was doing at the institute would now come to light in an earth-shaking way.

The TV report was taking place in front of Chapel Grove Hospital. The misspellings and butchered syntax of the closed-captioning annoyed her, even in the midst of her despair. A SWAT captain was telling how he had managed to get a pregnant ghoul-bitten young woman to the maternity ward. Badly shaken, he confessed that after she gave birth he had to dispatch her. "I had no choice. I had to prevent her from coming back," read the closed-captioning. The reporter's captioned response to him was her assurance that what he had done was no longer a crime since it was a measure that was vital to the defense of our nation.

In the background behind them on the TV, Dr. Traeger caught glimpses of mutilated corpses that were being piled up in the hospital courtyard. From an earlier report she had learned that drug addicts who had been thought to have OD'd had actually been in the beginning stages of the plague when they arrived at the emergency room, and when they died they became "reanimated" and attacked other patients. Some wandered outside with IVs hanging out of their arms, and were gunned down by policemen and civilian volunteers.

Her Skype conference finally booted up. The first to speak was the ranking board member, Colonel William E. Spence, a tanned, craggy-faced man who was all soldier. Her first clue that Homeland Security might be disposed to treat her leniently came when he started off by asking, "How did the delivery go?" With a sharp intake of breath, she at first thought he was referring to the baby delivered by the pregnant ghoul-bitten young woman at Chapel Grove Hospital, but was relieved when she realized that he meant the delivery of the convicted serial killer Carl Landry to the institute. Pleased that nobody was jumping down her throat right away, she felt her spirits lift and she said, "It came off without a hitch." Colonel Spence had always been one of her staunchest advocates, a career soldier with a West Point pedigree. He had ruthlessly dealt with enemy forces in Afghanistan, and often quoted the proverb that "desperate times require desperate measures." She emulated that same attitude, because otherwise she couldn't bear her own guilt.

The others present on Skype were Captain Pete Danko and Major Steven Thurston. At times, the major had been Dr. Traeger's adversary. Like Colonel Spence, Thurston was a career soldier, but ROTC, not West Point, so he didn't command the same respect as Spence did, and he knew it. He would most likely follow Spence's lead in whatever decisions had to be made, including whether she was to be exonerated in the matter of the missing needles. She figured that if the two officers of higher rank were swayed in her favor, then Danko would follow suit. Her ace in the hole, she hoped, was that HSD would have a strong desire to suppress any hint of their own culpability. They were already under fire for using truth serum and illegal interrogation methods on American citizens, and they were scared of getting any more heat. And what had happened today wasn't ordinary heat, it was a potential conflagration.

Colonel Spence said, "Dr. Traeger, it is our considered judgment that the Chapel Grove Medical Research Institute should issue a worldwide report stating that the current outbreak of the plague was spread by drug addicts using old needles that must have been infected by a decade-old epidemic in some town other than Chapel Grove. This will tally nicely with your initial briefing of Captain Danko and Lieutenant Curtis."

Major Thurston said, "We can state publicly that we haven't precisely tracked down where the needles came from, but are working hard to solve the mystery. So much is unknown about the plague that ignorance is our greatest ally."

Colonel Spence said, "That's true. Who can really question what we say anyway?"

"I agree," said Major Thurston. "But even so, Captain Danko, I'm worried about your man, Bill Curtis. Don't you think he knows too much?"

"Well, he only knows what he's been told. He's not a scientist, he's a layman. I can control him. And I can eliminate him if I have to."

"Satisfactory," said Colonel Spence.

"Yes indeed," said Thurston. "All the needles found at the nightclub and at that drug dealer's apartment have been destroyed. For good measure, we should burn the club down and totally sanitize it."

"Good idea," said Spence.

"I'll take care of it," said Danko.

Dr. Traeger said, "I can draft the language of my news release for proper approval before I release it to the media. If I have to go on television, I won't deviate. If things get too sticky, I'll stonewall, claiming issues of national security."

"Of course," said Colonel Thurston.

Dr. Traeger liked the way this discussion was going. Nobody was being accusatory toward her. Instead they were treating her as a colleague and a coconspirator, and they were all bent on working together to deflect blame.

Captain Danko said, "As you gentlemen know, in the midst of the carnage and confusion, four babies were born to mothers who came under attack in the maternity ward at Chapel Grove Hospital. The surviving spouses were told that the infants were still-born, which of course is not true, but their final disposition hasn't been decided yet."

Dr. Traeger said, "We were worried at first that the infants may have been infected in the womb, but blood tests, tissue samples, and brain scans showed us that they're perfectly healthy. Their mothers had to be killed, for obvious reasons, and we discussed euthanizing them as well, but decided it would be not only immoral but irresponsible. We need to study them as they grow up to find out if they might be carrying a genome that might mutate as they grow older. I feel that anything is possible, in light of what has already happened."

"That makes perfect sense to me," said Major Thurston. "The obvious question is, why didn't they become infected prior to birth? It could be because they were born too soon for the disease to take hold. Or perhaps they were protected by the amniotic fluid. It's certainly our responsibility to find out."

"I couldn't agree more," said Colonel Spence. "Who knows? We might even discover something that could lead to a cure."

"My thoughts exactly," said Dr. Traeger.

"I presume you'll need even more money to study the children," said Colonel Thurston. "Any idea how much?"

"I'll work up some new budget projections," Dr. Traeger replied. "I'm going to propose that we set up a program called the Foster Project, to be funded for seven years at the outset. It will place the children with adoptive parents of our choosing, who must agree to reside in Chapel Grove and utilize supervised facilities and professional services that we recommend. At the end of the initial funding phase, the project ought to have the option of applying for additional funds, depending upon what we may discover as the adoptees grow up."

"Yes, of course," Major Spence said. "I look forward to your formal proposal."

When the Skype conference ended, Dr. Traeger wiped her moist brow and un-muted her TV, jolted by the sight of Reverend James Carnes, on-screen waving around a wooden mallet and a sharpened cross. She turned down the volume as he shouted, "The dead must be spiked! The dead must be spiked!" She despised him. Last year some of his followers had accused an old woman of invoking satanic spells to cause the plague, and she had to lock herself in her house, fearing for her life. Carnes had shown up in the nick of time to make his followers disperse, but in Dr. Traeger's eyes he was the root cause of the fanaticism that had put the woman in danger in the first place. She hated the fact that science had to battle against the abysmal ignorance of nuts like Carnes who rejected the reality of global warming and evolution and the efficacy of stem cell research, yet whose unmitigated belief in supernatural forces obscured the undiscovered but undoubtedly *natural* causes of the Plague of the Living Dead.

One inadvertent blessing of the Chapel Grove outbreak was that it had furnished her new subjects for her experiments, in addition to Carl Landry, who was still undergoing test batteries. Some of the undead from the Rock 'n' Shock nightclub had exhibited the black spiderweb patterns, and some had not. Therefore it was easy to differentiate between those who had been punctured by infected needles and those who had been bitten.

Three persons had exhibited neither type of wound, and so the police must have shot them in the head by mistake. That sort of thing must not be revealed to the general public. It must not leak out. Dr. Traeger well knew by now that in any justifiable endeavor, there was always collateral damage.

CHAPTER 10

Three days after the disaster at the Rock 'n' Shock, Detective Bill Curtis had a few drinks with Pete Danko at the American Legion post that they both belonged to. They had to sneak in, using side streets and back alleys to avoid the media hounds who were always pursuing them. The streets and buildings in Chapel Grove were full of newspaper and magazine reporters, television cameras, and talking heads. Ordinary citizens stayed in their houses for the most part, but the vultures circled and circled. Politicians and media outlets were in an uproar. It was like that anytime there was a plague outbreak anywhere. There would be an all-out furor that lasted for weeks or months, then gradually died down to the customary despair and dread that everyone was living under.

Because Bill Curtis and Pete Danko were central figures in the Chapel Grove situation, newshounds were all over them. Danko had briefed Bill the morning after the outbreak and told him in no uncertain terms not to divulge anything but just keep saying "No Comment" till the media leeches got tired of hearing it and went away. Bill stuck to that protocol. But it was early days yet, too soon for anything he said or did or *didn't* say or do to discourage them.

After they snuck into the Legion, wearing civilian clothes, Bill and Pete huddled in a corner of the long oval bar. On the wall behind them there were two four-by-six glass display cases of mementos such as uniforms, helmets, medals, and so forth, donated by the families of members who had been killed in America's wars. Blue-and-gold banners were hung all around the ceiling of the club, bearing the names of living members and the branches of the military that they had served in.

Pete seemed friendlier toward Bill than he ever had before. Maybe, Bill thought, it was because they had fought together and backed each other up effectively at the Rock 'n' Shock, and this made them brothers-in-arms in Pete's eyes. Bill welcomed the change. It would be nice not to be treated like a total underling anymore.

On the other hand, he was not immune to the realization that Pete wanted him to stonewall the subject of the infected needles and not say anything that might seem to contradict the official version of events. But Bill was uneasy with that, and he voiced a possibility that was nagging him. "Pete, I know we have to deal tactfully with the media, but I can't help wondering just how forthcoming Dr. Traeger was being when she told us that the infected needles came from a disease control facility in Kentucky. She contradicted herself when she announced publicly that it isn't exactly known where they came from. Why would she shade the truth?"

"Get off it. It's a minor discrepancy," Pete said adamantly.

"But obviously she wants to deflect blame from herself. She never admitted in any of her press conferences that the needles were stolen right from the institute. She put it all on unknown drug addicts from an unknown place."

"That doesn't really bother me," said Pete. "She's doing valuable work that has to continue. Ignorant people could tear it down if they go off on a tangent."

"Who knows what kinds of experiments she's actually doing? What if the needles somehow picked up an infection in her own laboratories?"

"Don't even think that way," Pete said. "I guarantee you,

heads will roll, including our own. Bear in mind that Homeland Security authorized Dr. Traeger's press conference and what she would say. It would be madness to doubt HSD. Their prime responsibility is to keep our nation safe from any and all threats, including not only foreign and domestic terrorism, but also potential pandemic diseases."

"Well," Bill said, "I hear what you're saying, but why shouldn't we at least go back and ask Dr. Traeger the hard questions I mentioned? She should fully cooperate if she has nothing to hide."

"We wouldn't get far with that," Pete said. "She's a dedicated scientist, and I have no doubt she's telling the truth. Like I told you, I know her personally, and her integrity is solid. I think she'd rather die at the stake, like Galileo, than stoop to violating her commitment to science, which to her is as holy as any religion."

"Galileo wasn't burned at the stake," Bill corrected, "but he was threatened with it and made to renounce his belief that the sun, not the earth, is the center of the universe. He was put in prison for the rest of his life. Another free-thinking scientist, Giordano Bruno, *was* burned to death in 1600 for the same beliefs, because he *wouldn't* renounce them."

"How do you know all that?" Pete asked.

"I was a liberal arts major at Pitt. I didn't know what kind of career I wanted, and went into the army because I had a bug up my ass about terrorism. The other bug up my ass was religion, starting with the medieval church and its persecutions, and I broke away from it. I'm a nonbeliever, even though I was raised Catholic. Too many of the folks who claim to know the mind of God have a penchant for torturing and killing other people for disagreeing with their theology."

"Same with politics," Pete said. "Bucking the system can still get you killed. You'd be a fool to go up against Homeland Security."

Bill said, "I hate that name the neocons gave it. It sounds like nomenclature straight from the Third Reich."

Pete chuckled and sipped his beer, then started talking about the prospects of the Pittsburgh Steelers in the upcoming season, with practice starting in August, only two months from now. He didn't stay much longer in the bar, because he said that he needed to be with his wife, Wanda. Bill didn't blame him. He felt that he really shouldn't stay long either. Both their wives had been severely traumatized at the Quik-Mart, and of course Lauren was pregnant. He knew that women often spontaneously aborted under extreme duress, and it was a wonder that her fear of losing another baby thus far hadn't come true.

Unwilling to let go of his desire to learn more than what Dr. Traeger and the HSD had let out, Bill hit on the idea of speaking with Ron Haley. Ron and his girlfriend had been rescued from right inside the Rock 'n' Shock where the whole outbreak must've started.

Bill tossed down the warm dregs of his beer and headed for the Municipal Building to do some research. A check of Ron's drug arrest records revealed that he had been living with his parents right in Chapel Grove, on School Street, one block behind the elementary school. Bill called the listed phone number, spoke to Mrs. Haley, and quickly ascertained that Ron was still living there.

"I hope you're not a reporter," she said. "Ron doesn't want to talk about any of the bad things that happened."

Bill reassured her that he was a police detective, not a media hound, and that he was the one who had helped rescue her son and his girlfriend. Mrs. Haley called Ron to the phone, and Bill asked if they could meet at the American Legion. He didn't mind heading back up there, rather than asking Ron to come to the station, since he did not want any of his fellow officers to tumble to the fact that he was pursuing something that the chief had told him to stay out of. If he got spotted with Ron Haley at the Legion, no big deal, because it was common for folks to meet up there, even if they were going from there to someplace else, like a basketball or football game. To get in you had to be a member, which eliminated most of the out-of-town reporters.

Bill bought beers for him and Ron, and they went into the

back room where they could be by themselves. He almost didn't recognize the former Hateful Dead guitarist when he first came in. Ron no longer had the scrawny look of a rock-and-roll druggie. He was wearing clean khaki trousers, a Metallica T-shirt, a wide, studded belt, and black sneakers. The new, neater look appeared to signify a resolute transition point between his forsaken Hateful Dead persona and his more hopeful aspiration of settling down and marrying Daisy.

What Bill wanted from Ron was clarification of the events that had led up to the outbreak at the Rock 'n' Shock. Some of the facts, if they could truly be called facts, had come out of the mouth—or the screwed-up mind—of Jackie Shaheen. Bill recapped Jackie's drug-addled spiel, then asked Ron if he could fill in any missing details.

Ron said, "Screwed up as Jackie was, it seems like he got most of it right. What he didn't know is that Sissy and Ferdy laid some shit on me before they went down into the basement. I blew them off, I thought they were sniffing glue or something."

"They told you what happened at Fishhead's place?"

"Yeah, I was like a big brother to Ferdy. He had a good brain when he wasn't stoned. I was trying to help him get his life together, get off of drugs and enroll in the junior college or something, but he idolized the band, he wanted our kind of wacked-out lifestyle. I knew we were going strictly nowhere, partly because of our drug addictions and partly because we weren't really that good—but Ferdy thought we were the next Metallica or Black Sabbath or something. Sissy was coming down off of her starfucker thing with Hal Rotini. She wanted to be a mommy and she really took her pregnancy seriously and he didn't. Her real name was Sally Hensley but he started calling her Sissy Space-Out—a pun on Sissy Spacek, an actress who won an Academy Award way back when. Everybody knew Hal knocked her up, but he said she couldn't prove paternity as long as he refused to give up his DNA."

Bill asked, "Did either Sissy or Ferdy talk about the needles?"

"He was babbling about the needles somehow turning Fishhead into a zombie. It didn't make much sense to me. Ferdy said Fishhead seemed to be dead, and then he got up and bit Ferdy before he could wrestle him for his gun and shoot him in the head."

"What do you think about what the whole country's been told? That the outbreak at the club was caused by old infected needles from some place in Kentucky?"

"It could be the truth, for all I know. The plague infection had to have some kind of cause, and maybe that's it. I was pissed off at the band and I was gonna quit, but I didn't want Ferdy to go off the deep end. I didn't buy into his rap about zombies and infected needles, but I didn't expect him to start shooting people either."

"Did you see how the outbreak began?"

"No. Daisy and I only started to tumble to it when we heard the shots from the basement."

Ron was fidgeting and perspiring, obviously shaken by remembering what he and Daisy had gone through. There were tears on his cheeks, so Bill stopped questioning him and they both fell silent. Ron said, "I gotta use the men's room," and got up and went around the corner.

Bill didn't think Ron would skip out, and he didn't. When he sat back down, his face was wet and he blotted it with a paper towel. "I wish we were back in high school. We didn't know how good we had it."

Bill clinked his glass against Ron's, then asked him if he had spoken with any of the investigators from Homeland Security.

"Nobody other than you. I figure I owe it to you 'cause you got me off the hook with my drug bust. Plus, Daisy and I would've been done for if you hadn't show up at the Rock 'n' Shock."

Bill thought it was strange that no one from Homeland Security had questioned Ron. A thorough inquiry into the Chapel Grove outbreak should have entailed an interrogation of anyone who had been on the scene. HSD might've reasoned that Ron's being there when all hell broke loose did not mean that he would know how it originated. It was also possible that they really didn't want to stumble upon a witness who might contradict Dr. Traeger. For that matter, if any kind of intrigue was afoot, how could a small-town detective poke a hole in it? His prodding of Ron Haley seemed to have taken him about as far as he could go.

Or had it?

In spite of Pete's warning that he should back off, he knew it would eat at him if he didn't at least try to speak with Dr. Traeger. After Ron left, he got her on his cell phone, and without any stonewalling or hesitation she agreed to see him at the institute.

With a wan smile, she greeted him in her office and offered him coffee, which he declined. He jumped right in and said, "I'm hoping you might tell me if you've discovered anything more about the Chapel Grove outbreak. Is there anything you held back from the media?"

"No, I gave full disclosure. To do anything less would have been unethical. The needles were contaminated when they were sent to us, and they got stolen. The matter is cut-and-dried. We tried our best to avert a catastrophe, but we failed. I'm doing my utmost to see that such a thing never happens again."

"I have great respect for scientists such as yourself," Bill told her, in an effort to make her open up more.

She said, "It's refreshing that you believe in science. There are too many people, even some in high places, who think the plague is going to be cured with prayers, either to God or to the devil."

"I'm not religious, nor superstitious," he said. "Police work solves crimes by evidence, not speculative beliefs."

"That's for certain. Superstition and religion are two sides of the same coin. Superstition is belief in things unsupported by facts, and religion is a superstitious belief in a god or gods who meddle in human affairs."

"That's a good way of putting it," Bill said. "But you must realize that most people in this town would call you a heretic."

"Or worse," she said. "But they're not going to stop me unless they burn me at the stake. And I don't think you and Pete Danko will let them do that. The causes of the plague have proven to be more enigmatic and more elusive than the pathogens that cause cancer. But I've dedicated my entire career to finding a cure, and I believe that in the end science will triumph."

"I saw you at the American Legion memorial service. Are you a member of the Ladies' Auxiliary?"

"No, but my husband belongs. He served in the first Gulf War, as a battalion psychiatrist. In his civilian practice, he specializes in cases of mental and emotional trauma. We attended the service at the Legion out of respect for all the suffering people have been through."

Bill admired her passion for her calling and her empathy for others. But he could see that he wasn't going to get any more out of her, if indeed there was anything more for her to give.

"Does Captain Danko know you're here?" she asked, shooting him a piercing look.

"I'm not trying to agitate, just trying to soothe my conscience," he told her. "I'd feel guilty if something I did or didn't do contributed to the outbreak."

Seeming to buy that, she said, "If you and Captain Danko hadn't tracked the needles down so quickly, the epidemic would have gone totally out of control. I can't say it publicly, but in my estimation you were both heroes."

"Thank you," he said. "I wish you great success in your endeavors."

They parted cordially, he thought. But early the next morning, when he was heading to the police gym, he was summoned to Pete Danko's office.

"You went behind my back," Danko said angrily. "You had no business grilling Dr. Traeger after I told you *not* to."

"I didn't exactly grill her, and you didn't explicitly say not to. You just said that it might not be a good idea."

"You knew what I meant, so don't pretend to be obtuse. If you *are* that obtuse, maybe I should demote you."

Bill gritted his teeth to rein in his temper.

Pete glowered at him, then finally snapped, "Dismissed!"

His face red, Bill went to the gym as planned, and worked hard on the machines to exorcise his worries and his anger. Nobody else was there, something that used to be an unusual occurrence. Some of his fellow policemen had given up their regular exercising, which seemed to be a further sign of the general despair. As if there was little use, even for them, of staying fit and prepared for a better tomorrow.

Bill didn't think he was actually going to get demoted, but he wasn't ready to take that chance. Not with a baby on the way and his wife already traumatized by the ghoul attack at the Quik-Mart and the mass funerals that followed, including the ones for her father and for Pete and Wanda's son.

Lauren was worried more than ever about having another miscarriage. Bill had tried to talk her into getting grief counseling, a service that was provided pro bono for family members of policemen, but she refused. She suffered extreme mood swings that seemed to come without the typical manic highs but with only the bottom end of the bipolar spectrum. Still, Bill hoped for positive changes after their daughter was born and at the same time was scared that she might succumb to postpartum depression. Or worse.

CHAPTER 11

As it turned out, Lauren managed to carry the baby to full term, in spite of the fact that in the aftermath of the plague she was more emotionally damaged than ever before. She and Bill were at Applebee's enjoying seafood dinners and a rare get-together with Pete and Wanda Danko—and two hours later, after they had gone to bed, Lauren was awakened with labor pangs. They both got dressed in a hurry and he drove her to the hospital. She was in labor for eighteen hours. Bill resolutely stayed by her side the whole time, partly because she would have been frightened if he left her, but mostly because he didn't want to take a chance on anything going wrong. A nurse told him that he should watch the gauges that Lauren's uterus was hooked up to, and that if the needles took a plunge, it would signal an emergency and he should immediately call for assistance.

After ten or twelve hours, the head nurse said it would be safe for Bill to take a break now, but he still didn't dare; he wanted to stay till the finish and not be sorry he didn't.

All of a sudden one of the gauges took a plunge, his heart leapt into his throat, and he pressed the emergency button and two nurses came running, along with a doctor who said that the umbilical cord was wrapped around the baby's neck, and they had to break Lauren's water. They did so, and Bill and Lauren hoped they'd saved the fetus, but the couple remained in suspense till the baby was delivered, and it had to be done by C-section because, according to the doctor, if her brain had been deprived of oxygen during the time that the umbilical cord was wrapped around her neck, she would have been born brain-damaged.

Thankfully, the delivery was successful, and Bill experienced the greatest relief and the greatest happiness of his life, even more euphoric than making it through combat situations alive and in one piece. He and Lauren named the baby Jodie. She was born healthy, six pounds two ounces. In Bill's eyes, she was one of the prettiest babies ever, but he was aware that most other parents felt that way too. He had been awake for thirty-six hours, but he didn't want to stop looking at his child. Neither did Lauren. She was weak, but beaming. It was the most loving moment they had ever experienced in the entire history of their marriage, hugging each other and looking down at their little newborn. Bill drove home only to hastily shave and shower, then drive right back to the hospital to look at the infant again. He remained sleep-deprived, visiting his wife and baby bright and early before he had to report to police headquarters, every single day that they were in the hospital.

Sadly but unavoidably, the joy of becoming parents was muted by the cloud hanging over them and their beleaguered small town. Their aspiration toward becoming a happy little family was dimmed by the horrible memories of what they had been through. Of course they were not alone in this. It was seldom talked about, as if it might go away by avoiding it, but many of the survivors were still scarred psychologically by the horror and the losses.

After the baby came home, Bill hoped his little family might achieve a semblance of normality. Lauren immersed herself in the duties of a young mom, cooking and cleaning and breastfeeding and diapering and sandwiching her exercises in between. Meanwhile she took to worrying over every detail of little Jodie's well-being—her eating, her napping, her sleeping, her clothing, her bouts of fussing and crying. She couldn't be away from the baby for five minutes without heading back into the nursery to check on her. Bill tried to ease her mind by putting a monitor in the crib to guard against sudden infant death syndrome, but she kept on checking and hovering.

By the time Jodie was a toddler, Lauren was uptight that Jodie wasn't safe in her crib anymore but was now crawling or walking all over the house where she could get herself into more danger. Even though Bill had inserted plastic plugs into all the wall outlets and had done all the other recommended "baby proofing" that Lauren insisted upon, she still hovered over Jodie like a watchdog.

Bill said, "You're going to have to back off and let her grow up, you know."

But Lauren said, "You don't get it, do you? I worry about her because I'm her mother!"

But he knew that at all times her concern verged on panic. Many times in the middle of the night he would be jolted awake by Lauren's feverish outcries and pitiful sobs and he had to stroke and soothe her because of her recurrent nightmares about her father's death in the Quik-Mart, her own brush with doom at the hands of the undead, and the horror of seeing Wanda Danko bitten by her own son and that son, Jerry, being shot by Pete.

The little things about Lauren that had made him fall in love with her ten years ago were still locked in his heart. Her sense of humor and sarcasm, her quirky laugh, her way of telling jokes lamely because she forgot or screwed up the punch lines, the look in her eyes when she wanted him to make love to her, and the unabashed pleasure she used to take from it. Even though those parts of her were submerged now, he still could relive them with wistfulness and compassion. And he still entertained hope that those endearing qualities in her would return.

He went along with Lauren when she wanted to sell their split-entry on the outskirts of Chapel Grove and move into town. She said that she and Jodie shouldn't be left alone while he was away all day, on the job. She was afraid of who might turn on them both if there should be another outbreak. So they sold their old house at a slight loss, which they could absorb because of a modest inheritance from her father, and moved into a two-story brick on a residential avenue, not far from the police station.

After that, for a time, Lauren's spirits picked up. She and Bill started paying a babysitter so they could go out together at least once a week. There were more smiles and touches between them when they were able to enjoy themselves now and then. It gave him hope that they could slowly begin to rediscover each other, in spite of the horrors they had endured and feared might hit them again.

CHAPTER 12

For the first year of the Foster Project, everything went along as smoothly as Dr. Traeger could have hoped for. The necessary personnel were hired, adoption agreements were signed, and the adoptees were put under rigid observation and frequent medical and physical exams and evaluations. She generally had complete control over all logistics involving not only the adoptees but relationships between them, their parents, and the community. But of course Captain Peter Danko was her on-site control officer, with oversight by high-ranking officials of the Homeland Security Department who were beholden only to Congress and the president. But the majority of senators and representatives were not given an all-encompassing "need to know," not even those on select congressional committees. Thus leaks were relentlessly controlled.

Dr. Traeger had the foresight and fortitude, not to mention the absolute dedication to her mission, to take one of the special children into her own home and adopt her. She and her frail older husband, Daniel, who suffered from asthma and degenerative arthritis, named the child Kathy. She was the "control" subject needed for valid and proper experimentation. Three of the four Foster Project adoptees were placed with ordinary Chapel Grove families who did not know the children's true origin. The fourth one, Kathy, was the adoptee who would be more closely and intimately observed each and every day of her life by Dr. Traeger and her husband, a retired psychiatrist, who knew exactly where she had come from. Thus their evaluations of their adopted daughter would have extraordinary value.

She could detect nothing wrong with the child over her first two years. The others born of infected mothers seemed to be getting along well also.

But two years and three months into the Foster Project, one of them drowned, a toddler named Tommy Stratton. He had slipped into the family swimming pool unnoticed by his adoptive parents while they did backyard chores, thinking he was safely in his playpen. It was ruled an accident, but it was really an abdication of the obligations they had assumed when they signed the Foster Project adoption agreement.

However, the chance for Dr. Traeger to learn as much as she could postmortem could not be passed up. She purposely delayed little Tommy's autopsy for three days on the chance that the little boy might prove immune to a normal death. After the third day of wary observation, she was pleased that she had learned something invaluable: Though born of a ghoul-bitten mother, the child had died without becoming undead.

Like his peers, two-year-old Tommy had been subjected to comprehensive mental and physical examinations every three months, and as luck would have it his last regularly scheduled exam had taken place just two weeks prior to his death. Therefore Dr. Traeger would get to compare postmortem results with the results of the very recent tests performed while the boy was still alive. Even though she lamented the death of the little boy, from a scientific standpoint she couldn't help strongly looking forward to the comparison.

Kallen's Funeral Home, on the main street of Chapel Grove, was the facility where the Foster Project children were to be autopsied and where burial services for them were certified to be carried out should any be required. When Dr. Traeger arrived there, she rang a bell in the back and was let in by Pete Danko who said, crudely, "He's all yours."

The little boy was nude and laid out on an embalming table. Danko was there to observe the procedure and note whatever he thought might be of interest to the Department of Homeland Security. The owner of the funeral home, a handsome black man named Steve Kallen, was also present and was one of HSD's plants in the community. His daughter, Brenda, who lived with him in the apartment above the viewing rooms, was not one of the Foster Project adoptees. Kallen was in his mid-forties, tall and trim with a goatee and mustache, wearing a short-sleeved white shirt and gray slacks this evening, instead of the dark suits he habitually wore when greeting mourners.

Dr. Traeger said, "As you both know, this is the first adoptee who has died. None of them get sick. Not even so much as a common cold. I'm going to examine Tommy's bodily fluids, organs, and brain. If we're lucky, I'll learn something new."

"Good luck with that," Danko said dismissively.

"I almost can't believe we actually have one in this condition," said Kallen. "I'm glad my daughter, Brenda, wasn't adopted, know what I mean? I'd hate to think she might be one of these."

Danko said, "Isn't your daughter in the same day care center where Tommy's parents used to drop him off?"

"Well, yeah," said Kallen. "There aren't too many choices of day care places in Chapel Grove. I wanted Brenda in the best one. Since my wife died, I've been trying to raise her the best way I know how."

Dr. Traeger said, "A lot of the kids play together. That's the main idea of the Foster Project—to observe and study the adoptees in a natural environment, not someplace rigidly controlled."

She put on rubber gloves and took the first step in the autopsy, making the Y-shaped incision from Tommy's narrow little chest to his soft and vulnerable thorax, so she could extract the internal organs. She had to steel herself to perform such a hideous procedure on a little boy, but it had to be done for the good of humanity. It pained her to have to carry her work forward in ways that circumvented the normal tenets of law and democracy, but there was no other way. Although she believed heartily in government of, by, and for the people, at the same time she wished martial law could be temporarily instituted till she could find a cure for the plague. She knew the precedents for it. Lincoln had done it during the Civil War, and Roosevelt had done it during World War Two. Civilization was direly threatened during those historic times, but the plague was far worse and deserved the harsher measures.

She meticulously carried on with Tommy's autopsy, and was disappointed when it did not yield any further discoveries. She found no anomalies, no abnormalities. Though anticlimactic, this was totally in line with what she had expected. She said to Kallen and Danko, "Nothing unusual was going on inside the boy. I think the adoptees are perfectly normal. Maybe even *better* than normal, in fact."

Danko said, "How so?"

"Well, they're unusually healthy and affliction-free. I'd like to discover the cause of that. It's gratifying that poor Tommy didn't exhibit any signs of becoming undead. Perhaps he lacks the animating force, or else it was weaker in him, but still was strong enough to prevent disease."

"Pretty far-fetched," said Danko, with a scornful snort.

"Everything that we don't understand seems far-fetched to us, until we unlock the scientific reasons," said Dr. Traeger. "Isaac Asimov famously remarked that the technology of any sufficiently advanced society will inevitably seem like magic to the *less* advanced."

"Eggheaded drivel," said Danko.

"The secret of the plague is how it somehow reanimates corpses," Dr. Traeger said. "So, what if the cause of it could be deciphered and controlled? Maybe then it could be regulated so that human beings reap immunities from it but also don't become mindless creatures out to devour all of humanity."

"A stupid pipe dream," Danko said. "We're better off blasting them down."

"We need to move beyond that," said Dr. Traeger. "Maybe the secret of the plague is also the secret to a longer life."

"Dream on, Doctor," Danko said.

CHAPTER 13

On the third anniversary of the first outbreak of the plague in Chapel Grove, Bill Curtis's American Legion chapter held another memorial service that was attended by many of the survivors, including Ron and Daisy Haley, who had married soon after the outbreak and now had a cute little girl, Amy, about the same age as Jodie. Lauren and Daisy showed each other wallet photos as they mingled over coffee and cookies, Ron and Bill in suits and ties, their wives in their best dresses. The Haleys seemed happy together, and Bill had a fondness for them because of how well they appeared to be doing since their harrowing ordeal at the Rock 'n' Shock and how hard Ron had fought to escape from addiction.

As speeches got underway, Bill and Lauren sat at a large round table with Steve Kallen and his daughter, Brenda, Pete and Wanda Danko, and Ron and Daisy Haley. Pete was the Legion Commander. He stood behind the podium, welcomed everyone, and spoke briefly about the somberness and appropriateness of the occasion. Then he turned it over to Reverend James Carnes, the clergyman who went around preaching that the dead needed to be spiked. Bill was annoyed that Carnes had gotten himself elected to chaplain of his American Legion post. He considered Carnes to be an anachronistic fear-mongering fool. But it wasn't

hard to get elected to a Legion office; all you had to do was ingrati-
ate yourself with enough voting members by always showing up at
meetings, helping to put flags on veterans' graves for Memorial
Day, and volunteering to do such things as roasting corn or grilling
burgers and dogs at the annual picnic. Bill wasn't intolerant of all
religious people, just the ones he called *religionists*—those who
pretended to have a direct pipeline to God. To his relief, Carnes
didn't let loose with his usual blather. Instead he read the same
prayer that was read each Memorial Day for soldiers who had
given their lives in America's wars.

Bill held Lauren's hand and glanced at her warmly. He reminded himself that she had good reason to be traumatized, in
light of all she had been through, and maybe someday, hopefully,
she'd be able to put it behind her. She had lost her father that
day, but Wanda Danko had lost her son, yet seemed to be recov-
ering in a faltering way. As for Pete, he never let on that he was
suffering. Maybe he wasn't. He had the coldest thousand-yard
stare Bill had ever seen, colder and deader than the eyes of badly
wounded soldiers. Was he battle hardened? Or was he immune to
his own suffering as much as he was to the suffering of others?

Bill suddenly noticed that Dr. Marissa Traeger was sitting with
a rather frail elderly man in the back of the room, at a table for
eight that held only those two. He wondered why they hadn't
mingled with anyone, not even Pete and Wanda Danko. Still, he
thought, it was nice that they had come here to show support for
the community, and he said to Pete, "Should we go over and say
hello to Dr. Traeger and her guest?"

"Stay away from them," Pete said. "They're very private
people."

"Then why are they here?" Bill said.

But Pete shrugged and walked away, which contributed to the
strangeness of this already bizarre occasion.

In many ways, Bill found the loss of life from the plague
harder to deal with than the deaths of his fellow soldiers in Iraq
and Afghanistan. He realized that some of people in the community, who had never gone into combat in an "ordinary" war, were

scarred just as terribly, or even worse, by the losses they had suffered during the battle with the undead. Some of these folks, not just Wanda Danko, had been attacked by their own sons or daughters who had secretly been into drugs and had fallen prey to the infected needles.

Bill knew that he wasn't immune to the freakish fears that had engulfed other people. He didn't like to believe that he might have a touch of PTSD, but ever since his combat tours, he had endured flashbacks and nightmares in which he was about to die, totally surrounded by enemies armed with machine guns and mortars while he possessed only a rifle with an empty clip. But lately the nightmares had morphed. The beings about to kill him were now heavily armed corpses in varying stages of decay. He would clutch his empty gun and try to run, but he couldn't. His legs were as heavy as concrete in quicksand. He would wake up drenched in sweat, and Lauren would be shaking him, then soothing him the same way he often had to soothe her, hugging him, terrified by his cries in the night.

He believed that if a second outbreak should ever happen, the little town of Chapel Grove might not be able to withstand it. The living people might vanquish the undead as they had done before. But the psychological damage next time would be even worse. People would be overwhelmed by repetitive terror. They would believe that rebuilding their lives could never work, and they would always feel threatened, no matter what they might do to survive here. Fleeing from Chapel Grove would do them no good either. The plague could strike anywhere, at any time.

Bill spent "quality time" with Jodie as often as he could. He pushed aside thoughts of how futile it might be to teach his child how to play checkers or ride a tricycle on a tree-lined avenue, in the shadow of impending doom. He read her stories and drew pictures for her, even though he didn't have much art talent. Sometimes the stories were of his own invention, and she liked those best. Her favorite was about her and her imaginary friends, Lucy and Ethel, going on a hike to pick raspberries and having to tame and befriend a purple polka-dotted Raspberry Monster who was trying to take their berries away from them. All the stories Bill made up had lessons to them, and what Jodie was supposed to learn from the Raspberry Monster story was how kindness can combat meanness. Jodie would gleefully color his badly drawn pictures as she sat in his lap, and he would jump up with her in his arms and dance around the room with her and make her giggle, trying to show her how much fun life could be, as opposed to what he felt that Lauren was often teaching her—that life was dangerous and threatening at every moment.

He believed that there were only two things anybody could ever give a child: dreams and wounds. He wanted to be the bearer of dreams, and he hoped he had overcome the wounds of his own childhood so he wouldn't pass them on. His father had been a brutal alcoholic who made him and his mother live in terror. He would beat her up and rip the phone out of the wall when she would try to call the cops. Sometimes he'd land in jail. Bill's mother would threaten suicide. His worst memory, worse even than some of his combat memories, was of himself as a terrified six-year-old kid, running down the cellar stairs after his mom, crying and trying to pull the clothesline out of her hands so she couldn't hang herself.

In first grade, he thought he was the only kid in the room who didn't have a father like the ones on TV. His dad didn't show him how to make a birdhouse or take him to feed pigeons in the snow or teach him how to make a kite. *His* dad beat his mom up so badly she wanted to kill herself.

His parents divorced just before he got out of the army. His father fled to California and never kept in touch, and his mother moved to Alabama with her second husband, and Bill didn't blame her for getting away from Chapel Grove and its bitter memories. But he was glad when, as soon as she found out that Jodie was born, she rushed up to see her in the hospital and was as delighted as any other woman with a brand-new grandchild.

Bill and Lauren both had gone through unhappy childhoods. Lauren's parents were congenitally bitter. Her dad was the unchallenged boss of the family, gruff and reluctant to show affection. Her mom never questioned him, just cooked and cleaned and meekly did his bidding. He made Lauren take over his wife's chores after she died of pneumonia. He also made Lauren start working at the Quik-Mart at age thirteen, as soon as he inherited it from his more clever brother. But the store did not do so well under his bean-counting stewardship, so he bullied Lauren more and more, as if it were her fault. When Bill first started dating her, she was still working there. Because he made her feel safe, cherished, and protected, he brought her out of her shell. She revealed a verve and a sense of humor that she never showed to her father. But nowadays those special qualities were lying dormant under a blanket of fear, and he wished he could revive them again.

CHAPTER 14

On Christmas morning, when Jodie Curtis was only four years old, she was playing under the tree when she bit into a piece of store-bought fudge—and immediately started choking. Forcing himself to remain calm, Bill applied the Heimlich maneuver, but it didn't work. He thought of CPR, but was afraid he might force the gooey fudge farther into her windpipe. Frantic to save her from choking to death, he probed with his index finger inside her mouth and couldn't feel any fudge lodged in her throat. While Lauren panicked, paralyzed with fear, he bundled the child into a quilt and broke all speed limits driving her to the hospital, with Lauren in the back seat, cradling Jodie, whimpering and shaking. Luckily, Bill found a drugstore that was open on Christmas, flung a twenty-dollar bill on the counter to pay for an over-the-counter antihistamine, then jumped back into the car and yelled at Lauren to make Jodie swallow some of it while he continued to drive like a crazed parent.

Jodie was wheeled into an operating room while Bill sweated it out, along with Lauren, in the waiting room. He was more scared than he had ever been, even in combat. Lauren had gone into the hospital's little chapel and knelt and prayed. But he could not. Even though he was under a desperate agony of despair mixed with hope, he wanted to stick to his principles and

not surrender to what he felt was a useless belief in divine inter-
vention. He just sat there with his arm around his wife's shoulders, comforting her the best he could, while he himself felt no
spiritual comfort. Finally a doctor came out and gave them the
good news that Jodie's life was saved by a tracheotomy. Bill felt
relief flood his mind and body as he hugged Lauren and they
both cried, wetting each other's clothing with their tears.

The doctor explained that Jodie had suddenly developed life-
threatening allergies. Of the long list of potential culprits, tree
nuts were the worst, but she was also highly allergic to peanuts,
almonds, milk, wheat, and many other normally harmless and
nutritious foods. There had been walnuts in the fudge, and that
is what had sent her nearly all the way into anaphylactic shock.
The medicine Bill had thought to grab on the way to the hospital
had partly opened her breathing passages, or else they would
have closed up tight and she would have died. From now on she
must avoid the many, many foods she had become allergic to. According to several allergists, there were no sound medical explanations for her sudden sensitivity to substances that had previously
caused her no problems. Now she must always carry an epineph-
rine pen and be ready to inject herself to save her own life.

Bill was proud, as was Lauren, of the bravery Jodie had shown
at the hospital. But in the weeks following the incident, she
began suffering panic attacks and flashbacks that morphed into
agoraphobia, separation anxiety, and fear of being abandoned.
She wouldn't play in her room by herself anymore; she always
had to be at Bill's or Lauren's feet. If they went out into the yard
or onto the patio, she would run after them as soon as she noticed
their absence.

She threw tantrums everywhere and anywhere, even at the
American Legion picnics that should've been a lot of fun for her
because there were all kinds of games for kids, with prizes and
even pony rides. Everybody thought that Jodie was a brat and Bill
and Lauren were terrible parents. People would stare at them,
shake their heads, and mutter disparaging things, not caring if
they were overheard.

A child psychologist told them they needed to set limits, establish a consistent daily routine, and create a pleasant and orderly home life for Jodie. But Lauren, in Bill's judgment, was part of the problem, not the solution. When Jodie threw a tantrum, Lauren appeased her. Bill kept trying to make her see that she was placating, not parenting, but she insisted she was doing it right and refused to make any changes. She argued that she should be able to tell Jodie what to do and Jodie should obey, and if Jodie did not, then it was Jodie, not she, who was to blame. She blamed Bill, saying that if he would back her up, Jodie would be easier to handle.

"Fathers are supposed to support mothers," she said.

She bristled when he said, "I can't back you up when you're wrong, because it'll make her feel that *both* parents are ganging up on her."

When things didn't improve, Jodie was given a psychiatric examination that led to a diagnosis of post-traumatic stress disorder, and counseling and prescription medication were recommended. Bill had always associated PTSD with the suppressed fears of combat, and had dreaded the thought that maybe it would hit him when he came home from the Middle East. It used to be called "combat fatigue" or "shell shock." But because of what his daughter was going through, he had to realize that not just the trauma of war could cause PTSD, but also some of the fears and dangers of civilian life.

One day when he was about to punish Jodie, she said, "Daddy, I'd rather have people think I'm a brat instead of letting them know I'm scared." What she said opened his eyes all of a sudden, and at that moment he finally grasped the reason for her terrible tantrums. Because she had behaved so well in the emergency room, he had wanted to believe that she had overcome her near-death experience, but now it was clear to him that it had traumatized her more severely than he had thought. It had festered inside her and had led to her multiple stresses and fears. As a defensive measure, she was always trying to avoid the things that scared her the most, and she would scream, kick, and throw things if that's what it took.

Bill tried to explain this insight to Lauren, but she refused to accept its direct cause-and-effect explanation. "That's not it!" she snapped back at him. "You give in to her instead of taking *my* side, so she knows she can work one of us against the other!"

"That's absolutely not true. That's not what is really going on."

Lauren ran up to their bedroom, slammed the door, then sulked for the rest of the day. He almost felt that he was dealing with two children instead of one. He felt that he was the only one of the two parents who truly understood their child. Since Jodie's tantrums were not her fault, it would do no good to punish her for them, and so he resolved to listen to her with patience and kindness. But Lauren wouldn't buy into that. She thought he was coddling Jodie instead of disciplining her like a father should, and worse, he was turning Jodie against her by being the easier parent, the one she could always run to.

It worried Bill that disagreements over how to raise children was one of the main reasons for divorce. As discouraging as his marriage got, he felt that he couldn't consider that option because one of Jodie's worst manifestations was separation anxiety, which a divorce would only reinforce and make worse. Lauren was in denial and wouldn't acquiesce to family counseling when Bill got the nerve to suggest it. He wished she would go back to being the cheerful, loving person she used to be, but that person seemed to be gone now.

CHAPTER 15

Jodie was six years old, playing in a sandbox while her mom kept a close eye on her. Lauren had brought a book to the playground, but it was useless because her eyes kept going over and over the same paragraph. How could she concentrate when she didn't know what Jodie might be getting into?

She was annoyed with Bill for always harping on her to "give the kid more space." Well, how could she do that? Weren't little children always in need of a mother's love and protection? When little birdies learned to fly, the mother bird watched over them. Didn't she have a right to feel worried and upset? How could Bill forget what a close call she had had in the Quik-Mart? She had watched her own father being torn apart and she herself had almost been bitten and turned into something unspeakable. Her constant nightmares, jolting both of them awake in the middle of the night, should be enough to remind him of what she had been through.

She had badly wanted to have a child and had been sure that if she could only have one, she'd be a good mother. But now, no matter what she did or how hard she tried, it never seemed to be enough for the two most important people in her life. She only wanted them to return her love and make her happy, but Bill told her that nobody could "make" another person happy, it had to come from within. He said she had to love herself before she could love anyone else, and she had to put her troubled childhood behind her. But she did love him and Jodie, she really did. She thought he was just too critical of her. He wouldn't even let her put away Jodie's toys. But if she didn't put them away for her, who would? Same with Jodie's clothes. Lauren always put them away for her after she washed them, but Bill said Jodie needed to learn how to take care of them herself and pick up after herself, not leave her clothes on her bed or on the floor and go to the drawer for fresh ones even when the ones she already wore weren't dirty. Lauren did actually agree with Bill that Jodie made too much work for her, so much that she couldn't attend to her own wants and desires.

In *Cosmo* she had read that the purpose of marriage is to keep people together during the times when they're not in love with each other. It rang true to her. Every marriage waxes and wanes, but Lauren always loved Bill even when her love for him wasn't at the top of her mind. She didn't think he completely understood her, even though they still had their moments of tenderness. She wistfully remembered how they had felt closest when they were standing over Jodie in her crib, looking down at the innocent little miracle they both had wrought.

She kept hoping that this terrible stage Jodie was going through would play itself out. Maybe then their family life would stabilize. She hoped she and Bill would find each other again, and grow old together, and have grandchildren.

She looked up from her novel with a tremor of anxiety when a little boy named Darius Hornsby got into the sandbox with Jodie. They were both six years old, both wearing sandals, shorts, and T-shirts. To strangers they might appear to be two cute little blond-headed kids—but Lauren knew that Darius was a brat, and by that she didn't mean that he misbehaved once in a while like Jodie or any other kid, she meant that he really was a "problem child." She had to be on guard in case Darius acted up and did something bad to Jodie, so she moved closer to the sandbox. She didn't see Darius's mother around; she let the brat do whatever he pleased most of the time. That was why he was so spoiled, in Lauren's estimation.

So far, the two kids seemed to be getting along fine—but still Lauren glanced around and tried to spot Mrs. Hornsby by the swings or coming out of the ladies' room or something. Then suddenly Jodie let out a scream. Lauren jumped up and saw that Darius was trying to take her little tin shovel away from her. She wouldn't let go, so Darius bit her on her arm. His mother appeared from somewhere and shrieked, "Darius!" And Lauren ran over, yelling, "Oh my God! Jodie!"

The two moms grabbed at their kids, trying desperately to pull them apart, mortified by their children's failure to "play nice." Darius was unhurt, while Jodie's arm was bleeding. Lauren freaked when she saw a fleck of blood on Darius's lips. It seemed to her that the little brat was defiantly leering at her even as his mother yanked him by his arm and started scolding him. Jodie continued to wail. Lauren grabbed tissues from her purse and tried to stop the wound from bleeding. She was so upset that she bit her own lip, and it bled a bit too.

Mrs. Hornsby, a tall, bony, gray-haired woman in a limp house-dress, kept apologizing all over herself and saying that she was going to take Darius home and punish him. This didn't seem to faze him. He kept staring at Lauren and Jodie with a snotty expression on his face, even as his mom dragged him toward her SUV.

Lauren immediately took Jodie to her pediatrician, Dr. Miller, who was considered by most parents to be tops in his field, partly evidenced by his being on the board of the Chapel Grove Medical Research Institute. She figured that the bill from him would help document the incident in case Bill wanted to sue for medical costs, or in case the wound got worse, festered, and developed complications. Fortunately, after examining Jodie's sore arm and applying salve and a gauze bandage, Dr. Miller said, "There isn't any sign of infection. Nothing to worry about."

"Will she have a scar?" Lauren asked anxiously.

"I don't think so. Not much of one anyhow. Children heal marvelously at her age."

"That little Darius is a brat," Lauren said. "Why do some children bite other children?"

"It's a form of aggression that they lose as they get older. It's pretty common, actually. Teeth are a natural weapon, and children can readily figure that out."

"Well, I think his mother could curb his behavior if she tried harder," Lauren said adamantly.

That afternoon, when Dr. Miller reported to Dr. Traeger that the Curtis girl, Jodie, age six, had been bitten by Darius Hornsby, the director of the Chapel Grove Medical Research Institute was deeply concerned. Little Darius was one of her special children, and Dr. Miller was aware of it since he was one of the HSD plants in the Chapel Grove community.

Dr. Traeger needed to find out what might be at the root of little Darius's impulse to bite another child. She had to somehow figure out if it could be a trait inherited from Darius's infected mother, because there was no doubting what she would have turned into if she had been allowed to survive and become transformed. But on the other hand, many children threw tantrums and bit their playmates when they were too young to control their angry impulses, and eventually they realized it was unacceptable behavior and simply outgrew it. Dr. Traeger wanted to believe that Darius's "acting out" would follow this same pattern. She clung to her knowledge that her intensive studies of the Foster Project children, including brain scans, blood and tissue samples, and every other advanced scientific procedure that federal money could provide, hadn't revealed anything in the least abnormal.

She further reassured herself by reflecting upon the unfortunate little boy, Tommy Stratton, who had drowned at age two. None of his autopsy findings had been unusual or alarming. And so, relying on that precedent, Dr. Traeger had every reason to believe that even though Darius Hornsby had bitten the Curtis child, it probably did not carry with it any disturbing ramifications beyond the act itself.

Three weeks later, during the boy's regularly scheduled evaluation, tests for pathogens and abnormalities proved negative, and she was greatly relieved. It seemed to be holding true that the children were perfectly normal in spite of the unique circumstances of their births.

CHAPTER 16

As the Foster Project passed its seventh anniversary, Dr. Traeger got approval for eight more years of funding so it could continue till the remaining three adoptees could matriculate through puberty. She felt this was necessary and pragmatic because so many changes would take place in developing human beings during the preteen and teen years, so many complicated hormonal transformations and wild mood swings, that if anything were to go wrong in the adoptees' maturation, this would be the time of most danger.

She had already made a troubling observation. The special children were developing a strange, almost eerie affinity for one another, even though such cliquish behavior doesn't usually manifest strongly prior to the onset of adolescence. Even as early as first and second grade, they did not integrate well with their other classmates.

But they continued to have very strong immune systems, highly resistant to all types of illness. One of Dr. Traeger's goals in continuing to study them was that she hoped to discover how that same kind of disease resistance could be conveyed to *all* children, perhaps even while they were still in the womb.

She had plenty of highly important, intellectually stimulating things to do at the institute and was as deeply motivated as ever, but unfortunately, in her personal life she was not happy. She and her husband were having constant behavioral problems with their adopted daughter, Kathy. Dr. Traeger felt thwarted in her hope of having a warm, comforting family, the kind she had always yearned for, that would help her put the nightmare of her mother's savage death behind her. She was always dispassionately objective even when analyzing herself, and so she readily understood that what she had experienced as a child had adversely colored her disposition and her path through life.

She always was inhibited about love and romance. She did not marry until late in life, age forty-three, and Daniel was the pursuer, not she, even though he was twenty years older. She was not highly sexed, absorbed as she was in her calling, and so a much older man suited her. She had grown attached to him during psychotherapy appointments with him while she was still in her twenties, and she could admit to herself that, having grown up as an orphan, perhaps she had a father complex. When they started dating, he stopped being her therapist, which was of course the ethical thing to do. Even after their wedding, she remained immersed in the science of pathogens and the search for cures. They were a compatible if not passionate couple, both working professionals, until his age and his infirmities forced him to give up his practice.

He became a stay-at-home father after they adopted Kathy, who at first seemed like a bright and bubbly child. But gradually, being with her all day every day, Daniel began to suspect that something was not right with her. Dr. Traeger hated to entertain that thought, for she had come to love Kathy as deeply as she would have loved a child who was biologically hers. She suspected in the beginning that Daniel wasn't warming to their adoptee as readily as she herself was. She overcompensated by lavishing affection upon Kathy, and Daniel criticized her for it. "You realize," he said, "that one can smother a child with a blanket of love as easily as one can smother it with a blanket of wool. And any kind of smothering will only make her pull away from you all the more."

As time went by, Dr. Traeger had to struggle more and more for her daughter's respect and obedience. And the more she fought, the more she lost. The distance between the two of them was palpable. She did not feel that she and Kathy had ever fully bonded. She lay awake night after night, hoping that an explanation would come to her. The child did not know that she was adopted, and therefore the distance that she kept could not be due to animosity felt because she was not being raised by her birth parents. Dr. Traeger had to come to grips with the realization that Kathy seemed to treat her and her husband as mere providers of food, shelter, and spending money, instead of as the willing couple who loved her and took loving care of her.

They had a live-in British nanny, only nineteen years old, and Kathy and the nanny got along fine, better than Kathy got along with her parents. Perhaps it was because the girl was so much closer to Kathy's age, Dr. Traeger thought, and told herself that she shouldn't be jealous. At the same time, she tried to fight off the nagging sense of alarm that haunted her when she reflected upon the fact that emotional coldness toward one's parents was the classic trait of a sociopath. But she didn't want to believe that about her own daughter. Even if it were somehow to prove true, she felt that it was not necessarily a product of Kathy's unusual biological parentage. Many, many children went bad who were not born of a plague-diseased mother. So what was going on with Kathy? To search out the answer to that heart-wrenching question was just one of many reasons that the Foster Project must continue. Dr. Traeger needed to find out all those things that she currently did not know, not only about the other adoptees but about her own daughter.

She longed for a healthy family relationship, which had been denied her after she was orphaned and placed in foster care. The pressures put on her by her crucial work at the institute, coupled with pressures in her own home, were sometimes almost too much for her. It seemed grossly unfair to her that she was such an intelligent, dedicated, and accomplished woman, and yet true happiness eluded her.

CHAPTER 17

On a Saturday morning when Bill Curtis was supposed to have the day off, he was jolted out of a fitful sleep by a phone call from Pete Danko. "Bad news. Dr. Traeger's husband has fallen down a flight of stairs. She says he has no pulse, and she thinks his neck is broken. I'll meet you at their place. Coroner is on his way."

When Bill got to the Traegers' home, a large Tudor with a four-car garage, there were two squad cars parked in the wide driveway, along with the coroner's van. A patrolman guarding the front door admitted him into the living room, where the coroner was at the foot of the stairs examining Daniel's body. A three-pronged aluminum cane lay next to him, as if it had tumbled down the stairs with him.

Bill realized that Pete Danko must have arrived not long before he did, because Dr. Traeger, who was wearing a gray skirt, a blue blouse, nylons, and high-heeled shoes, was just now clueing him in. "I was about to leave for work," she said shakily. "Our daughter witnessed the fall, but I heard the noise. She told me my husband tripped over our pet cat. You can talk with Kathy if you wish, but treat her gently, she's only seven years old. She's in her room. We have a nanny, but she's in Pittsburgh for the weekend, with one of her friends."

Pete turned to Bill and said, "We'll have to question the little girl, much as we might not want to. I'll talk with Dr. Traeger, Bill, and you talk with Kathy. We'll compare notes."

Bill tapped lightly on the little girl's door, which was slightly ajar, and she said, "Come in, Mommy." Her eyes widened when she saw it wasn't her mommy. She was sitting on her bed. The room was full of stuffed animals and expensive-looking furniture, and also contained a computer and a PlayStation. Bill thought it looked like a bedroom that would belong to one of Hollywood's child stars, definitely more high-end than Jodie's room. He hesitantly approached the pretty seven-year-old, reminding himself that he should be as tactful as possible, but before he could ask her anything, she said, "Is my daddy dead?" He didn't see any tears, and her flat way of asking that question seemed strange. She rattled on, in an emotionless monotone. "Kitty was on the steps, and Daddy didn't see her at first. He tried not to step on Kitty, and then he fell. His cane missed the step."

Dr. Traeger interrupted right then, peeking into the room with Pete at her side. "Please don't push my daughter too hard," she pleaded. "At Kathy's age I witnessed my own mother's death, and I didn't get over it for a long, long time. I had nightmares from grade school on, even through medical school."

"I'm deeply sorry to learn that," Bill told her.

"Likewise," said Pete. "Step outside, Doctor, and we'll talk some more. You too, Bill."

Bill stepped into the hallway and pushed Kathy's bedroom door all the way shut.

Dr. Traeger said, "This happened because my husband is so frail. He has degenerative arthritis, among other things, including osteoporosis. We were scheduled to have a chairlift installed next week. If we could have gotten it earlier, this probably wouldn't have happened."

"The coroner says he's going to rule it an accidental death," Pete said, lowering his voice so Dr. Traeger's daughter wouldn't overhear. "I don't see anything that would contradict his assessment. It's sad that poor Kathy had to be there to see it."

Bill thought to himself that if Kathy were an adult witness

Pete wouldn't so readily accept her statement, but would dig deeper. Instead he had interrupted Bill's chat with her before she could be questioned in depth. All right. She was only a child, in third grade. But Bill had the nagging thought that she might know something more. However, there really didn't seem to be any strong reason to suspect the child of pushing her elderly parent down the stairs even though it was conceivable that she would have had the strength. But what possible motive?

Still, Bill didn't want to let it go. "Pete, why don't you let me finish talking with Kathy?" he said. "That way I can put everything she says into my report, and inquiring eyes will see that we did everything by the numbers."

"No," Pete said adamantly. "The child has been through enough. We already know what she told her mother, and we don't need to put her through any more trauma."

Bill could concede that maybe that sounded reasonable. But the way Pete was squelching him made him think back to the hunt for the missing needles and the outbreak at the Rock 'n' Shock. Pete had seemed less than candid back then, too, as if he knew something that he wasn't telling. When Bill tried to probe more, he felt like he was walking on dangerous ground and might fall into a pit with sharpened stakes.

After the detectives left and Daniel's body was taken to Kallen's Funeral Home for cremation, Dr. Traeger fell to pieces, crying uncontrollably, soaking three hankies and a sheaf of paper towels. Was it possible that the child she and her husband had adopted could be more tainted than she ever wanted to believe?

Trying to pull herself together, she considered the fact that from Kathy's earliest childhood she had seemed unnaturally close to the other children of the Foster Project. In reports to Homeland Security, and in her personal journals, Dr. Traeger had gone so far as to use the word "eerie" when puzzling over the unique affinity that the children had for one another. But she had not wanted to use language stronger than that until she was more certain of her findings.

She had also noted that the close-knit circle of Kathy's friends was definitely widening. She had to ask herself if her daughter, as well as the others like her, might have a special charismatic power over other children, even those of normal birth, a charisma not unlike that of certain cult leaders or religious zealots like David Koresh, Jim Jones, or even Reverend Carnes, the pastor of his stupidly named Church of Lazarus Risen.

In her grief, Dr. Traeger decided that, now that her husband was gone, she needed to redouble her efforts to form a deeper bond with Kathy. She needed to be warm and welcoming, not judgmental or accusatory in any way. She had to try to nurture the human empathy that usually comes naturally to humans.

She understood well the workings of the human brain, for it had been the major focus of her studies and experiments. Most laymen think of the brain as just one organ. But scientists had learned that down through the millennia, the most primitive part did not evolve further; instead, as evolution created mammals and then man, more advanced parts were added onto the basic reptile brain that humans still retain. The reptile complex is the seat of aggression. The limbic system, which began to show up in early mammals, is the seat of nurturing and caring about others. And the neocortex, the last part of our brains to evolve, gives us our power to discriminate and reason.

When the neocortex loses its control over the reptile complex, we become creatures devoid of ethics and morality. Who was the tempter in the Garden of Eden? The serpent. The reptile. In other words, the reptilian side of *man*—that's who the devil *is*. That is what Dr. Traeger firmly believed. She had long looked at the plague as an enigmatic disease of the neocortex, the seat of reason, coupled with an impairment of the limbic system. The people afflicted with it were not much different from reptiles, driven by the urge to kill and eat. Therefore, she had reasoned, the cure for the plague, if she could someday find it, would most likely involve discovering some way to revitalize and rebuild the neocortex and the limbic system, thereby reviving the power to think as well as to empathize.

Over the past several years, several outbreaks in various parts of the country had provided her with specimens to continue her studies. They were immobilized with paralyzing darts, like zoo animals, and brought to her for her purposes. A crude way of doing it, but a necessary procedure, of course. Desperate times require desperate measures.

It had occurred to her, with a flash of insight, that the unfortunate disease Alzheimer's might be related to the disease of the undead. The most horrible thing about Alzheimer's was that one could feel one's brain being stolen away. Were not the undead similarly afflicted? Their brains were partly alive, but only to animate them and imbue them with an implacable craving for human flesh.

Therefore, for some time now, Dr. Traeger had been studying sufferers of Alzheimer's as well as captured specimens of the undead. She became excited when she thought of how wonderful it would be if she could find the cure to *both* diseases! She believed that the solution, when it came to her, would likely be elegantly simple. But arriving at it was not simple at all. It was frustratingly elusive, as were her attempts to break through to her own daughter.

She left her study, gently knocked on Kathy's door, and asked if she might come in. When she got no answer, she entered anyway, and sat on the edge of the bed. "Tell me once more how Daddy's accident happened," she began. She hoped that they would be able to cling to each other through this time of grief, so that healing could begin to happen for them both.

But Kathy turned her head away and said, "Please, Mommy, leave me alone."

She decided that she just needed to give her little girl more time. So she backed away and softly closed the bedroom door. She wished Kathy would display more emotion about her father's death. She didn't want her to start blaming herself, she only wanted her to at least shed some tears or give some sort of sign that she could behave in a normal way. In spite of the fact that she was an adopted child, and one with strange origins, Dr. Traeger had come to love her as she had wished she would, and she longed for her love to be returned. She knew from the tests she had performed on Kathy that the child's neocortex was healthy and uncompromised. She was highly intelligent and creative, so perhaps her superior intelligence was what made her standoffish to children outside of her own close-knit group.

Still, Dr. Traeger wondered if Kathy's limbic system, the seat of caring and empathy in all mammals, was damaged in some scientifically undetectable way, leaving an unfathomable emotional void. And if this should be true of Kathy, was it also true of *all* the special children?

CHAPTER 18

Jodie was nine years old when, on a Friday in May, Lauren texted Bill that she had gotten great news and was coming to the police station to tell him about it. He was immediately excited because she almost never came to his workplace because she hated to be around Pete, and now she had texted that she and Jodie both would be there in fifteen minutes. They arrived in even less time, and barged right in with big smiles on their faces.

"We just came from the allergist!" Lauren blurted happily. "Jodie's allergies have cleared up! She may not even need to carry her EpiPen anymore!"

"How could that be?" Bill asked, maintaining skepticism at first, not daring to be too quick to get his hopes up. After five years of wondering when or where Jodie might inadvertently eat something that would send her into anaphylactic shock, it was hard to believe that the ordeal might end. From everything he had been told or had read online, the defect was genetic and had no known cure.

"The allergist can't figure it out," Lauren told him. "He says her body chemistry must've changed, but he hasn't a clue why. He's going to consult with some of his colleagues, but he's sure they've never seen a case like it. He said if they did come up with an answer, they'd patent it and get very, very rich."

Jodie was beaming, and Bill got up from behind his desk, hugged her tightly, and said, "I'm glad, honey. You've been through a lot, we all have, and now everything will start to get better."

"I'm already better, Daddy," she said, smiling the sweet unblemished smile he remembered from her earliest childhood but hadn't seen for several years. It made his heart ache.

Lauren stepped closer for a hug too, and he folded her and Jodie both into his arms, in a loving cluster that included the three of them.

Pete Danko peeked in and gruffly demanded, "What's going on here? Too much levity in my police station?" But he smiled to show he was just kidding—for him a rare display of good humor.

Lauren said, "We got great news today, Pete. Jodie's allergies have cleared up. The doctor doesn't know why. It's almost like magic!"

"Great, I'm happy for you. I hope it lasts," Pete said.

Within the hour, Dr. Marissa Traeger learned about Jodie's miraculous reprieve, not only from Pete Danko, but also from Dr. Miller, who forwarded her a copy of the allergist's report. She studied it in detail. The findings seemed to have been verified, and she had mixed feelings about that. It was definitely good news for the Curtis family, but from a scientific standpoint she didn't know how to feel or what to think. She was puzzled because allergies as severe as Jodie's didn't simply go away. Usually they got worse. It could take a long time for the immune system to break down, but once it happened it couldn't be undone. Gene therapy might help someday, but right now anything like that was on the far horizon.

Dr. Traeger considered the fact that the children of the plague were remaining disease-free up till now. Could that anomaly, that unique trait, somehow be passed on to an ordinary child? Jodie Curtis had been bitten by Darius Hornsby when she was six years old, and Darius was a Foster Project adoptee. Was there something unusual in his saliva? Contemplating the fact that rattlesnake venom was actually a form of saliva that was poisonous, but could also be used to cure certain diseases, Dr. Traeger wondered if, by some stretch, a cure for the plague might possibly be hidden in Darius's saliva. But if so, why hadn't any anomalies been revealed throughout all of his many tests? Could there be something happening here that modern science couldn't detect?

Dr. Traeger realized that she had no choice but to more closely monitor the Curtis child as she grew older. Luckily, Dr. Miller was on hand to help, and as Jodie's pediatrician he was in a trusted and very close professional relationship with the Curtis family. It was a good thing that Homeland Security had done a thorough job of infiltrating the community with well-placed professionals, including pediatricians like Miller.

That night, Bill made love to Lauren with renewed joy and abandon. A weight had been lifted from their shoulders. They confided their doubts as to whether their good fortune would last, but for now they were able to push aside trepidation and surrender to the moment. They cuddled after their lovemaking and talked intimately and unreservedly, opening up to each other the way they used to. For the first time in years, they dared to think that happiness might lie ahead.

Jodie's fear of being in school and away from her parents slowly subsided. Her grades improved, and she started making the honor roll. Bill bought her a smartphone, and just having it with her eased her anxieties considerably because now she could readily get in touch with her mother, her father—or an ambulance, if need be. Thanking Bill for the phone, she said, "I never told you this, Daddy, but the school nurse and some of the teachers didn't believe me when I said I would use my EpiPen if I had to, but they would still have to get me to the hospital within twenty minutes. The nurse called me a liar, she said there was nothing wrong with me and I just wanted attention. So I was scared that if something bad happened to me, they wouldn't call an ambulance."

"You should've told me, honey," Bill said angrily. "I would've gone straight to the school board. I would've made them apologize and do the right thing."

"I guess I knew that. But I didn't want the kids to keep making fun of me."

"Did you tell your mother what the nurse said?"

"No, I was sure she'd freak out. She freaks out over everything."

"I don't think she's going to do that so much anymore," Bill said. "I think a lot of our problems are behind us."

"I think so too, Daddy."

Bill kissed Jodie on her forehead and gave her a hug, holding her tightly. She was the most precious thing in his life, and he never wanted to lose her.

CHAPTER 19

When Jodie turned thirteen, she was on her way to becoming such a typical teenager that she was constantly giving her mother a hard time. On the way to the pediatrician's office, she kept complaining, "Why do I have to waste my time seeing Dr. Miller? There's nothing wrong with me, Mother! I haven't been sick in two years!"

"He's not supposed to only treat you while you're sick, Jodie. He's supposed to do regular checkups so you don't *get* sick."

"Well, I'm not going to. I feel fine."

Lauren was glad when Jodie put on her earphones and started making her fingers go like mad on her smartphone. It was a tactic she used to block her mother out, but this time Lauren found some relief in it. People talked so much about the "terrible twos," but the teen years were far worse in her estimation. Jodie could be a pain in the butt. She was exceptionally healthy now that her allergies had gone away, and her self-image had improved a great deal as well. But now she thought she deserved to be treated like an adult without demonstrating much of the necessary maturity.

As soon as they both got out of the car, she started up again. "Mom, I *hate* coming here! I'm *thirteen!*"

"I don't like to change doctors if I don't have to. Dr. Miller knows your whole medical history."

"*What* medical history? I never get sick anymore. If my friends find out I'm still going to a *baby* doctor, I'll curl up and die!"

"A pediatrician's normal practice covers children from birth to age eighteen. So you shouldn't find it embarrassing to come here."

"Well, I'm sorry but I *do!*"

After arguing all the way across the parking lot, they entered the building, which was a ranch-style home converted to a small clinic. Jodie slinked sulkily into the waiting room with a sour look on her face that instantly brightened when she spotted her friend Tricia Lopez sitting with her mother, Hilda.

"Tricia! What are *you* doing here?" Jodie sang out.

Lauren said, "Hi, Hilda. Hi, Tricia."

Tricia said to Jodie, "C'mon, let's sit together by the window."

They immediately moved to where they could be apart from their mothers. Watching them and pursing her lips, Hilda said, "They're both showing too much midriff. There's too much sex stuff aimed at teenagers these days."

"What're we supposed to do?" said Lauren. "They're young and pretty and the boys flock to them. They could pass as sisters, or twins even."

"Except Jodie's a blonde and Tricia's a brunette," Hilda said. "I wish they wouldn't wear their jeans so butt-hugging tight and low on their hips, and their blouses showing so much bare midriff."

"Me too," said Lauren. "Jodie waited to get dressed and out of the house till it was too late for me to make her go back in and change into something more modest."

Hilda's eyes widened and she shook her head, saying, "Gosh, Tricia did exactly the same thing!"

"Sex, sex, sex!" Lauren exclaimed. "It's all over the Internet and the movies and TV! Not to mention those lurid and violent video games. Isn't life scary enough?"

"I know," said Hilda. "I feel like throwing my hands up."

"Amen!" said Lauren. "By the way, Tricia has such smooth, blemish-free skin. She takes after you, doesn't she?"

"Why, thank you," Hilda said. "My husband is darker. He's Cuban. His name is Umberto but he goes by Bert, for the sake of his insurance business. It's a shame that people can be so prejudiced."

Lauren said, "Jodie's just here for a routine checkup. It bugs her to come so often, but Dr. Miller insists on it. She's been very healthy the past few years."

"Same with Tricia. Do you think Dr. Miller is just especially good at what he does? I don't know what he puts in those vaccinations of his but sometimes I wonder if they'd work on *me*."

They both laughed.

Lauren said, "Our two girls seem to really like each other. It's a relief to me. Jodie used to be shy around other children."

"Sometimes Tricia shies away from kids her age," said Hilda, "but then with certain others she really hits it off. She likes Jodie, though."

Both mothers smiled and glanced toward their daughters on the other side of the room, who were lost in their own teenage world.

Out of their parents' hearing, Tricia asked Jodie, "Can I see your scar?"

"I guess so, if my mom doesn't freak."

"She's not watching right now," Tricia said.

Eyeing her mom, who had her head turned, Jodie held out her arm.

Tricia asked, "How old were you when it happened?"

"Six. It was at the playground. I didn't *start* the fight."

"With who?"

"Darius Hornsby. That snotty brat!"

"Well, he's far from a brat now, Jodie. He's a hunk!" Tricia whispered, "I'd let him do me. Wouldn't you?"

"Tricia!"

"Well, it's the truth. Almost. I think."

They both giggled.

Jodie said, "I can't think rationally about him. I've been seeing him in my nightmares for too long."

"He must've bit you pretty hard. Did it hurt?"

"Sure it hurt. It bled a lot, too."

"Do you know Amy Haley? She goes to our church. She has a scar like yours on her shoulder. I think Darius must've bitten her, too, just like he bit you."

"Well, he's not a little kid anymore. Maybe he doesn't act like that anymore. But he still thinks he's God's gift to every girl he sees."

"He could tie himself in a bow and be a gift to me anytime he wants to," said Tricia.

"Why isn't anybody being called in?" Jodie griped. "Where the heck is the doctor? I want out of here."

Dr. Miller was in his office, putting off seeing patients because Dr. Traeger was sitting in front of his desk, confiding in him about a personal matter that might also have a bearing on the Foster Project. After listening in patient silence, Dr. Miller voiced his surprise. "You're telling me you're afraid of your own daughter?"

"Not afraid . . . suspicious," Dr. Traeger said. "The kids she hangs around with seem nice enough, almost too nice. I can't quite put my finger on it. They stick together in their own little clique, and now even the Curtis girl seems to be becoming part of it. They give each other sly, sneaky looks—and strange smiles."

"Kids think they know everything at their age," said Dr. Miller. "To them, all parents and authority figures are either invisible or else riding herd on them all the time. Kathy will grow up and change. Don't let it bother you so much."

"Well, her friends are all she cares about. Ever since my husband died, she acts like I don't even exist. She shows me no warmth or affection whatsoever. She was like that before, but now it's worse."

"Does she blame you for her father's death?"

"Maybe she blames herself. But she was only seven, and she wasn't responsible."

"Even though it wasn't her fault," said Dr. Miller, "she still could be carrying a lot of guilt. I think you should try not to be so uptight about her. The poor kid probably doesn't know how to please you, so she keeps her distance."

Those words hit home with Dr. Traeger. She knew she was hard to live with because she was so preoccupied. Her mind was always on her work. Yet she believed that her experiments would turn out to be a tremendous boon to people everywhere, including her own daughter. Wasn't that a worthy sacrifice?

She said to Dr. Miller, "The funding for the Foster Project is going to run out in two years, after the children reach age fifteen. I've applied for another grant, but I don't think it's going to go through. The Homeland Security Department has other fish to fry, and the consensus is that our studies haven't uncovered anything worth pursuing. I think they're wrong, but nobody is listening to me."

Dr. Miller said, "I promise you I'll back you up if anything goes drastically wrong and they try to lay it at your feet."

"Let's hope it doesn't come to that," said Dr. Traeger.

CHAPTER 20

Detective Bill Curtis parked in front of a modest ranch-style home ringed by crime scene tape. A police car and a coroner's van were already there, in the driveway. He took a deep breath, steeling himself against the horrors of what he was about to face.

Pete Danko was standing with the coroner in front of a big maple tree in the backyard, and Ron Haley's body was hanging from a rope tied to a thick lower branch. A picnic bench was lying in the grass under the body's legs, the bench tipped over onto its side.

Ron Haley had hanged himself.

Ron's wife, Daisy, and his daughter, Amy, age sixteen, were also dead.

Bill had great respect for the way they had moved on with their lives, up till now, and so what had happened to them today was especially devastating to him. Amy was the same age as his own daughter, Jodie. It was sixteen years since the plague outbreak caused by infected needles, when Bill had helped rescue Ron and Daisy from the swarming mob of undead at the Rock 'n' Shock. Since then he had seen Ron and his family fairly often, for instance at the American Legion Hall for the memorial service some years ago and since then at softball games or Legion picnics. Ron had become an English teacher at Chapel Grove

High School and also gave private guitar lessons. Daisy had been a wife and homemaker and also a volunteer at a church-run day care center. Bill sadly wondered what could have caused Ron Haley, a decent family man, to kill his loved ones and then himself. Anytime he had seen them together, the Haleys had struck him as a cohesive and loving family unit. He had attributed that to the rough, drugged-out life Ron and Daisy had led and their resultant thirst for normality. It had looked to him that they had successfully separated themselves from the Hateful Dead and their groupies and hangers-on and had built a more rewarding life. And now it was suddenly and disastrously over.

Pete ordered Bill to have one of the uniforms show him into the house, telling him, "I've already doped out how it must've gone down, but you need more exposure to this kind of thing, so get with it."

Bill thought, *Maybe I haven't investigated as many homicides as you have, Pete, but I'm not a total novice and you shouldn't treat me like one.* He vowed that someday he was going to tell Pete off. Probably he would do it in a tactful way. Or maybe not so tactful.

The sergeant in uniform led him up to the master bedroom, where Daisy lay in bed, a bullet hole in her forehead, her blood soaking the pillow and mattress. There were no casings in sight; either a revolver had been used or the shooter had picked up the ejected shell. Bill moved around the room and took in everything of note, of which there wasn't much more to analyze. The photos of Bill, Daisy, and Amy on the nightstands on either side of the queen-sized bed showed smiling people who appeared to be immune to this kind of tragedy.

He didn't see any bloodstains on the carpets or on the stairs as he followed the sergeant back outside. He saw no bloodstains on the grass, either, as the sergeant led him dutifully to the side yard and showed him where Amy had fallen. She was wearing filmy pink pajamas and had been shot twice in her upper body, one a direct bullet hit to the chest that pierced her right breast, and the other a large bloody exit wound that must have come from a bullet in her back.

Bill had to fight back tears. He had seen many young corpses in Iraq and Afghanistan, and yet he never got over the deaths of those who should have had long lives to live, lives of joy and purpose instead of brutality.

He was also a bit shaken when he saw an old scar on Amy's shoulder that looked like teeth marks. It reminded him of the similar scar on Jodie's forearm, from the bite by Darius Hornsby at age six. Jodie's scar was now less pronounced than Amy's, so Amy's was probably more recent.

Bill came around the side of the house and looked toward Pete, who was watching the coroner's men take Ron Haley's body down from the tree. He walked over as they were zipping up the body bag.

"What do you make of what you saw?" Pete asked sharply, as if giving a pop quiz.

Bill parried with, "Where's the gun? Did you find it?"

"In the garage, on the workbench. A .38 revolver, Smith & Wesson. A six-shot cylinder with three cartridges expended."

"Okay," Bill said. "A revolver is what I figured. He likely shot his wife first, then he went to do his daughter, but she ran out of the house and he had to chase her. Brought her down with a bullet in her back, then finished her off with one to the chest."

"Why did he hang himself?" Pete challenged. "He had three rounds left."

"We'll probably never know the answer to that. People behave in strange ways when they're under extreme duress, and he must've been. Sometimes suicidal people don't think they can pull a trigger on themselves, but hanging only takes an instant of enough gumption to jump off a bench."

Pete's follow-up question was "It looks like Ron Haley was the shooter, but how will we know for sure? Somebody could've strung him up, right? It's been done before."

"Did anybody do a GSR test?" Bill asked. "If not, his hands should've been bagged so they can be tested for gunshot residue at the morgue."

"Already done," said Pete. "Positive for GSR."

He didn't question Bill's deductions on chain of events, so Bill supposed that he agreed with it. Otherwise he'd have picked holes.

Just then they were interrupted by a loud, angry voice, and they turned around and saw Reverend James Carnes storming onto the crime scene and halting behind the yellow tape. "Allow me to do the Lord's work!" he demanded. "The dead will arise unless they are spiked!"

Bill's feeling about people like Reverend Carnes was still that, in the face of something they could not understand, they naturally gravitated toward easy religious or superstitious explanations, like primitive peoples did when they could not understand lightning and thunder, not to mention the many revelations of modern science. In the absence of a cure for the plague, they resorted to prayers, charms, and potions so they wouldn't feel utterly hopeless. The plague was a great boon to Bible thumpers like Reverend Carnes because it was so unfathomable that it *seemed* supernatural. Thus it seemed to validate a belief in gods, devils, angels, and miracles.

The reverend started chanting, "The dead must be spiked! The dead must be spiked!"

Pete sneered at him from behind the crime scene tape and said, "It's been sixteen years, Reverend. Let it go. Get a life."

True, it had been sixteen years since the Chapel Grove outbreak, but many other towns across the United States had been hit since then. The plague was far from being wiped out.

And Reverend Carnes had recently been indicted for conducting a burial service in which a deceased child had been spiked while she lay in her coffin, with the consent of the mother and father.

Eyeing the cross-shaped spikes and the wooden mallet in the bitter, gray-haired cleric's thick fingers, Bill said, "You're already facing charges for this kind of thing, Reverend Carnes. Please turn around and leave peacefully so we won't have to arrest you again."

Carnes shouted a warning. "You are standing in the way of the Lord's work, and you will pay with your immortal souls!" He stepped back from the yellow crime scene tape and began muttering prayers as he eyed Bill and Pete with disdain.

Just then a black van pulled up in the alley that ran past the backyard. The van was spray-painted with silvery satanic symbols and emblazoned with the name of a rock band: DARIUS & THE DEMONS.

"For Christ's sake!" Pete growled. "Just what we need!"

"My sentiments exactly," Bill adamantly agreed.

A dismayed look on his face, Reverend Carnes turned and called out to the blond, handsome, insolent-looking teenager behind the wheel. "What are *you* doing here, Darius?"

"On my way to school. Got a police-band radio in here. Thought I'd stop by and scope out what's goin' on."

"There's death here. Show some respect. Be on your way."

Darius snickered, pointedly eyeing the mallet and spikes that Carnes was wielding. "What's the matter, Reverend? Afraid of another plague?"

"That's exactly what I'm afraid of."

Darius flashed a flippant grin and said, "They're coming to get you, Reverend!" Then he peeled out and sped down the alley.

Pete and Bill shook their heads ruefully. They suspected that Darius Hornsby and his clique of "bad boy" wannabes were behind a rash of break-ins in some of the more upscale neighborhoods of Chapel Grove, and the cops felt it was a matter of time before they would do something worse.

Bill went up to Carnes and asked, "What was that all about, Reverend? You probably know that Darius Hornsby isn't one of our favorite people."

Carnes didn't answer right away. He seemed to be mulling something over. Then he said, "I need to have a word with you. I have some crucial information about the Haleys, and it has to do with that devilish young man."

Bill said, "Don't think you can hit me with unfounded suppositions or biblical revelations. If you want to make a statement that has a foundation in reality, come down to the station."

"I'll do that," Carnes said. "I assure you I'm not your enemy, Detective Curtis. There are ominous things transpiring behind your back."

He gestured for Bill to duck under the crime scene tape and follow him out toward the alley. Then, lowering his voice to a confiding level, he said, "I can tell you how Amy got the ugly scar on her shoulder. Ron and Daisy became good God-fearing folks after they extricated themselves from the clutches of that perverse band they were hooked up with. They returned to Jesus and were reborn. I welcomed them into my congregation. Daisy was a volunteer at my day care center. In return for her help, I enrolled Amy free of charge, and now the poor little girl is dead. The whole family is dead, and I think I know why."

"How did you *know* the whole family was dead?" Bill shot back at him.

"Darius isn't the only one who listens to police calls. Anytime there's a death, I have to try to get permission from family members to pray over the body and make sure it doesn't arise."

"With those damned spikes of yours!"

"You shouldn't disparage the Lord's work, Detective. Don't you believe in God?"

"My beliefs are my own business."

"Well, I can tell you for a fact that when Amy Haley was about four years old, she got into a fight with Darius Hornsby, and he bit her quite hard. Bit her till she bled."

"Did you take her to a doctor?"

"She stopped crying after I put medicinal salve and a gauze bandage on her little shoulder, and Daisy was there and didn't want to make a big fuss over it. She was anxious to be liked by the other parents, including the Hornsbys. I phoned Darius's mother and told her what he had done, and she sighed and dismissed it by saying he was a just a willful child. Spoiled brat was more like it, in my mind. From that time on, I've always felt that there's something wrong with Darius, something congenital. And he's become quite the juvenile delinquent, hasn't he?"

Pete Danko ducked under the crime scene tape and said, "Sure has. Petty theft. Bullying. Vandalism. If I had my way, he'd be in juvenile court, but his old man bails him out every time."

"He's spoiled rotten," said Carnes. "Too much money for his own good. His parents spent a fortune buying him and his snotty friends guitars and drums and weird costumes."

"They let 'em play in bars, too," said Pete. "I heard them once and had to walk out. They made my ears hurt."

"It's the devil's music!" Carnes spat. "They dress up like a bunch of satanists! Darius still comes to my church with his parents, and to my great surprise he has joined my youth group— but I don't welcome him. He's a bad influence. Kids gravitate to him as if he has a mystical hold over them. The Bible tells us about evil spirits, and I'm afraid he's got one inside him. Not just him, but his friends, too."

"Listen, Reverend," Bill told him, "we don't need evil spirits to make us do evil. We come up with plenty of it on our own."

"Too deep for me," Pete said. "I'll see you at the station, Bill. Don't go anywhere without talking with me first."

Bill wondered if he should say, *Yes, master.* But he kept his mouth shut.

Carnes said, "Your boss is a good man. This town is lucky to have him."

Grudgingly, Bill supposed that was true. But he didn't say so.

"Come to my church at seven tonight," Carnes pleaded. "You really need to hear what I have to say. I sense that you, too, are a very good person, Detective Curtis, even though you act like an unbeliever."

"It's not an act," Bill said bluntly.

He really didn't want to give Carnes the time of day, mainly because he didn't believe that religious fanatics had a habit of living in the real world. But his curiosity and sense of duty got the better of him, and he showed up at the so-called Church of

Lazarus Risen that evening, hoping that Carnes actually might have something pertinent to tell him. He sat in one of the pews and listened while the clergyman stripped his soul bare, speaking fervently and breaking into tears. He revealed that after he left the Haleys' home that afternoon, he prostrated himself before the altar and prayed till he felt like he was sweating blood. "I'm under a terrible load of guilt," he told Bill. "I hold myself greatly responsible for what happened to the Haley family."

"Don't be too hard on yourself, Reverend. Nobody made Ron Haley do what he did. He must've been mentally ill."

"No! It was I! I planted the seeds and stood back and let them grow!"

"What exactly do you mean by that?" Bill said, more interested than before.

"It was just three weeks ago," Reverend Carnes said, "that I asked Ron to come to the church, and I conveyed my suspicion that Amy's soul might be unclean. I told him that, as the family's pastor, I had been keeping a close watch over her ever since, as a little girl, she was bitten on her shoulder by Darius Hornsby. Then I asked him to look out for any signs that Amy was in thrall to the Evil One. He denied that any such thing could be happening. But I insisted that in case she might give herself over to Satan, or even if he should have some fear of that inclination taking root, then he and Daisy *must* let me perform a preemptive exorcism, and in the meantime we must all pray for her immortal soul!"

"Look, Reverend," Bill said, "you've let the fear of the plague make you paranoid. You're an intelligent man. If there's a God, and if he's as merciful as you claim, he wouldn't let Satan take over the soul of an innocent child."

"But Satan preys on the vulnerable among us," Carnes said. "There is an eternal battle between God and the devil, and sometimes the devil wins."

"I don't believe in any of that," Bill said.

"I know you don't, but Ron Haley did. What do you think of

this? Just three days before his death, he came to me sobbing that his daughter seemed to be more and more distant from him and his wife. He said that Amy and Daisy used to have fun to- gether, doing things like going shopping or cleaning the house, or going to the movies. But now Amy had changed for the worst. He caught her ripping the pages out of her hymn book and trying to flush them down the toilet, but the toilet got clogged up and he had to call the plumber."

Appalled by these fantastic speculations, Bill Curtis wasn't sure what to say. He knew it wouldn't do him any good to point out to the reverend that the Bible contained much that was worthwhile, but was also riddled with Iron Age superstitions.

Carnes said, "Ron was in extreme anguish, and we both agreed that I would perform an exorcism this coming Sunday. But now, just days before the exorcism would've taken place, the entire family has been wiped out. Ron must have felt it necessary to kill Amy and the demon inside her." He rolled his eyes toward the heavens and pursed his lips tightly, as if questioning his own words. Then tears rolled down his cheeks as he said, "But what if I was wrong? What if the poor little girl wasn't possessed at all, but was suffering from some sort of mental illness?"

Bill wanted to say that it was rather too late in the game for Carnes to have that insight, but it would be cruel to grind it in. The damage had already been done. It was quite plausible that the worm of doubt that the Bible-thumping pastor had planted in Ron Haley's mind indeed had caused Ron to destroy himself, his loving wife, and his cherished little girl. Bill wished that he could console Carnes in some way, but the truth, as he saw it, was that the guilt that Carnes felt on his conscience was well placed. Fa- natical religion was to blame for much of the evil in the world, on and on and down through the centuries, forever and ever, amen.

Meanwhile, Satan got blamed for the evil in the hearts and minds of men.

Most people did not want to face the fact that we're down here on our own, and it's up to us to make the best of it and stop slaughtering one another.

Now our own dead had turned against us. And if the undead were to be cured, or at least defeated, it would be done by rational methods, not by superstition.

CHAPTER 21

The day after the Haleys' murder-suicide, when Bill came home for dinner, Lauren told him that the scar on Jodie's arm was suddenly acting up again. It hadn't bothered her ever since that wonderful day when her allergies had cleared up, but now it was itching and stinging.

Hearing this was like a slap in the face to Bill. Over the years since Jodie was pronounced allergy free and had recovered so much from PTSD, he had dared to cautiously hope that the anguish of the past would stay buried.

He asked Lauren, "Do we still have any of the salve Dr. Miller gave us?"

"It got old, and I threw it out," she said, biting her lip nervously. "The scar is inflamed. Oh, God! Things were going so well! I should've known it wouldn't last."

He hugged her and caressed her face and hair, her tears wetting his own face as he did so. When he stepped back to take off his jacket and put his gun and holster in a locked cabinet, she continued to weep softly, looking utterly dismayed. It made him feel helpless. He said, "Try not to overreact. Maybe the inflammation will go away overnight."

"We're never going to be a normal family!" she wailed. "We're *snakebitten*, no matter how hard we try!"

"Don't freak out. I'll go up and see her."

"She's so upset she wouldn't even talk to me," Lauren said. "I made roast beef and mashed potatoes with gravy, her favorite, but she won't even come down and eat."

With considerable trepidation, he went upstairs to see Jodie. He knew that any hint of an allergic reaction to *anything* might cause her to be hit with a flashback. Might even plunge her back into full-fledged PTSD. *Why* did this have to happen, he asked himself. He was aware that Jodie still carried her EpiPen at all times, just to be safe, but her latest blood and skin tests had continued to astonish her allergist. For the past several years now, she had stopped reacting to substances that used to make her blister. But now Bill was afraid that the sudden burning and itching of that old bite mark was a very bad sign.

Jodie was in bed in her darkened bedroom, and when he quietly opened the door and she saw him silhouetted by the light in the hallway, she cried out, "I *hate* Darius Hornsby! I wish he'd get crushed to death in that silver van of his!"

Bill went to her bedside, saying, "Come on, honey, you don't mean that. He was just a child. He didn't know what he was doing."

Looking down upon her, he felt his love for her aching in his chest. She was so innocently beautiful and feminine, it seemed a travesty that she should be anything less than flawless, in a physical sense. She had her sore arm lying outside of the covers, and in the ambient light Bill could see pus oozing from the remnants of her scar.

"It's all over school what happened to the Haleys," she snapped. "And all the kids know Amy had a scar on her shoulder—and do you know who gave it to her? Darius Hornsby, *that's* who! I *hate* him!"

"It was a long time ago," Bill said. "You were just a little kid."

They both fell silent for a long moment. Then she blurted, "Darius is insufferable! Half the girls in school are hot for him! He acts like he can have any one of us with a snap of his fingers!"

"Well, you don't need to pay attention to him. In fact, I'd prefer if you didn't. He's off to a bad start in life, and who knows where he'll end up."

"Well, I hate him!" Jodie said.

"Your mother said she'll call Dr. Miller," Bill consoled. "I'm sure he'll have something that'll soothe your blister."

"I hope so," said Jodie. "But I doubt it."

He kissed her cheek, then went back downstairs, sat in the kitchen with Lauren, and told her the gist of the conversation between him and Jodie. He tried to sound comforting and not reveal how upset he really was. He somehow had a gut feeling that worse things were about to happen to him and his family, and he was trying to ward it off by reminding himself that he didn't believe in ESP or paranormal glimpses into the future.

Still looking terribly distraught, Lauren said, "I'm glad she still dislikes the Hornsby boy. I still hear lots of bad things about him. I'd like to give him the benefit of the doubt, but I can't. I don't trust him."

"Neither do I," Bill agreed. "He's still a bad boy, but he's older now and can do even more damage. Good thing I'm a cop. I have ways of getting in his face."

The next day, while he was at his desk at the police station, he got a phone call from his wife, and he was surprised that she didn't sound so badly shaken anymore. "Jodie just got back from an appointment with Dr. Miller," she said brightly, "and we both a feel a lot better now. He examined her scar, swabbed it and applied an antibiotic ointment and a gauze bandage, and said there was nothing to worry about."

"Is he sure she's going to be okay?"

"He sounded very confident. He said the scar was just irritated by something. Maybe even just sunlight, or possibly the soap we're using. He said the irritation will go away."

"I'm glad you sound calmer and more at ease, honey."

"Well, Dr. Miller was reassuring. I always feel better when Jodie is under his care."

"I do too."

"It would be so nice if Jodie could get herself on track and you and I could both relax a little. We deserve it. Don't you think so, Bill?"

"I sure do. I love you. I love you both."

That afternoon, he was scheduled to testify in a robbery case, and had to shoulder his way through a throng gathered in front of the courthouse. Reporters and camera crews were covering a large crowd cheering for Reverend Carnes and his lawyer, Bennett Stein, who had appeared on the courthouse steps. It turned out that Carnes had been acquitted of a past charge against him of Mutilating a Corpse.

Appalled by these kinds of goings-on in a supposedly civilized society, Bill looked on as Attorney Stein made a short, lawyerly speech, aimed at convincing the crowd and the reporters, in his words, that "justice was done today and freedom of religion was protected." Then Stein stood back as Carnes ranted, "If we fail to heed the Word of God, the dead will rise again! All sinners must repent! The dead must be spiked to prevent them from arising before Judgment Day!"

Although Carnes and Stein obviously shared the same religious beliefs, in appearance they were a study in contrasts. The reverend was tall and gaunt, with a shock of startlingly thick black hair dotted with gray and pulled into a long ponytail. The lawyer was short, jowly and rotund, with a bad comb-over blowing in the wind, revealing a pink pate. They were both fervent speakers, and Bill could easily see how convincing they could be in the pulpit or in front of the bench, by the sheer force of their impassioned certitude.

He had never been a religious man, even when his life was on the line in Iraq and Afghanistan. He had scoffed at the oft-repeated platitude that "there are no atheists in foxholes." Though he was sarcastic about Reverend Carnes, he couldn't help pitying him for allowing himself to be so tortured by his beliefs. Bill had noticed that there was a segment of the clergy who almost gloated over the plague itself as a true sign of the vengeance of Almighty God, and Carnes seemed to be one of them. Because the dead had been coming back to "life," they thought it was an affirmation of satanic possession. It made them all the more certain that their calling was valid and that their faith rested on solid spiritual ground. They built sermons around the story of Jesus casting out demons. According to the Bible, He had banished them into the bodies of pigs, then drove the pigs into the ocean to drown. Sincerely religious people, as well as the ones that Bill called religionists, prayed that Jesus would come back down to earth and perform a similar miracle to wipe out the plague.

CHAPTER 22

Pete Danko came into Bill Curtis's office, shaking his head in consternation. He said, "Bill, you're not going to believe this. Three bodies have been stolen from Kallen's Funeral Home—the Haley family, Ron, Daisy and Amy. Their autopsies were supposed to take place this morning, but now they're gone."

Bill didn't say anything, just stared at Pete, knowing he wasn't kidding, wasn't making a macabre joke. He wasn't the type.

"I want you to get on this right away," Pete said. "Go over there and push Steve Kallen for any leads he can give you. His daughter Brenda, too. He's been teaching her the business."

"Do you think she could be behind some kind of teenage prank? Her or her friends?"

"At this point, anything's possible. I wouldn't rule out Reverend Carnes or members of his flock. They all think that Jesus wants them to burn the dead, shoot them in the head, or drive spikes into them."

Bill thought it was bad enough being a lawman when the worst you had to deal with were ordinary crimes like robberies, rapes, home invasions, and homicides. Not that they had much high crime in Chapel Grove, which was why he had been able to convince Lauren that if they stayed there his becoming a cop wouldn't be such a dangerous choice. But the plague had changed everything, creating more danger for policemen everywhere, even in the small towns. And the theft of three corpses seemed to fit right into the new reality.

Luckily, he recalled grimly, when the outbreak happened at the Rock 'n' Shock they were able to control it before it went much further. In other localities, when an epidemic had spread rapidly and had run rampant, people had often been in danger not just from the undead but from looters and marauders taking advantage of the breakdown of law and order.

He checked a black-and-white out of the motor pool. It was a sunny morning in mid-July, and as he drove to the funeral home, on the main drag, seven blocks from the police station, he once again marveled at how pleasant and peaceful the town looked, on its surface. Not much had changed since his childhood, except a dollar store had replaced the five-and-ten, and some of the saloons got facelifts. Chelsey's Diner was still flourishing, and Chelsey Turner was much older now, but still working the tables and the counter with the same brisk bustle Bill had known as a youngster on a lunch break from school. As he drove past, it was nine a.m., the early rush was over, and Chelsey was probably distributing place mats, napkins, and silverware, getting ready for the lunch crowd. He had had bacon and eggs there at around seven, and had immersed himself in the good smells of the coffee and the grill and the muted banter of the customers, which would probably never regain its former level of cheerfulness till the threat of the plague was somehow over and done with.

He couldn't look at the streets of the town anymore without remembering friends and acquaintances he would never see again. Mr. Barone, who had owned the hardware store, had sold it to a newcomer and moved to Pittsburgh after his teenage daughter was killed at the Rock 'n' Shock. Bert Swantner, who tended bar at the American Legion, had a son who had worked as an ER nurse and was bitten at the hospital, then had to be dispatched by a member of the SWAT team. He could go on; the list of personal tragedies was a long one, and the town was permeated by muted despair. People didn't go out much anymore, so there weren't as many pedestrians as there used to be in the nine blocks of business section. A shoe store, a clothing store, and a mom-and-pop grocery store were still in business, but several of the folks that he saw going in and out of the post office or the other businesses had either lost a loved one or had come very close to it during the Chapel Grove outbreak.

He parked in front of Kallen's Funeral Home, which was once lived in by a large Italian-American family, the Corrados. There were five brothers and four sisters. He had graduated from Chapel Grove High with Esther Corrado, but all the boys were a couple years older than he, and the sisters, other than Esther, were several grades behind him, so he hadn't hung out with them. When Steve Kallen bought the large brick home with plans of turning it into a mortuary with viewing rooms on the ground floor and an apartment for him and his family on the second floor, all of the Corrados left town.

He got out of the squad car, locked it, then opened the trunk and took out his fingerprint kit so he wouldn't have to come back for it. The funeral home had a large front porch with white banisters and white columns and a beautiful green lawn totally free of dandelions and weeds. Visitation hours for the Haleys, scheduled for tomorrow morning, were posted in a glass frame to the left of the porch. Except now they wouldn't have any visitation hours unless he could somehow recover their bodies. He had the strange, rather unnerving thought that if Carnes and his flock had taken the corpses and spiked them, Steve Kallen would be obliged to use his facial reconstruction skills, employing derma wax and cadaver cosmetics, to make them presentable for a rescheduled viewing.

He didn't know whether he should ring the doorbell or go around to the asphalt driveway in back, where the dead were delivered for autopsies, embalming and cremation. He opted for going up onto the porch and ringing the bell. Steve Kallen opened the door, wearing a dark suit, black tie, and crisp white shirt, his habitual uniform for greeting mourners, but in the face of the bizarre theft this morning, his lugubrious composure had deserted him. "Come in, come in, Bill," he said, "this is terrible." Like most people in town, Bill had shaken hands with Kallen at many, many funerals, but they weren't drinking buddies. "Where can we talk?" he asked, getting right down to business. He took out his ballpoint pen and spiral-ringed notepad and the funeral director said, in his usual hushed voice, "Let's go into my office."

The office was nicely appointed. The oils on three of the walls were scenic pastorals in large gilt frames. Two leather-upholstered armchairs faced the ornately carved oaken desk. The desk blotter was green, and so was the carpet, which looked freshly vacuumed. There was a framed photo of Kallen's daughter on the desk, which showed her to be light-complexioned whereas he was very dark. So maybe she took after her mother, Bill thought, but he had never met her because she passed away before Steve and Brenda had moved here. Sitting in front of the solemn-looking funeral director, he said, "Tell me how you discovered the bodies were missing."

"They were going to be autopsied, and they were still in their body bags last I saw them. I figured that by later today I'd be done working on them, and my handyman, Sam Kent, would help me get the coffins up here and into the viewing room. He's here now. But there's nothing for him to do, unless we quickly re-cover the bodies. I already phoned Ron Haley's mother and let her know what happened. Naturally, she's horribly upset. She's up in years, and it's another very hard blow for her to take."

"When you got to the basement, what exactly did you see?"

"My heart jumped into my throat. All three body bags were gone. And all the doors were locked. No signs of breaking and entering."

"Well, I'll have to take a close look," Bill told him. "Although, if a lockpick was used, I may not be able to spot any evidence of it. Who has keys, besides you?"

"Sam does. And my daughter, Brenda. That's all."

"By any chance, does Sam Kent belong to Reverend Carnes's church?"

"I don't know what church he belongs to or what religion he

practices. In any case, why wouldn't they simply spike the bodies right here in my basement, if that's what you're driving at, instead of carrying them off?"

"What about your daughter?"

"Brenda? We're both Presbyterians, but not sticklers about it. In our business, it helps to be ecumenical. She did join Carnes's youth group, but only because her friends belong to it."

"Do her friends believe all the things that the reverend preaches?" Bill inquired, trying not to sound sarcastic about it. "Spiking the dead, for instance," he added more pointedly.

"I suppose that some of them do, but my daughter definitely isn't a true believer. Like I said, she joined the youth group just for the social aspect."

"Well, I'm going to have to question Sam Kent. And Brenda, too. Not that I suspect them of anything. But it's my job to cover all the bases."

"I'll make them both available," Kallen said.

"First, let's you and I have a look at the crime scene."

They didn't use the elevator, but instead took the stairs down to the basement. Bill pulled latex gloves out of his pocket and put them on before scrutinizing the doors and the locks. There were two windowless garage doors, large enough to accommodate ambulances or hearses, and a side door made of steel, with a deadbolt. He didn't see any scrapes or nicks, so he dusted the doors, the jambs, and the locks for fingerprints, but got only smudges, too blurry for identification purposes. He then dusted all three of the gurneys that had supported the Haleys' body bags, got several legible prints, and used his phone to photograph them. He knew he would have to fingerprint Steve Kallen, Brenda Kallen, and Sam Kent for comparison with the prints he had gotten. He found nothing else of evidentiary value in the basement.

"Where's Sam?" he asked Kallen.

"Still sitting in one of the viewing rooms, unless he went outside for a cigarette."

"I'll find him," Bill said. "I'll talk with him first, then your daughter. She's here, isn't she?"

"In her room. I'll be in my office while you're with Sam. Let me know when to get her down here, and I can buzz her on the intercom. There's a meeting of Carnes's youth group at the church today, but I made Brenda stay home. I knew you'd want to talk to her."

"I want to question Brenda and Sam separately, and in private," Bill said.

Kallen went back into his office and closed the door, and Bill found Sam Kent sitting in the viewing room that had been meant for the Haleys. A lanky, rawboned white man who looked to be in his sixties, Sam had long gray hair pulled back into a ponytail and held together with a rubber band. He was wearing bibbed coveralls and yellow clodhoppers. He smelled like cigarette smoke, and his fingers were brown from nicotine. He looked up when Bill entered, but remained seated on one of the chairs lined against a wall, waiting for the mourners who weren't coming. Three satin-draped pedestals stood at the front of the room, devoid of coffins. Floral arrangements, with sympathy cards attached, surrounded the empty pedestals, emphasizing the creepy feeling Bill got over the fact that the three guests of honor were absent.

Sam Kent said, "I know who you are. You're the Curtis boy. Your parents were Bill and Mary. Do I recollect rightly?"

"Yes. How did you know them?"

"Painted their house for 'em, when you were little. Too little to remember, I guess. You married the Stanski girl, didn't you?"

"Lauren Stanski."

"Uh-huh. I thought so."

This sort of banter was obligatory in Chapel Grove, a kind of ritualized tail-wagging before people would warm up and get down to the business at hand. After Bill figured he must have schmoozed Sam long enough, he asked him if he had any gut feelings about the missing bodies.

"I ain't got no idea who took 'em. If'n I did, I'd tell ya."

"What do you think of Reverend James Carnes?"

"He's a Bible-thumping fool! He drives spikes in people's heads after they're dead. A stupid waste of time! If he did that to my old lady or my daughter, I'd knock all his teeth out, or I'd spike *him!* There's nothin' magical about the plague—it's just a disease that we ain't figgered out yet—like AIDS or cancer. By 'n' by, the scientists'll come up with somethin'. But meanwhile spikin' or burnin' the corpses ain't gonna help. It's only the ones that we *know* are carryin' the germ that need to be put down. If they're just ordinary dead folks that ain't gonna jump back up and bite us, we should bury 'em and leave 'em alone. Leave 'em rot in their graves."

Sam had made some good points, Bill thought. In his rude but pragmatic style, he had cut right to the heart of the matter. He obviously didn't have much formal education, but there was nothing wrong with his intellect. Bill couldn't picture him teaming up with the kind of people who wanted to steal dead bodies.

He went back upstairs to ask Steve Kallen to let him talk to Brenda. Kallen turned his desk over to Bill after buzzing Brenda on the intercom, then left the office after she came in. Bill eyed her for a few minutes in silence, just to put her on edge in case she had anything to hide. In person, her skin was a shade darker than how it appeared in the photograph. Her oval face was framed by shiny black hair down to her shoulders. She had a gleam of insolence in her black eyes and a hint of scorn in her tightly pursed smile.

She sat in front of Bill and he said, "Thanks for talking with me, Brenda. Do you have any idea who could have broken in here?"

"If I did, I'd tell you," she said huffily. "I know the bodies were stolen, but I don't have a clue who did it."

"How did you find out?"

"My father told me. Stealing dead bodies? Why would anyone *do* that?"

"Some people believe in spiking or burning them," Bill said.

"Well, yeah," Brenda said. "But why wouldn't they just spike them right where they found them?"

"Good question," said Bill, "but I don't have the answer yet. I didn't find any indication that the doors or the locks were tampered with. Your father says that, besides him, only you and Sam Kent have keys."

"I never loaned my key to anyone. I can't speak for Sam or my father."

"Is there any chance one of you could have failed to make sure the doors were locked and dead-bolted? Including the doors up here?"

"I wasn't down here last night. I was in my room studying and listening to music. Then I took a shower and went to bed."

"Are you sure? You didn't come back downstairs for any reason?"

"Not that I recall, no."

"I understand you joined Reverend Carnes's youth group. What's that all about, Brenda?"

"Carnes is a cartoon. I only joined his little club so I can hang out with my friends. We smirk and laugh behind his back. But he buys ten pizzas and a bunch of cases of pop for us when we go to his Bible meetings and pretend we're listening to him."

Bill said. "Is there any chance you could have set your purse down at Carnes's church, and somebody could have taken your keys and made copies of them?"

"I suppose anything's possible. I wouldn't put anything past some of the true believers who want to drive spikes in people's heads. That's why I never leave my purse unattended."

Bill decided he'd have to get a list of the members of the Church of Lazarus Risen so he could do background checks. It was conceivable that some of them might have prison records, might even have been sent up for burglaries that involved skillful lock picking—the kind that left no scratch marks. To Bill, the theft of dead bodies seemed less likely to be a teenage prank than the work of religiously deluded adults. Unless the good Reverend Carnes wasn't above using brainwashed kids to help him in his misguided mission.

After fingerprinting Brenda and Steve Kallen in the funeral director's office, Bill got back into the squad car and drove to Carnes's church, which was on a hilly side street, three blocks from the business section. Its gravel parking lot was filled with vehicles, and Bill noticed that Darius Hornsby's garishly decorated silver van was among them. The church proper was over a hundred years old, and he had always admired its beautiful stonework, done by Italian artisans in the early 1900s. He headed for the front doors, but changed direction when he heard voices coming from the cemetery on the far side of the church, opposite the parking lot.

Making his way among the gravestones, he saw that a prayer was being chanted by a group of thirty-odd young people led by Reverend Carnes himself and by his attorney, Bennett Stein, who must be a deacon or something of that sort. Stein's wife, Margaret, was standing next to him. Bill knew her from seeing her with Stein at quite a few fund-raisers and social functions, including the Memorial Day services and picnics held by the American Legion.

Other than the three adults, the prayer group was comprised of teenagers ranging in age from about thirteen to eighteen. Their chant seemed to have been lifted from the King James version of the Old Testament, then modified into an incantation against the Plague of the Living Dead. The final stanza was a direct plea to Saint Lazarus:

> *We beg thee, our dearly beloved patron saint,*
> *To let all these souls rest in peace.*
> *May their bodies turn to dust.*
> *May their bodies never rise again.*
> *May their souls enjoy the bliss of heaven.*
> *May they be bathed in perpetual light.*
> *Forever and ever. Amen.*

Bill wondered why they were reciting a prayer designed to keep their dead and buried parishioners from coming up out of their graves. No such thing had ever happened during any of the plague outbreaks. Only walking, talking people aboveground had been dying, then coming back to life to attack the living.

There were three boys standing shoulder to shoulder with Darius Hornsby, two of them black and one of them white, all with smirks on their faces, aloof from the proceedings. Several badass-looking girls were clustered around them, including Tricia Lopez, a close friend of Bill's daughter, Jodie. He figured that the three boys huddled around Darius must be members of his rock band, and the girls must be groupies. Their openly disdainful attitude seemed like typical adolescent insolence, unwarranted and disdainfully aggravating, but usually harmless unless it led to something worse.

The vast majority of the other kids in the prayer group seemed to piously believe in what they were doing here, and the looks on their faces plus the way they gazed so reverently at their pastor indicated that they were awed to be in his presence. At the end of the prayer Reverend Carnes made the sign of the cross. "In the name of the Father, the Son, and the Holy Ghost. Amen."

Then Bennett Stein said, "All right, boys and girls! I'll see you at next week's youth group meeting."

As the teenagers began to disperse, Margaret Stein called out, "Do your homework! Be good in school! And be good to your parents!"

Bill heard a few snickers as the kids disbanded in groups of three and four and Darius, Kathy, Tricia, and Darius's boy buddies remained clustered together as if joined at the hip. As they shouldered past him with scornful looks on their faces, he wished he could stop them, put some pressure on them, and fire questions at them, but he had no grounds for doing it.

He went up to Carnes and said, "Reverend, may I have a word with you?"

The reverend said, "Surely you're not going to arrest me again?" And he turned toward Attorney Stein for moral support.

Stein put his hand up as if warding Bill off and said, "As his legal counsel, I won't let him answer any questions that might—"

"Don't get your ass in an uproar," Bill barked. "He hasn't been charged with anything, at least not so far. But if I start to think either of you might be obstructing a police investigation, that would be a different matter entirely."

"I know nothing about the bodies missing from Kallen's Funeral Home," Reverend Carnes blurted.

"Well, you've just made it clear that you know *something*," Bill shot back at him. "How did you even find out about it?"

"In Chapel Grove, everybody knows everything."

"Don't say anything further," Stein warned.

Bill said, "I won't take up too much of your time if you'll be truthful with me."

"My husband *always* tells the truth!" Margaret Stein said indignantly. "And so does my pastor! We're *God-fearing* people!"

"I have no doubt of that," Bill said, although inwardly he meant it sarcastically and not as a compliment. Maybe Margaret picked up on that, because she kept working her mouth as if wanting to say something nasty to him. He wished she wouldn't because she had a shrill voice that made his teeth hurt and was in perfect apposition with her garish red dress, red plastic spike-heeled shoes, and gaudy red smears of lipstick and rouge.

Attorney Stein said, "Go ahead and ask your questions, Detective, but I reserve the right to instruct my client not to answer." Turning to his wife, he said, "Margaret, why don't you wait for me in the church till this is over?"

"Surely you won't let him arrest you!" Margaret shrilled. And she shot Bill a distasteful look. Then she huffily stomped out of the cemetery.

He said to Carnes, "I'd like to have a look inside the church, if you don't mind. And in that storage shed over there."

"You'd have to show us a warrant," Attorney Stein said.

"Why?" Bill said. "As long as you have nothing to hide."

"This is police harassment!" Carnes shouted. "We've done nothing wrong!"

"What about your followers?" Bill shot back at him. "You have them in thrall. Perhaps some of them took it upon themselves to do something they thought you'd approve of, even if you didn't tell them to do it. That way you could have plausible denial."

"Oh, I get it!" Carnes scoffed. "We're talking tacit conspiracy here, like when King Henry supposedly implied to his henchmen that he wanted to get rid of the Archbishop of Canterbury!"

"Something like that, but not so grandiose," Bill said. "It's obvious that you've got your people thoroughly indoctrinated."

"I fulfill their spiritual needs," Carnes said. "They've flocked back to the church because they can no longer deny that the supernatural is real. They pray that the dead will not arise."

"Hah!" Bill scoffed. "Do you believe they're alive under the ground? How are they going to break out of their vaults and coffins and push through six feet of hard-packed dirt?"

"The same way they will do it on Judgment Day!" Carnes snapped.

"This interview is over right now!" Bennett Stein declared vehemently. He grabbed Carnes's arm to lead him out of the cemetery, but Carnes shrugged him off and said, "It's all right, Bennett, this detective can't hurt me. The Lord protects me with the power of sanctifying grace."

"You're convinced Jesus is on your side," Bill told him, "so you think you can get away with anything. You and your parishioners with your handy mallets and spikes."

"If you have hard evidence against us, file your charge," Stein said. "Otherwise, get off my client's back."

Carnes said, "What happened to the Haley family was the devil's work. I had nothing to do with it. My advice to you, Detective, is to shed your atheistic ways, get down on your knees, and pray that Almighty God doesn't send the plague down on us all over again."

CHAPTER 23

On the TV in her office at the institute, Dr. Traeger watched intently as a major media event unfolded. Kelly Ann Garfield, the infamous "Pickax Killer" from Texas, was about to be executed. A rowdy crowd was gathered outside the prison walls. An anti-death-penalty gospel singer was belting out "Amazing Grace," while a pro-death-penalty group was chanting, "KILL THE BITCH! KILL THE BITCH!"

Dr. Traeger had followed Kelly Ann's story from the moment she was arrested and all through the trial, as much as she could, while still carrying out her daily responsibilities at the institute and at home with her daughter. In a jealous, vindictive rage fueled by drugs, Kelly Ann had used a pickax to chop up her ex-boyfriend and the girl he was in bed with, and had left the vicious weapon buried in the other girl's chest. At trial, Kelly Ann boasted that each time she penetrated flesh and bone with her heavy weapon, she had an orgasm.

But in prison she claimed she had been born again. She said she was no longer the evil person that she used to be. She was now, in the eyes of many, a saint, a Joan of Arc, who had undergone a divine transformation. Evangelical ministers, movie stars, and even the pope advocated for her. They said that she had been touched by the hand of God and should not now be executed, which would be a travesty. God had chosen her for a divine mission, to save the souls of other death row prisoners by blessing them, hearing their sins, and convincing them to accept Jesus. But the governor of Texas had decided to let God be her final judge, and he allowed her execution to go forward. This was after fourteen years of appeals and stays granted by what Dr. Traeger felt was a stodgy, convolutedly perverse legal system.

She believed in the death penalty and agreed with the governor, and not because she coveted Kelly Ann for her experiments. She had never bought into the preposterous claim that the infamous "Pickax Killer" was no longer the same person who committed those heinous murders. She *was* the same person! Her views may have changed, her personality may have changed, but that did not mean that she should evade responsibility for her past actions. If she were truly enlightened, truly remorseful, she should have willingly gone to her own death. Dr. Traeger would have more strongly believed in the "new" Kelly Ann if she had instructed her lawyers to end her appeals and speed up her execution. Instead she became a centerpiece for the endless debate over capital punishment and whether or not it was a deterrent.

Those who would excuse her and commute her sentence had tirelessly pointed out that she was led into a life of prostitution and drug addiction at the tender age of eleven, and by her own mother. This was, of course, a sad and woeful mitigating factor that was considered with a certain amount of empathy by the judge and jury during the penalty phase of her trial, and for years afterward by higher courts and judges all the way to the Supreme Court. Dr. Traeger agreed with the final decision. She believed that society needed to teach people that, no matter how angry or mistreated they may feel over their lot in life, they must not kill another human being unless their own lives were threatened. But with the added caveat of: *unless it is for a good cause.* For instance, when in warfare against the enemies of one's country. Or, as in Dr. Traeger's own case, when fully authorized to carry out experiments to preserve mankind.

Soon Kelly Ann would be delivered to her, like the others

whose executions had been faked over the years. It would be justice delayed, but in the end still accomplished, after she learned all she could from her.

She had discovered how to stimulate early-onset Alzheimer's by means of injection, and she had this in mind for Kelly Ann Garfield. She wanted to find out if follow-up injections of serum extracted from the brain of an undead specimen would actually delay or stop the slow deterioration of mental acuity in Kelly Ann once she had instigated the dementia in her.

CHAPTER 24

Driving back to the police station in the squad car he had checked out of the motor pool, Bill Curtis radioed ahead and asked to speak with Captain Danko. "Gone already," the desk sergeant said. "I think he was gonna grab some restaurant chow on his way home."

"Okay, thanks," Bill said.

He pulled over to the curb when he spotted Pete's black Mercedes parked in front of Chelsey's Diner. It was past six o'clock, he was tired and frustrated after spending all day on the case of the missing bodies, and he was going to be late getting home. Lauren would probably have something ready for him to microwave. He thought he remembered her saying something about roast beef and mashed potatoes. Good. It'd be his excuse for not spending any more time with his boss than he really needed to.

Pete looked up at him as he entered, and motioned for him to have a seat in his booth.

"You going to have anything?" Pete asked.

"Just coffee. Lauren cooked."

Pete was working on a plate of Chelsey's beloved Southern fried chicken and potato salad, which made Bill almost sorry he wasn't going to eat there. Chelsey, as pleasantly plump and cheerful as ever, came over with an order pad and poised pen, and he told her he just wanted some coffee with sugar and cream. "Piece

of my wonderful coconut cream pie?" she teased, and with re-
grets he had to tell her no.

When she went away, Pete said, "Tell me what brings you
here."

"The case isn't going well. I don't have any leads, just a few
suspicions."

"Did you speak with Steve Kallen?"

"Of course."

"His daughter?"

"Yep."

"Sam Kent, his handyman?"

"Again, yep."

"Don't be smart with me, Lieutenant."

"I wasn't trying to be."

"Then be careful how you speak to me."

"Yes, sir."

Bill wanted to bite his tongue when he had to kowtow that
way. It should've gone without saying that he would have done
all the things Pete had grilled him on. He wasn't an incompetent,
and for about the umpteenth time he resented being treated that
way. To forestall any more derogatory questions, he told Danko,
"I've already been to the so-called Church of Lazarus Risen.
What a name for it! Carnes and his lawyer clammed up on me.
I'd like to obtain a search warrant for the church, the toolshed in
the cemetery, the tractor shed, Carnes's house, and any other
place we can think of where they could hide three coffins."

"You're barking up the wrong tree," Danko said.

"Why?"

"The good reverend is already under our watchful eye. And
he's not a fool. If he commits another offense, he's looking at jail
time."

"I think his fanaticism gets in the way of his good judgment,"
Bill said.

"Be that as it may, no judge is going to give us a search warrant
without probable cause."

"I think we already have probable cause. His past history."

"Inadmissible."

"Are you sure?"

"I don't speak unless I'm certain of what I'm saying."

"I thought that maybe because of your position, you could pull some strings. Don't you play golf with a judge or two?"

"I do, and that's why I can't push for special favors. It wouldn't look right. It could get me fired, or it could get a judge impeached."

"My other possible suspects are Darius Hornsby and his groupies," Bill revealed. "But I've got no evidence."

"Right. So don't grasp at straws," Pete said.

"I'm going to get surveillance footage from the different places around town that have mounted cameras," Bill said. "Just to see if any of them recorded Darius's bizarre silver van bopping around in the right time frame. The funeral home doesn't have surveillance. I already checked."

"That would make it too easy," Pete said.

"Yeah, I wonder why Kallen doesn't at least have a camera above that steel door in back."

"Probably because nobody is going to want to steal corpses."

"Well, not before now," Bill said.

"Don't go making a pain in the ass of yourself with the merchants around here. Don't bug them and get them all upset just to collect a bushel full of surveillance videos. The Chamber of Commerce will get on my ass."

"Point well taken," Bill said, rather than arguing. "It bothers me that Darius Hornsby and his hangers-on would join Carnes's youth group. They seem like the kind of snots who would make fun of religion, not buy into it."

"The plague has got everybody in town scared shitless," Danko said. "Even our rebellious teenagers."

"Yeah, I guess so," said Bill. "See you tomorrow."

"Hang in here for a minute. I want to ask you something."

Bill sat back and waited. It would be unusual for his boss to ask his opinion on anything that much mattered.

"Do you know much about the history of the first plague outbreaks here in America?" Pete asked.

"The first one happened way before I was born, but I've read up on it and watched old news footage and documentaries."

"If you recall, they experimented on some of the undead back then," Pete said.

"That was before those kinds of experiments were made illegal, thanks to religious protest groups, mostly right-to-lifers. Their argument was that the undead were still human and could not be treated like lab animals."

"In other words, they could not be operated on against their will," said Pete.

"Right. That was the gist of it. The AMA fought it, but the law was upheld by the Supreme Court."

"What do you think of that ruling?" Pete asked.

"I tend to think that the experiments should've been allowed to continue. I believe in stem cell research and all other forms of scientific enquiry, within ethical boundaries. I would be against potentially damaging or life-threatening experiments upon live human beings. But the plague victims *are* technically dead. *Un*-dead, but still animated somehow—we just don't understand how. Whatever we can learn from them might lead to a cure."

"I agree," said Pete. "And I would call that an enlightened attitude."

"Like I've told you before, I'm against ignorant people who always want to put barriers against scientific advancement."

"Again, an enlightened attitude," said Pete. "You can go now. I was curious about what you might say."

Getting up from the booth, Bill said, "See you tomorrow, boss. I'm going home and microwaving my dinner."

Pete said, "Tell your wife I said hello."

After Bill left, Pete considered whether Bill's "enlightened attitude," if patiently stroked and groomed, might actually make him a good candidate for recruitment by Homeland Security. Although Bill seemed to harbor some vague suspicions about the official explanation for the outbreak in Chapel Grove, he was at heart a pragmatist. It might be rather easy to make him see the light and keep his mouth shut. If not, well, there were always quicker and more decisive ways to get rid of the problem.

Three years ago, when Pete first took over as chief of police in Chapel Grove, he had resisted his instinct to get rid of Bill Curtis and replace him with someone who was ex-CIA, like himself. But Colonel Spence and Major Thurston didn't want the kind of shake-up that would alarm the community, so it was decided that Bill Curtis and most of his fellow officers would have to stay on the force. Any of them, including Bill Curtis, could be eliminated in a timely manner, if the need should arise. In the meantime, Pete had to keep tabs on fluctuations in their thoughts, habits, and behavior patterns so he could determine when and if he must get rid of them.

Pete also kept a watchful eye on the mayor, the town councilmen, and other notable citizens such as doctors, lawyers, and educators. He couldn't allow anything to fester under the surface and erupt in a calamity.

He thought about what Bill had said about the kids in Reverend Carnes's youth group, and he wondered if Bill's so-called "gut feelings" were somehow on the mark. Knowing that Darius and a couple of the others were adoptees from the Foster Project, Pete wondered if, by some stretch of the imagination, they were actually behind the theft of the dead bodies from Kallen's Funeral Home. Perhaps they were now true believers in Carnes's crackpot rants. Maybe they were as pliable and gullible as most other teenagers and if so, perhaps that nutty preacher had actually succeeded in brainwashing them.

Pete got Dr. Traeger on his secure line and told her about the theft of the dead bodies, then asked her, "Do you think an old fart like Carnes could become some kind of guru for the special children?"

"You mean like that Heaven's Gate cult leader who got all his followers to suffocate themselves so they could be transported to an alternate universe ruled by Jesus?"

"Something like that, yes."

"I think our special children really *are* special intellectually and psychologically. They're too aloof and independent to blindly follow anyone."

"You don't think they'd steal dead bodies? Or help Carnes spike and burn them?"

"Absolutely not. What would be the point? My studies of them have not shown them to be cannibalistic in any way. Their mothers weren't either. They didn't get a chance to be, even though they were attacked and bitten by carriers of the disease."

"That makes sense," Pete said.

But after he got off the phone he wondered if the special children really might be behind the theft and disposal of the dead bodies, and if so, might it not be a good sign instead of a bad one? It might indicate that they must have a normal *revulsion* toward death, instead of an affinity for it, even though what they were doing was foolish and unnecessary.

CHAPTER 25

For the first three days after Kelly Ann's "execution," Dr. Traeger followed the institute's policy concerning the handling of death row inmates who were sent to her. A nurse and an orderly were delegated to take care of all of the murderess's needs and get her adjusted to her new surroundings. They understood that they were to give vague answers to any of Kelly Ann's questions about where she was, how she got there, and why she was not dead. She was allowed to think that she was in an ordinary hospital. She was told that her death by lethal injection had failed and she had been reprieved—which was a semblance of the truth. Her reprieve would not last very long, but she did not need to know that.

At her bedside in a hospital-like recovery room at the institute, Dr. Traeger took notes on her laptop while also digitally recording Kelly Ann's initial diagnostic interview. She wanted to learn all she could about the patient's psychological complexities and how they had evolved. She needed to understand how past history and behavior might affect a person's transformation into one of the undead. Would a poor wounded soul like Kelly Ann, who had already killed two human beings in a horrible fit of passion, carry some of her deadly inclinations forward into the strange, flesh-hungry "new life" she would live after she became trans-

formed? In other words, would she be harboring a powerful innate urge to utterly destroy, not just devour, those whose living
flesh she was bound to crave?

Kelly Ann was wearing the institute's standard white hospital
gown, a blandly baggy garment that made her look petite, almost
childlike. The skin of her face, arms, and lower legs still retained
prison pallor, yet there was a freshness and even, surprisingly, a
wholesomeness about her. Her dark brown hair was worn in
bangs cropped above a clear, smooth forehead, and the pigtails
on either side of her head were tied with red ribbons, one of the
braids longer than the other by an inch or so, probably due to a
shaggily chopped institutional haircut.

In this first interview, Dr. Traeger pretended that she knew
nothing about the crimes that had caused Kelly Ann to be condemned. She wanted candidness, not reticence. She made it
clear that no matter what thoughts or secrets might be divulged
to her, she would never be judgmental. She didn't want to make
Kelly Ann feel like a specimen under the prying lens of a microscope.

Dr. Traeger had a medical degree; her focus was on psychiatry.
She had honed her penetrating knowledge of the human psyche
on the condemned prisoners who had previously been delivered
into her custody. She needed to be perceived by Kelly Ann as a
compassionate medical doctor, not as an interrogator, and she was
relieved when Kelly Ann soon seemed greatly comforted and put
at ease by that deftly contrived misperception. She opened up in
much the same way as she had done with the many others who
had been swayed by her when she was on death row, and she
talked freely and without overt malice about her cruel upbringing, her sexual exploitation by her stepfather with her mother's
collusion, her abandonment by those two cretins, the sordid relationships that followed, including two failed marriages, and her
descent into drugs, alcohol, and prostitution. She spoke with
what seemed to be unblemished honesty, and Dr. Traeger was
prone to conclude that her anger over what had been done to her,
and her drive for vengeance, must have been softened by the

gradual self-awareness that had come over her during her long, torturous years of incarceration.

Kelly Ann asked, rather timidly, in her soft Southern accent, "So, Dr. Traeger, now that you know all about me, does it make you hate me?"

"No, no, quite the opposite," she replied gently.

She couldn't help thinking that in spite of her previous skepticism, perhaps she should not have been so cynical about Kelly Ann's conversion and her motives. It seemed that she actually believed that she had "found God." Dr. Traeger knew that her belief was delusional, brought on by her desperation and intense fear of the death chamber, yet Traeger could see that these terrifying factors had probably instigated a true epiphany. The young woman had a beatific glow about her. It was the sort of glow that lights up the faces of saints, martyrs, and charismatic cult leaders.

Still, Dr. Traeger was aware that she must preserve scientific detachment. The evil rages that Kelly Ann had been capable of in her wretched past, coupled with the transcendence of her conversion, contributed to an aura, a mystique, that made her seem not only mysterious but enthralling. But Dr. Traeger knew that she must retain her objectivity. She could not permit herself to be charmed in the way that Kelly Ann had charmed the movie stars, the clergymen, the pro bono lawyers, the smitten mass of supporters who had advocated for her, fervently believing that she should not have gotten the death penalty. While her case was intriguing and even fascinating, perhaps motivating Dr. Traeger to keep her alive longer than she had most others, still the final outcome would be unpleasant.

In a tremulous voice, as the interview was nearly ended, Kelly Ann asked, "Will my reprieve last? I hope so, but God's will be done. I've put myself in His hands."

Dr. Traeger didn't blame Kelly Ann for not trusting the bureaucracy that had strapped her onto a gurney. In prison, she was allowed to read newspapers and magazines with the parts that the officials did not want her to see blacked out, but there was one long-running story that probably should have been redacted, but was not, and she felt that they wanted to torment her with it and that's why they had left it intact. The article told of a condemned man in Oklahoma whose lethal injection went horribly wrong, and he writhed and screamed while the executioners were desperately trying to kill him for over an hour of excruciating agony. The poisons were dissolving his blood vessels and internal organs without making him die, but the executioners kept upping the dosages till he convulsed for the final time, bleeding from every orifice.

Kelly Ann asked why the state of Texas hadn't carried on with her own failed execution in the same relentless manner. Dr. Traeger said that the public outcry over the botched procedure and horrible death of the condemned man in Oklahoma had caused the Texas governor to decide that she deserved to be spared.

"What's going to happen to me?" Kelly Ann asked anxiously. "Am I going to be sent back to prison?"

Dr. Traeger had to give her an answer that was a combination of truth mixed with palatable lies, and she told herself it was the humane thing to do. "No, you are not going back to prison, you might even be paroled, if I recommend it. Your case history is quite valuable to me, from a psychiatric standpoint. I've been commissioned by the federal government to find out why people perpetrate horrible crimes, and even more so, why many of them seem capable of being rehabilitated."

"Do you believe I've been rehabilitated?" Kelly Ann asked hopefully.

"I don't know for sure yet," Dr. Traeger told her.

She blanched at having to be so deceptive, but there was no other way. Although she had to lie, her lies were merciful ones. Kelly Ann would never know that the other death row inmates who were sent to the institute, like the serial killer Carl Landry, were selected within a matter of days or weeks either to be experimented upon, or else to become sustenance for some of the patients who required further study. It was an unfortunate but necessary protocol, and Dr. Traeger had to steel herself to carry it out.

CHAPTER 26

Tricia Lopez hated her father because he was different. Chapel Grove was a white-bread community, and he didn't fit in. Like many adolescents, Tricia didn't want to be different in the eyes of her friends. None of them had immigrant fathers. Umberto was born in Cuba and spoke with a Cuban accent. He was always trying to get Tricia to learn Spanish as a second language, from the time she was little. But she didn't want to be different, like him.

Not really wanting to take part in family doings, Tricia was reclining in a lounge chair in her bikini, her body already oiled with suntan lotion, listening to rock music funneled into her earphones, and eyeing her father snidely through her amber sunglasses as he grilled hot dogs on the patio. He was wearing denim cutoffs, his belly bulging over his waistline, where a belt would have been if he had worn one. Tricia thought that even his feet were too chubby for their rubber thongs. He had an olive tan, but she thought, contemptuously, that his Cuban skin would've been brown even without sun exposure.

She glanced at her mother, who was finished setting the picnic table with paper plates and plastic knives, forks, and spoons. Hilda turned toward Bert when he said, "We should move back to Miami before summer's out so Tricia can start the new school year there. She'll love it—the ocean, the beach. Look how much she loves to sunbathe."

"But I don't want to move again," Hilda said.

Neither did Tricia. She hated how her father flat-out said what she would love or not love without asking her opinion. He persisted, bringing up the subject of her baby brother to try to bolster his side of the argument. "Listen, Hilda, when Emilio gets bigger, he can play baseball year-round when we're living in Florida. I almost made the minor leagues. Maybe he inherited my skills. He probably did, as a matter of fact. He might make the majors if he can practice all the time as he grows up."

That's nothing but a pipe dream! Tricia thought to herself. *You're trying to relive your youthful ambitions, and making us suffer for it.*

"But Umberto," Hilda said, "I love it here in Chapel Grove. I really do. And we haven't had another attack here, since that one sixteen years ago. I don't think lightning is going to strike twice in this town."

Tricia snapped, "Can't you call him Bert instead of Umberto? It at least makes him *sound* American."

"He's as American as you are," Hilda snapped back. "He has his citizenship papers, and he had to study hard for them. He knows what this country is all about—better than you do."

"Hmph! Just because I don't like history class. Who cares about that ancient stuff?"

"*You* should care about it, Little Miss Smarty-Pants!"

"Who says so?"

"I say so!"

Tricia glowered at her mother, her mouth pinched tight but her angry eyes hidden behind her amber sunglasses.

Hilda said, "I don't think I could ever go back to Miami now, Umberto. They have to fear the plague, just like everyplace else, but they also have those terrible hurricanes. And we're comfortable here, honey. Tricia has close friends, and she doesn't want to leave them. I think we should stay here at least till she graduates from high school."

"But that's two more years!" Umberto said. "By that time, I

might get downsized. My company is offering me a transfer with higher commissions. I can't just sit still and wait for the worst to happen. I've got to be proactive."

Hilda came closer to him and whispered, "But what about the papers we signed?"

But Tricia overheard, and although she didn't understand what her mother was referring to, it sounded like something fishy that involved her, or else why would she be whispering? Her ears perked up and she listened keenly.

"Red tape," Umberto whispered to his wife. "She's grown up enough now. I don't think they can hold us to anything we signed."

Angry that she couldn't comprehend what her parents were being so hush-hush about, Tricia got up in a huff and started across the lawn.

"Where are you going, dear?" Hilda called out. "Food's almost on the table."

"My hands are yucky from suntan lotion. I have to wash them."

She let herself in through the sliding glass door, but she didn't really need to wash her hands. She had lied about it. She sneaked into her father's little office and extracted a tiny key from under the leatherette corner of his desk blotter. Then she rummaged in the back of a file drawer, and got his pistol. She took it into her bedroom and hid it in her dresser, inside some frilly undergarments.

CHAPTER 27

Dr. Traeger went to Kelly Ann Garfield's room and found her sitting up in bed eating her lunch from a tray. "This is much better than the usual hospital food," she remarked. "Better than prison food by far."

"We do our best here," Dr. Traeger said with a slight smile, and was gratified when Kelly Ann smiled back at her, in spite of what she had to keep hidden about the young killer's fate and her own part in it. She had the power of life and death over Kelly Ann, true enough, but Kelly Ann had a certain glow about her that drew her in, which she hated to admit, because she liked to consider herself superior to all the others who had been hoodwinked or co-opted. She told herself that Kelly Ann's magnetism was born of her deep, single-minded passion for a God that did not really exist. And yet she was finding herself far from immune to the sad young woman's beatific aura. She knew that psychopaths believed so strongly in their delusions that they could overwhelm others with them and gain their belief as well. Perhaps that explained why so many people had not wanted Kelly Ann to be put to death.

Ever since the death of her husband, Daniel, and because of the alienation between her and Kathy, Dr. Traeger felt deprived of emotional and intellectual companionship. Of course, she could never share *anything* about what actually went on at the institute with her own daughter. Ruefully, she told herself that if Kathy could only appreciate how important and how dedicated her mother was, perhaps their relationship would improve by leaps and bounds. But this was doomed to never happen because of the dictates of utmost secrecy. Dr. Traeger had few ways to share and celebrate her achievements in the laboratory except in the dry letters and reports that she routinely submitted to Colonel Spence and her other overseers at HSD. This was especially galling at this very moment, because during the previous night, working late, she had confirmed a startling new breakthrough. She was bursting to tell it to *someone,* but she knew she must restrain herself. She wished she could share it with Kelly Ann, if with no one else right now. Kelly Ann was bright enough and intuitive enough to understand it but would not be able to go out into the world and blab.

So excited was Dr. Traeger about her newest discovery that she had almost opened up about it to Pete Danko, who did not deserve to be the first to know, and in her judgment was too obtuse to fully appreciate it. He was an enforcer, a bully, not a highly sensitive and deeply introspective human being. He was a walking advertisement for the observation by Socrates that "the unexamined life is almost not worth living." His level of intellectual passion was so dull that he had to kill and torture people in order to feel fully alive. He might even deride Dr. Traeger for being so thrilled that she could barely contain herself.

Her excitement derived from her late-night discovery of how the dead could become reanimated in spite of the fact that they did not have any blood circulation! Somehow their brains and nervous systems had been rendered active, while their circulatory systems had not. Their blood had been coagulated in their veins and arteries. But their brains and nervous systems were still alive, or at least partly so. This was remindful of a phenomenon exhibited by male quadriplegics: that they can still achieve erections and have sexual intercourse even though their bodies are inert, "dead" so to speak, from the neck down.

For a long time it had been well known in medical circles that the part of the nervous system that operates the sex organs is separate from the operations of the spinal column. In the case of the undead, the brain and the nerves were working, and also the digestive system that fed the nerves, without needing to rely on nutrients conveyed to the nerves by human blood. This seemed contradictory, even difficult to believe, but nevertheless it was so. That was the amazing thing that Dr. Traeger's latest experiments had proven! And solving its perplexities was a task that loomed excitingly before her, giving her a multitude of avenues to explore.

As Kelly Ann ate her lunch, Dr. Traeger questioned her about her teen years, how she had spent them on the streets, how she had managed to survive in her sordid world of drugs, sex, and prostitution, and how she felt about those things right now. She recorded the girl's responses on her digital recorder and took backup notes on a secure laptop. None of Kelly Ann's stories of her past life embarrassed her, and she was able to talk quite freely. She had come to terms with her ordeal and all its inequities and terrors. And so it struck Dr. Traeger that if Kelly Ann had never been through any of that, if she had had a decent upbringing, the kind of upbringing that Dr. Traeger was trying to give to her own daughter, who actually resented her for it, then Kelly Ann would have likely turned out to be a delightful human being. A young woman whom any mother would be proud of.

It occurred to Dr. Traeger, with a degree of wistfulness, that if her own life had followed the pattern that used to be considered normal for any young woman, she would not have waited till she was forty-three to get married, and would not have wed a man so much older. She would likely have been in her mid-twenties when she gave birth to her first child. And if that had happened, she would have had a biological daughter who by now would have been close to Kelly Ann's age—instead of a girl who was *not* biologically her own and seemed to hate her.

Kelly Ann put her tray on the bedside table and said, "Excuse me, I have to pee."

Then, as she tried to get up, her left foot caught in the thin white blanket, and she almost fell back onto the bed, but Dr. Traeger caught her. For a moment, they were so close their faces were only inches apart, and Dr. Traeger couldn't help herself— she kissed Kelly Ann lightly on her cheek. Kelly Ann pulled away, regained her footing, and stared at Dr. Traeger, who was already reproaching herself for her impulsive act.

"I was raped by a prison guard the first time I got arrested for prostitution," Kelly Ann said. "I don't want that to happen again anywhere, even here. I'd much rather be dead."

She turned away and went into the bathroom, and Dr. Traeger crept out of the room, ashamed that she had momentarily broken the boundary between patient and scientist and that it had been mistaken for a sexual advance, rather than a motherly impulse. She reminded herself of how wicked Kelly Ann used to be and perhaps could be again, under the right circumstances. Keeping herself mindful of this would help her to rein in her feelings. She knew that she must not feel any unusual warmth for this killer or ex-killer, however one wanted to look at it, because in the end it must come to nothing.

CHAPTER 28

Tricia's father was going over some of his clients' insurance documents when she came into his office at around midnight. "What are you doing up, honey?" he asked. "Are you thirsty? Want a glass of milk to make you sleep?"

She closed his office door and bolted it, then gave him one of her most angelic smiles. Smiling back at her, he said, "What's up, Tricia? Why lock my door? You got a secret to tell me?"

"I don't want to leave Chapel Grove, Daddy. And you're right, I have a secret reason. If you close your eyes, I'll whisper it in your ear."

"But you'll get used to a new place. You'll learn to love Miami. Don't you want to be closer to your grandmother?"

"Close your eyes, Daddy, and I'll whisper my secret."

He shrugged, then smiled again, closing his eyes and leaning his right ear toward her.

She eased his pistol out from under her nightgown and placed it against his temple.

His eyes came open when he felt the cold barrel—but before he could do anything, she pulled the trigger. It was only a little .22 and it didn't make a whole lot of noise. But the impact jerked him sideways and he slumped over.

She looked around, listening, in case her mother had been

jarred awake. She heard nothing, not even cries from her baby brother. Hopefully, she would be able to tend to him before she went back to bed.

She used the edge of her nightgown to wipe her prints from her father's pistol, then pressed it into his right hand and let it drop from his limp fingers onto the floor.

She slid open the top middle drawer of his desk and put the insurance documents he had been examining back in there. She was proud she had thought of it. If he were intending to kill himself, he wouldn't be looking over stuff like that, and the police would have probably tumbled to such a mistake.

The house was still nice and quiet. Good. She had time to creep into the nursery and smother her baby brother with a pillow. If she were lucky, the police would either think that her father killed himself because of grief over finding his treasured little son dead, or that *he* might have killed Emilio, before shooting himself in the head.

CHAPTER 29

Detective Bill Curtis had to choke back tears, looking down at the lifeless little baby in his crib. Nobody should have to see a thing like that, he thought, least of all a parent. Hilda Lopez was in the living room, sobbing her heart out. Poor little Emilio. Only seven months old, and he would never get to be a toddler, a pre-teen, or a teenager. He was survived by his mother and his sister, but not his father. Umberto had taken his own life while his wife and daughter slept.

Bill had to wonder, *Did he do it after finding his baby boy dead? Or did he do it because he was in some way responsible for his child's death?*

He realized how lucky he and Lauren were that their own child had made it through the perils of infancy. He remembered how they had so many times stood lovingly arm in arm over Jodie in her crib, after they brought her home from the hospital.

Choking back sobs, Hilda Lopez followed Bill from the nursery across the hall into Umberto's little home office. It contained a desk, a chair, a computer, some bookshelves, and not much else. Umberto had been Bill's insurance agent, a one-man operation. Bill and Lauren had bought auto and homeowner's insurance through him because he had been a member of Bill's American Legion post and had made a sales pitch at one of the monthly meetings.

Umberto was slumped in the chair behind his small desk, his right arm dangling down, a gun lying on the dark brown carpet, almost directly under his fingertips. There was a small bloody hole in his right temple. Bill felt his neck for a pulse, not expecting to find one, and was surprised when he did. It was so faint that he had to check two or three times—but for sure he felt it, it was not his imagination. "He's alive!" he urgently told Hilda.

She said, "Thank God!"

"Wait in the kitchen. This office is too small for the ambulance guys to do their job."

She reached out and touched Umberto on his forehead, where there was a sheen of sweat, then she backed out of the room. Bill radioed for an ambulance. Then he took latex gloves out of his pocket and put them on so he could pick the gun up and examine it. Just as he stooped down, Pete Danko peeked in. "He's clinging to life, still breathing," Bill said. "It looks like he may have found the baby dead, and couldn't take it."

"Be careful not to disturb anything."

"I know how to handle a death scene, Pete."

Pete shot Bill a sharp look, and Bill figured a scolding might come later, back at the station.

"You stay in the living room and wait for the EMS and the coroner," Pete ordered. "I'll question Mrs. Lopez."

"Should I collect the gun and bag it?"

"No, I'll do it. Leave me alone with Mrs. Lopez, in the kitchen. Who else is in the house?"

"She said her daughter Tricia is in her bedroom. She must've slept through it all."

"Well, get her up. I'll talk to her after I finish with her mother."

As usual, he was taking charge as if he had to or Bill might screw it up. Bill resented being treated like a rookie. He resolved to have a talk with Pete at the station as soon as he could. He was tired putting up with his crap.

There was a room with the door closed down the hall from the nursery, which he assumed to be Tricia's bedroom, so he tapped lightly on the door. Nobody answered, so he tapped again. Then he heard a young girl's voice, muffled by sleepiness. "Mom, leave me alone, I don't want any breakfast."

"I'm not your mom," Bill said through the door. "I'm a policeman. You have to get up."

"What the hell's going on?" she blurted.

Another snotty teenager. Bill was getting pretty tired of what seemed to be an epidemic of adolescent churlishness. He said, "Something bad has happened, and we need to talk with you about it."

"Oh, all right," she mumbled.

She came out of her room tugging a blue robe around her flannel pajamas. She didn't look as sleepy as she had sounded. She had a pretty face, but her hair was spiky and dyed purple, and there was a barbed-wire tattoo on her neck.

"Have a seat in the living room," Bill told her. "I'll stay with you while Captain Danko is talking with your mother."

She sat on the couch and Bill sat on an armchair. She seemed to be wide awake now, but laid her head back and closed her eyes as if doing some hard thinking. She didn't ask Bill what he was doing there or what was going on. Did she already know? Or did she simply not care?

He said, "I'm sorry to have to tell you this, but your baby brother has died. And your father is badly hurt. It looks like he tried to kill himself."

She sat up. Her eyes flickered, and she bit her lip. "Tried? How? Is he still alive?"

Bill thought, or maybe imagined, that he sensed something insincere about her. As with Brenda Kallen.

He said, "Apparently, he shot himself. But he's still breathing. An ambulance is on the way."

"Did he shoot himself with his own gun?"

So far she hadn't asked any questions about poor little Emilio.

"I suppose it's his own gun," Bill told her. "Do you know where he kept it?"

"In his file cabinet. Locked up. He showed it to me once. It's a little pistol. A .22 revolver."

"Did you ever fire it?"

"No, he wouldn't let me touch it, even when he showed it to me. Aren't you Jodie Curtis's father?"

"Yes."

"I like her a lot. We eat lunch together, in the cafeteria."

"That's nice. She didn't used to have many friends. Don't you want to know about the baby?"

"You already said he's dead. Did my father kill him?"

"It seems to be a crib death. Natural causes. But we'll have to do an autopsy."

"Will that tell us for sure?"

She seemed to hang on Bill's answer. Or, again, was that his imagination?

He said, "Sometimes a crib death is hard to diagnose. Even for doctors. They don't know all the causes."

"I hope my daddy recovers," she said.

But he didn't feel much emotion behind her words.

Pete Danko brought Hilda Lopez into the living room and asked Tricia to come with him into the kitchen.

"What about GSR?" Bill asked, figuring that neither mother nor daughter would know he was talking about gunshot residue testing.

Pete mulled it over. They both knew that proper procedure would be to swab the hands of everyone in the house, except for the baby.

Bill said to Pete, coaxingly, "We can do it quickly. I have my kit in the car."

Then they heard doors slamming outside and footsteps headed for the front porch.

"Yeah, let's do it," Pete said. "Hurry up and swab Umberto, too, before they put him in the ambulance."

When Bill turned around, Tricia wasn't there. She had gone into the kitchen already. And he could hear water running in the sink. It was too late to stop her from washing her hands.

CHAPTER 30

When Pete Danko came to the institute to tell Dr. Traeger about the crib death and the attempted suicide at the Lopez home, she was thrown into a quandary. What could have gone amiss? Was it possible that something was seriously wrong with the children, something that modern methods could not detect? She had to allow for that, because science presently had its inadequacies, or else the plague would already be cured.

Pete said, "Gunshot residue tests were performed on all three, the mother, the daughter, and the father. His hands were swabbed before he was taken to the hospital. All three tests were negative."

"Are those kinds of forensic tests completely reliable?" Dr. Traeger asked.

"Not one hundred percent, but close to it. GSR seems to indicate that Umberto Lopez did not shoot himself. That leaves Hilda or Tricia as potential suspects."

"Tricia was one of our special children!"

"I know. That's why I'm here."

"Do you think she tried to kill her father?"

"Maybe. It's quite possible that she killed the baby, too, by suffocation. The ME has listed the cause of death as undetermined. That's a common ruling in crib deaths. Hilda says she found Emilio lying face down."

"That's how SIDS babies usually die," said Dr. Traeger. "They have trouble breathing unless they're lying on their sides or on their backs. Whether they died by intent or by accident often can't be medically proven. It can be almost a perfect crime. It doesn't sound like you're ready to charge anybody."

"Not unless I can get Hilda or Tricia to confess or rat each other out. They could be in collusion. There's a $250,000 insurance policy that Umberto Lopez's company provides to all its agents, and unlike most policies it pays out in the event of death by suicide."

"Is it likely that Hilda or Tricia would've known that?"

"Probably Hilda. And maybe Tricia, if she's devious enough."

"I hate to tell you, but I think my own daughter, Kathy, could be that devious. And she and Tricia are close friends. Almost *too* close. They're more secretive than normal teenagers."

"Maybe if I put pressure on Tricia I could squeeze the truth out of her," Danko said. "But maybe the truth is exactly what it looks like on the surface. Umberto found the baby dead and was so traumatized by it that he tried to take his own life. Hilda said he doted on having a son. Tricia was even a little jealous about it."

"And jealousy is a powerful motive."

"Yes. But if I find out she's guilty and arrest her, and she goes to trial, the public outcry will be tremendous. I'll have reporters all over me. Things could go from bad to worse. If it comes to light that Tricia was adopted and that the names of the birth parents are fictitious, then everything we're doing here could come unglued. What the Homeland Security Department is engaged in could be exposed."

"Surely HSD could stop any reporters from gaining access to the adoption certificate," Dr. Traeger said.

"I suppose they could. In fact I know they could. But not for long. There's such a thing as the Freedom of Information Act."

Dr. Traeger said, "Sometimes freedom of the press is a curse more than a blessing. We *need* secrecy sometimes in order to *preserve* democracy, and the rabble rousers don't want to realize that."

"I think I'm just going to do my best to let the ME's ruling stand," Pete said. "Cause of death will remain undetermined for the Lopez baby. If Umberto comes out of his coma, maybe he'll tell us who shot him, whether it was himself or someone else. Until then, his condition can help me stall. I'll just maintain that we don't have enough evidence to go forward."

"Any chance of him regaining consciousness anytime soon? What do his doctors say?"

"They say it could happen. He has a small-caliber bullet in his brain, but it didn't fragment very much. Some people have lived a long time like that. The brain heals itself and they're able to go on, apparently without any adverse effects."

"But if he dies, wouldn't it be a lot easier to table the investigation?"

"Yeah. Detective Curtis doesn't feel that way. He says Tricia hustled into the kitchen and scrubbed her hands as soon as she heard us mention a GSR test. He's probably right. But he has to take orders from me, whether he likes it or not."

"He puts me on edge," Dr. Traeger said. "He's too nosy, too inquisitive, and frankly too damned smart. I hope you can continue to keep a tight rein on him."

Pete eyed her sharply, then said, "Now back to another subject. Your daughter, Kathy. Did she ever bite anybody?"

"When she was little?"

"Yes. Did she ever bite Amy Haley, for instance?"

"I don't think so. But I don't know for sure. I do know that Darius Hornsby bit Jodie Curtis when they were both around six years old."

Pete said, "I wish you would have done the autopsy on Amy Haley, instead of the Chapel Grove medical examiner. We should have had her bodily fluids and organs tested and kept the results under our control, and now it's too late unless we find her missing body."

"As far as I know, Kathy has never had a biting habit."

"Well, there was a bite mark on Amy Haley, and the ME noted it in his autopsy report."

"I don't have any idea who did it," Dr. Traeger told him. "I wish I did. I'll try to tactfully ask Kathy about it. But she doesn't confide in me. Not one bit, if she can help it."

"Just like Tricia Lopez," Pete said. "Bill said he couldn't get anything much out of her, and he's a pretty good interrogator. Not as good as me, though. I know how to shake people up. Maybe I should try with Kathy."

"Teenagers typically don't trust adults," Dr. Traeger said, "and our special children are even worse in that regard. Yet thus far they all test normal in every way, and that gives me comfort. I'm constantly monitoring them. If anything changes, I'll let you know ASAP, and I'll expedite a report to HSD."

"I'll let Kathy slide for now," said Pete. "If I came out and asked her if she ever bit anybody, she'd just look at me like I'm crazy and clam up." With a sly smirk, he said, "If she weren't your daughter, I'd torture her." Then he waited for Dr. Traeger's reaction, which came at him immediately, almost before his words were out of his mouth.

"Don't you dare! I'd kill you or die trying!"

"I wouldn't expect any less of you," he said. "But I was only jerking your chain. Let's keep as tight a watch on her as we can. Maybe she'll slip up, if she's doing anything wrong, and we'll learn something."

"This is exactly why I wanted funding for the Foster Project to continue," Dr. Traeger complained. "But Colonel Spence said that nothing really unusual had been discovered about the special children, therefore a further investment of substantial funds would be wasteful. I thought it was very shortsighted on their part, but HSD wouldn't budge. They said it made sense to close out the project because nothing has shown them that the kids are anything but normal."

"Well, maybe the powers that be were right for a change," Danko said. "Regular kids sometimes commit murders, even patricide and matricide, so in a way it's as normal as anything else in this crazy fucked-up world."

CHAPTER 31

Detective Bill Curtis had a gut feeling that the theft of the Haleys' dead bodies and the murder-suicide, or whatever it was, at the Lopezes' home were somehow interconnected. Why, he asked himself, did all these strange goings-on have teenagers either at the center of them or else tangentially involved?

Things had definitely gotten weirder in Chapel Grove, ever since the outbreak at the Rock 'n' Shock sixteen years ago. Ordinarily, police work was tough enough, but the Plague of the Living Dead had thrown so much fear and confusion into the mix that it was hard to know which end was up. To make matters even worse, Pete Danko seemed unwilling to take certain investigations as far as they ought to go. Either he yanked cases away from Bill and handled them himself, or he stopped Bill from going after things that Bill badly wanted to pursue. Bill had to ask himself why. And what might Dr. Traeger have to do with it? What did she know that she wasn't saying? Was she hiding something or not?

Bill was still bugged by the way events had unfolded, beginning with the theft of the contaminated needles. The official explanation of the contamination had seemed fishy to him, and at the time he would have tried harder to unearth more facts, but first he had had to face the immediate urgency of vanquishing the undead and then, in the aftermath, the desperate struggle to rebuild some semblance of normality in his town and in his own life while he and Lauren were about to have their first child. In any case, he'd had nobody to back him up, least of all Pete Danko, who was acting, then and now, more like a barrier than a facilitator.

He was nagged by thoughts of how he had been sent to sign out a patrol car while Pete dealt with Jamie Dugan on his own, without any witnesses except maybe Dr. Traeger. What had happened to Jamie after he confessed to causing infected hypodermic needles to get into the hands of the Hateful Dead? How much might Dr. Traeger know about Jamie's ultimate fate?

Were all these questions part of the same puzzle or not?

First and foremost, Bill needed to protect his own daughter, and more and more it seemed that the circumstances surrounding her were nebulous and perhaps dangerous. If Tricia Lopez had anything to do with the deaths of her baby brother, then Jodie should not be hanging out with Tricia or any of that girl's friends. Especially Darius Hornsby. The boy had been in trouble from grade school on up. He was suspected of much more than anyone could prove. But somehow he always managed to skate.

Bill figured he had to risk trying to interview Dr. Traeger again, even though he might get himself fired or demoted. She had been nice to him that other time, sixteen years ago, but then she had ratted him out to Pete Danko. He mulled it over for a couple of days, then took action and phoned her. Just like before, she readily agreed to see him. Once again they met in her office at the institute, and he hoped that she had mellowed over the years and would not turn on him.

Sitting in front of her desk, the same one of gray steel that he remembered, he began by saying, "Look, Doctor, I'm going to level with you. The chief doesn't know I'm here, and I hope you won't tell him. I just want to clear up some things. The Haley family needs closure."

With a wry smile she said, "I know their bodies are missing. Surely you don't think I had a hand in it? Like the grave robbers in an old Boris Karloff movie?"

"I wouldn't know," Bill said. "I'm not big on fictional horror when I have the everyday kind to deal with."

"We do sometimes use cadavers for medical purposes," Dr. Traeger said. "But we obtain them through proper channels."

"Well, here's what I'm wondering about," Bill said. "That fellow Jamie Dugan, do you know what happened to him?"

"Why would you worry about that after all these years, Detective?" she said with what sounded like genuine surprise.

Bill said, "There are so many things that seem off-kilter. Things I can't explain, can't get to the bottom of. And it's been going on for a long time."

"It's the plague. Fear makes people do strange things. Nothing is normal anymore, and won't be, until I can find a way to eradicate it."

"Can you tell me more about your research methods? Is there any chance that those stolen needles got infected right here at the institute?"

"No chance at all. I told you and Pete Danko the truth, and I told the truth in my press conferences as well."

"But it's exactly what you might say if you were doing something illegal here. Or if not strictly illegal, perhaps controversial."

"No comment."

"Does Pete Danko know more than I do?"

"Again, no comment."

"Why are you stonewalling me, Dr. Traeger?"

"This interview is over. And if you don't leave right this moment, I won't uphold my promise not to tell on you."

She whipped out her cell phone as if it were a weapon she could use against him.

He said, "You might have all the education, all the smarts and apparent sophistication in the world, but I suspect that you're more immoral and unprincipled than you let on."

For a long moment he enjoyed the shocked and flustered look on her face. Then he got up and left her office, certain that she'd be talking to Pete Danko before he even got out of the building.

CHAPTER 32

Pete Danko took the call from Dr. Traeger on his secure line, and she recounted her conversation with Bill Curtis, making sure not to leave out any salient details.

He said, "I hoped it wouldn't come to this, but we're going to have to eliminate him. Why did you even agree to meet with him? That was unwise, Doctor."

There was menace in his tone, and she got the hint that she herself might easily be eliminated along with Danko's lieutenant. Her mouth went dry and she was stunned to silence.

Danko filled the void with more menace. "You should have let me know he was coming there. We could have dealt with him right on the premises. Don't you still have some hungry ones in the cages?"

"Yes, a half dozen."

"Al Capone's boys used to rub people out and feed them to the pigs. They kept a hog farm about a hundred miles from Chicago, for that precise purpose. You already have quote-unquote patients, human garbage disposals, who can serve that same function for us."

"Maybe I can lure him back here by telling him I'm ready to cooperate."

"No, he might see through that."

"Then what are we to do?"

"I'll have to stage something at an advantageous time and make it believable. I'm not going to dress him down, like I did once before when he tried to pick your brain. I'll let him believe you never even talked to me. But I'll be biding my time for a proper shot at him."

"You're going to literally shoot him?"

"I don't think you really want to know."

"You're right, I don't," she said, and terminated the call.

CHAPTER 33

Even with the new tube of salve Dr. Miller gave Jodie, that stupid scar on her arm was still itchy. She tried not to scratch it when she was with her brand-new friends, Brenda Kallen and Kathy Traeger. Fleeing from a hot day in the classrooms of Chapel Grove High School they were wearing their school uniforms: tartan skirts, starched white blouses, and "sensible" black laced-up shoes; it was the dress code, and they hated it. Kathy hated it the most and was even more rebellious than Brenda, and on days when she wasn't going straight home after school but was going to hang out somewhere, like maybe the Play Room where they played video games, or the Snack Shack where they hung out and eyed the boys, she would duck into the ladies' room at the school and change into a T-shirt and jeans that she kept in her book bag.

As the girls bounded down Chapel Grove High's long flight of concrete steps, Jodie's arm was *so* itchy that she *had* to scratch it through the bandage, even though she didn't want to. Brenda and Kathy smirked at each other when they saw her doing it. She blanched at that. She always felt way inferior to them, even though they were only about a year older. They seemed more worldly, more sophisticated than she could ever be. No wonder! They had grown up free of the threat of anaphylactic shock, free of the bother and worry of having to carry an EpiPen every single day of their lives.

Jodie kept scratching even though Dr. Miller had told her not to. Her arm kept itching insanely. She wished she could rip the bandage off and really go at it, even if she made herself bleed. She almost swore at Brenda and Kathy when she saw them exchanging smirks, as if they somehow knew why she couldn't stop scratching and weren't about to tell me her reason.

"Hey! Wait up!" someone called out as they scampered the rest of the way down the steps onto the broad sidewalk. They stopped and turned. It was Tricia Lopez. She hustled to catch up with them. Then she winked at Brenda and Kathy when she saw Jodie scratching and said, "*We* know what that's all about, *don't* we!" Then the three of them giggled and smirked as if they knew more about what Jodie was going through than *she* did. It irked her that they seemed to delight in their superior knowledge while keeping her in the dark.

Brenda said, "Jodie, are you coming to the Honor Society meeting tomorrow after school?"

"I don't know. I was going to. But I don't feel well right now. I hope I'll feel better by tomorrow."

Tricia looked at her and said, "Arm's itchy, huh?"

Kathy said, "Prob'ly running a fever too, girl. You look flushed."

"Yeah, I feel hot all over," Jodie admitted, failing to suppress a shudder. "I've got the chills, too. Sometimes my old scar itches like mad, and other times it feels like it's on fire."

"Oh-oh!' Brenda said. "You're gonna start . . . *you* know." She winked and giggled.

Jodie said, "You're kidding!"

Tricia said, "Uh-uh, Jodie honey."

Kathy chimed in with, "Well, you're *old* enough, aren't you? Relax! You're entering womanhood, as my dad would say. Better late than never."

Jodie said, "If *that's* what it is, why would it make my *arm* itch?"

This made them laugh, and she was actually glad. She thought that if they got a kick out of her wisecracks it'd make them like her more. She desperately wanted them to like her, and it mostly seemed like they did, but she wasn't absolutely sure of it.

"When I got *my* period," Kathy said, "bright lights really bothered my eyes, even my skin. I felt like I was itching and burning all over. But it went away after a few days. My dad gave me some medicine. I know you go to Dr. Miller. What did he give you?"

"Some kind of salve. But it doesn't seem to help much. It feels like it's *festering*."

Kathy said, "Tell your mom to call my mom at the institute. She'll give you a prescription that'll really help. At least I think she will."

"How's *your* father doing?" Brenda asked Tricia.

"He's still on life support," Tricia said, with a snort. "He was going to make me and my mom move to Florida, and now we won't have to."

"Why would he want to do *that?*" Brenda said. "All your best friends are *here!*"

She stopped and stared at Tricia, her hands on her hips. As usual, she wasn't carrying any school books, and neither were Kathy or Tricia. Kathy didn't even have her book bag with her, the one that she hid a T-shirt and jeans in.

"Hey, Jodie," Kathy said. "Why don't you friend me on Facebook?"

"I'm not on it."

"You're *not?* You have a computer—what do you use it for, just schoolwork?"

"Well, that and playing games and stuff. My dad doesn't want me on it all the time. And he keeps warning me about predators. What can you expect? He's a cop."

"Booo!" Brenda moaned. "He's on your back all the time?"

"No, that's my mother," said Jodie.

"What about Facebook?" Kathy asked. "Can you friend me there? Or if not, can I friend you?"

"I don't have Facebook."

Brenda said, "You're out of it, girl!"

"You've gotta get on Facebook and Twitter," Tricia said. "I'll show you how. Your mother and father can't stop you. Just don't let them know."

"They're afraid it might interfere with my grades."

Jodie's three gal pals always got good grades without studying much, and Jodie got good grades too, but she had to study more than they did. She liked being on the honor roll right along with them. They got called the Four Aces by some of their classmates. When Jodie told that to her dad, trying to make him proud of her, he said there used to be a singing group by that name back in the fifties and sixties. That was way before even *he* was born, so Jodie didn't know how he even knew about it, except he used to listen to a radio station that played old-time music, because he was into history a lot, even the history of music.

Tricia said, "Sometimes parents need help doing the right thing. Like on the Florida move. I wasn't about to leave my BFFs!"

"Every now and then a blind pig gets an acorn," Kathy said.

They all laughed.

Tricia said, "The bullet is still in his brain. Didn't kill him, but made him a vegetable. In my humble opinion he'd be better off dead."

"Gosh, don't you *like* your father?" Jodie exclaimed. "You talk about him as if he's a stranger."

Tricia said, "Well, I guess I'm still kinda in shock . . . numbed out . . . it doesn't seem real to me. I was lying on a beach towel in my bikini, and my mom was putting paper plates, napkins, and stuff on the picnic table, and my dad was grilling hot dogs. I thought I must've heard him wrong when he dropped the bomb about how we were moving to Miami in time for the next school year! My mom said she loves it here in Chapel Grove and she wasn't in favor of leaving, so I thought that'd be the end of it. But it wasn't. My dad said his company was transferring him and he would be getting a promotion, and he had to take it. He said Emilio would grow up in a nice warm climate where he could play baseball year-round. My dad played minor league ball, but he got hurt and never made it to the big leagues, and he had fantasies of my little brother living out his dream for him."

Kathy said, "How could he know that your baby brother wouldn't want to be a teacher or a scientist or something?"

"Yeah, that's what *I* thought," said Tricia. "Anyhow, my dad's pipe dreams went up in smoke ... unless he comes out of his coma without any brain damage."

A horn honked as they reached the next corner, and Darius Hornsby pulled over to the curb in his silver van with all the satanic symbols on it. He yelled for Tricia to come over to him, and they talked, out of earshot, while Jodie stood on the sidewalk with Kathy and Brenda. All of a sudden Darius flashed her a smile—at least she thought he did because for a split second he seemed to be looking right at her. She saw his dimples, and felt her face turn red. The arrogant snob! He was so damned sure of himself, so terribly handsome and cool—and she despised him! She started fidgeting and scratched at her bandage, even though she didn't want to.

Tricia called out, "Darius wants to take me to the hospital to see my dad!"

Brenda and Kathy nodded at her, and then she got into the van and waved good-bye.

To her surprise, Jodie suddenly felt jealous of Tricia for being with Darius, even though Darius wasn't her boyfriend or anything.

CHAPTER 34

The next morning, when Bill Curtis came into the station, Pete Danko informed him that Umberto Lopez had died in the ICU without regaining consciousness. He said, "It pretty much puts the kibosh on any further investigation, Bill. I assume you agree."

It was rare for Bill to be asked if he agreed or disagreed on any of his boss's decisions concerning the disposition of cases. So he was taken aback a little. "We could hammer on the wife and the daughter," he suggested. "But I believed Hilda when she said she was in bed. As for the daughter, she's a hard nut to crack."

"You suspect *Tricia* of something?" Pete said, with a sharp look.

"Just uneasy about her," Bill parried, "but I can't say exactly why."

"Don't hit me with any crappy hunches," Pete said. "This is the scientific age, remember? Fingerprints, saliva samples, DNA."

"We don't have any of that," Bill said. "We only know that we have a dead father and a dead baby."

"There's nowhere else to go with it. So, case closed, conversation over," Pete concluded.

And he walked down the hall to his own office and closed the door.

Bill mulled over the fact that there had now been three strange deaths that Pete didn't seem all that interested in pursuing: the fall down the stairs of Daniel Traeger, what looked to be a suicide by Bert Lopez, plus the apparent crib death of his baby son. Furthermore, the Traeger case involved a girl of seventeen, Traeger's daughter Kathy; and the Lopez case involved a girl of sixteen, Tricia. But the true extent of their involvement seemed unknowable.

Bill had found out that Kathy Traeger and Tricia Lopez had been close friends as far back as grade school. And they both hung out with Brenda Kallen, who may have had something to do with the bodies of the Haley family going missing from her father's funeral home. But again, Bill couldn't prove it. So far, he hadn't found the missing bodies, and he didn't even know who else to question about them or where to go next.

He wished he could get a warrant for Tricia's, Kathy's, and Brenda's cell phone records so a police department techie could examine them and triangulate the towers that the phones might have pinged off of, on the night the bodies were stolen. But he didn't really have sufficient grounds for such a warrant. He clung to a vague hope that if the corpses had been dumped somewhere, maybe somebody would stumble upon them and call it in.

CHAPTER 35

Darius Hornsby was driving his silver van emblazoned with satanic symbols and the name of his band. Riding with him were Brenda Kallen, Tricia Lopez, and two teenage boys, Ben Kerr and Hank Lawson, both African-Americans, who were members of Darius & the Demons.

Ben was Brenda's boyfriend, and her father didn't know it; he would've disapproved of the long dreadlocks coiled like snakes all over the boy's head. The other boy had an Afro so huge it made his head look small. The kids were chattering away and messing with their smartphones, taking photos of one another and playing Internet games like Candy Crush Saga, except for Darius, who had a penetratingly thoughtful look on his face as he kept glancing in the rearview mirror. Finally, he turned the volume down on a Slayer song blaring on the radio and said, "Tricia, why would your mother be following us?"

"No clue," Tricia said.

"Better not mess where she don't belong," Ben Kerr said with a snicker.

Darius didn't think it was likely that Hilda would suspect them of anything. In his estimation, the woman wasn't particularly bright. Besides, how could she have figured out, on her own, what he and Tricia had done at the hospital?

They had made sure they looked like two nice, normal teenagers when they had stopped at the nurses' station. He was purposely wearing plain jeans and a plain T-shirt, and Tricia was still coming off like a girl fresh from school, in her tartan skirt and white blouse.

He hung back with an appearance of shyness as Tricia asked, "May we see my dad, Bert Lopez? He's in the intensive care unit."

"Only for a few minutes," the kindly gray-haired nurse said, "and only one of you at a time."

"We understand," said Tricia. "I just want to pat his hand and say a prayer."

"Me too," said Darius.

"Aren't you a cute young man," said the nurse. "You'll have the ladies head over heels when you get a little older, if you don't already. Mr. Lopez is in room 312."

Darius and Tricia smiled sweetly, then went down the hall. Outside the room, they stopped and whispered as they peeped in on Tricia's helpless father.

"I have the syringe," Darius said. "Lucky my mom is diabetic."

He took a hypodermic out of his pocket and unwrapped the clean white handkerchief that he had padded it with.

"Wouldn't poison of some kind work better?" Tricia asked.

"They'd find it if there's an autopsy. I'm gonna inject a tiny little air bubble. When it goes to his heart it'll work just like a blood clot. He'll flatline."

"Cool."

They went into the hospital room and hovered over Umberto, listening to the bleeps of the life-support system.

"Just a little bubble, Daddy," Tricia said to her father, getting off on the irony. "A tiny bubble, that's all. A tiny bubble to put you to rest."

It had worked like a charm. But right now it seemed that Tricia's mother was being too damned nosy.

"Your mom has been behind us ever since we left town," Darius said. "I've been watching her in the rearview mirror. That's her in the black Lexus, right?"

"Yeah, that's what she drives," said Tricia. "You saw her face, right?"

"Caught a glimpse," he told her.

Ben said, "Cool."

Hank said, "Floor it—let's lose her."

"It might be more fun not to," Darius said slyly. "Know what I mean?"

Ben said, "Yeah . . . cool."

Hank said, "Too much, man."

Tricia said, "She's been on my case more than ever now that my father isn't around. I think she might suspect something. I'm glad she had him cremated so he can never be exhumed."

Darius said, "We did her a big favor. She didn't have to wait forever and ever to collect the insurance money. Half a million—and if *she* dies . . ."

"I inherit," said Tricia.

The kids all laughed.

Hank said, "Don't worry, we'll help you spend it."

And Ben said, "Way cool."

The kids laughed again.

Darius pulled the van off the two-lane rural road onto a narrow one of dirt and gravel. After a mile or so, he parked in front of an old, dilapidated barn.

Chatting and laughing as if they weren't aware of anyone following them, the kids piled out of the van and entered the barn through a warped door that was hanging sideways on its rusty hinges.

Hilda gave them a few minutes. Then she got out of her Lexus and, to avoid the noise of the door slamming, she only eased it partway closed. She crept up to the rickety side door. The kids hadn't bothered to shut it, just left it hanging. She listened for whatever she might hear. It was strangely silent in there, for a bunch of kids fooling around, doing something, but she couldn't guess what. She moved toward the doorway and peered into the darkness within, but couldn't make anything out.

What the hell were they doing in there? Something sexual? Something weird?

Summoning her resolve to find out, she cautiously stepped inside. She told herself that she was an adult and they were only kids and she shouldn't be afraid to confront them.

A match was struck, a candle lit.

She gasped and nearly jumped out of her skin when she saw Darius sitting on a hay bale, staring at her. Smiling calmly, he said, "Hello, Mrs. Lopez."

"What are you up to?" she demanded. "Drugs? Booze? *What?* Where's my daughter? I saw her come in here. I think you're a bad influence."

Suddenly Tricia piped up. "I'm over here, Mom."

Hilda blinked her eyes, trying to peer into the deeper darkness. She finally made out an area with a bit of light from yet another lantern—and she moved toward it.

Tricia called, "Over here, Mom."

And a boy's voice said, "We're *all* over here, Mommy."

"Stop playing games with me!" she shrilled. "I swear I'll ground you for a month, Tricia! You're all juvenile delinquents as far as I'm concerned."

Another unseen boy said, "Well, you're an *adult* delinquent as far as we're concerned!"

The kids erupted in mocking laughter—but she couldn't quite see them. They were hiding in the murky darkness.

Then another match was struck and a third lantern was lit, casting spooky shadows. Now Hilda could see her daughter, Tricia, sitting on something, between two boys. Their laughter sounded incredibly evil, and Hilda angrily zeroed in on her own daughter. "Tricia, come on, you're coming home with me!"

"No, I'm not, Mom," Tricia said with utter calmness.

All of her friends brayed with laughter.

"Stay awhile," Darius said. "Have a seat, Mrs. Lopez."

"I certainly will not!" she snapped. "You kids are all hopped up on something, aren't you? Tell me the truth, Tricia!"

Tricia said, "We *are* telling you the truth, Mom. Look! Don't you want to see Ron and Daisy and Amy?"

Darius said, "They're *hungry* to see you, Mrs. Lopez."

"Come forth! Come forth!" Darius called into the darkness—and three shadowy forms shambled out into the lantern-lit area, and Hilda backed away, a scream lodged in her throat.

The three corpses—Ron, Daisy, and Amy Haley—were reanimated now, complete with the wounds and disfigurements that accompanied their deaths. They were wearing the clothing that they died in. Ron's face was bloated and purple, and Hilda could see rope burns above the collar of his shirt. Amy and Daisy both looked a little closer to how they had looked in life, due to the fact that their faces hadn't been shot and the bullet holes in their bodies were concealed by their clothes.

Darius had been wise to the fact that he had to get their bodies out of the funeral home before they were autopsied. He had not wanted the medical examiner or anyone else to see the wounds, the puncture marks, that would have revealed that Ron and Daisy had been bitten by their own daughter, Amy, who early in her childhood had been bitten by Darius and thereby set up to transform when she reached puberty. Which she now never would do. Having been killed by bullets, her ability to become a blood seeker had been aborted. Now she could only be one of the nearly brainless undead. Amy had bitten her parents while they were asleep in their bed. Thus she had revealed to them the terrible evil inside her. That was the truest and deepest reason why Ron had killed himself and his family.

Darius had wanted to get the Haleys out of Kallen's Funeral Home before their bodies could be undressed and washed. Kallen would have seen the bite marks from their daughter, even though much healing had taken place.

Luckily, it had taken them quite a while to revive as zombies—because of the severity of their mortal wounds. Also, Darius had taken the precaution of giving Brenda Kallen a syringe full of morphine, and she had injected them with it in the funeral home basement to keep them inert and looking dead until they could be allowed to transform.

Now, in their fully undead state, they shuffled toward Hilda, hissing and salivating.

She screamed at the top of her lungs.

The kids chuckled.

Tricia smiled in delighted anticipation as her mother looked at her imploringly and backed away from the three advancing zombies.

Hilda screamed again and started to run, but Darius tripped her by reaching out with the tines of a pitchfork.

Now that she was down on the ground, trying to crawl away, the three Haley zombies closed in on Hilda, rasping and drooling ravenously.

The kids' laughter became louder and more demonic as they watched her being torn apart.

Tricia started shooting video with her cell phone.

Darius said, "Way cool, babe!"

CHAPTER 36

Detective Bill Curtis went to Chapel Grove Hospital to see what he could find out about Umberto Lopez's death. He spoke with the gray-haired nurse who manned the station outside of the ICU wing. She told him, "Yes, such a pity. His daughter loves him so. She and her boyfriend, I think he was her boyfriend, came to see him in the afternoon on the very day he died."

"Was the boy's name Darius Hornsby?"

"Yes, so polite and handsome. I sort of know him because we've treated his mother here."

"How did Tricia act that day?"

"I felt so sorry for her, and I could tell Darius did too. She was very concerned about her father. She wanted to visit him and say some prayers, even though he was in a coma, and I let them both spend a brief time in the ICU."

Prayers? Bill asked himself. He had spent enough time with Tricia to be pretty sure she wasn't the praying type. It seemed she was in Reverend Carnes's youth group only for the social aspect. Same with a bunch of the other kids.

"What did Umberto's doctor say about cause of death?" he asked the nurse.

"He suffered a myocardial infarction."

"What is it and what causes it?" asked Bill.

"Basically, it's a heart attack caused by a blocked artery. There are two large arteries that deliver oxygen-bearing blood to the heart muscle, and if either one is suddenly blocked, the heart will be starved of oxygen, and that's what we call 'cardiac ischemia.' Unfortunately, if that condition lasts too long, the heart tissue dies."

"I know that cholesterol deposits can cause blockage," said Bill. "But are there any other causes?"

"There's something doctors call 'silent ischemia,' which is a sporadic interruption of blood flow. It's called silent because it's pain free, and we don't know why. It can be detected by ECG, and Umberto had that test, and it was negative. He wasn't a diabetic, either, and we know that people with diabetes often have episodes of silent ischemia."

"So, if he wasn't diabetic and he had a normal electrocardiogram, what else might you suspect?" Bill probed.

The nurse thought for a while, then said, somewhat reluctantly, it seemed to Bill, "For instance, if someone screws up and gets an air bubble into an injection."

"You mean it could be a hospital accident?" he said with some incredulity.

"Yes, or it could be on purpose. That's what I hate to admit, because a case five years ago brought disgrace to my profession. Too many elderly patients were dying in a hospital in Miami, and eventually it was discovered that a male nurse was murdering them by injecting them with air bubbles. He confessed to forty-three murders. The authorities believe he might've done even more."

"There was an old murder trial we studied at the police academy," Bill said. "Claus von Bulow, the husband of a wealthy heiress, was accused of killing her with an insulin overdose, but he was acquitted after a hung jury and a second trial."

"Sometimes diabetics do that to themselves by accident," said the nurse. "But there have also been people charged and convicted for using insulin as their murder weapon."

"Were Umberto Lopez's insulin levels checked during autopsy?" Bill asked.

"No, because there was no autopsy. His wife didn't want one, and his doctors didn't think it was imperative. They felt that he wasn't ever going to regain consciousness, so his death was merciful in its way and spared his wife from having to make the terrible decision to end life support."

"She or Tricia aren't diabetic?" asked Bill.

"No, neither one."

"You mentioned that you treated Darius Hornsby's mother here. Do you mind telling me what for?"

"I'm afraid that would violate patient confidentiality."

"Even to tell me if she's diabetic or not?"

"You'd have to ask her son or her husband, or else obtain a subpoena for the hospital to release her medical records. That's the only way the hospital wouldn't be exposing itself to a lawsuit."

"I don't have sufficient grounds for that," Bill said. "I'd just like to know, if she used hypodermics, who else might've had regular access to them?"

"If she did have any in the house, and I said 'if,' I imagine it would be her husband or her son," the nurse said with an intentionally coy look on her face. And Bill caught the hint. He was pretty sure she was telegraphing the answer to what he wanted to know.

The thought that a child may have committed not only a homicide but a patricide on his watch and in his own community sickened Bill. As mean as *his* father was, he'd never thought of killing him, except maybe if he had to defend his mother. From about ages nine to fourteen, he used to sleep with his hunting knife under his pillow. He was that scared. A hell of a way to grow up. And a wonder that he made it without any long-lasting hang-ups, as far as he knew.

When he was little, there were times when his mother would run away and not take him with her, and he wouldn't see her for several weeks, not knowing if she were alive or dead. His father would be sickeningly nice to him and give him his loose change and make him say what a "good daddy" he was. If Bill asked about Mommy, his father would say, "Don't worry, she'll be back." But Bill thought she may have killed herself. Then finally she'd come back one fine day, and he'd hug and kiss her, and his father would treat them both a lot better for a while, till his next binge and her next beating. He ruined every Christmas. He'd fly into a rage every time he had to put the tree up. He'd curse Bill's mother for buying a tree that shed needles. Then he'd work himself into a fit, scream at her and beat her up, and she would throw stuff into a suitcase and run out the door.

Now that all of it was in the past, Bill looked back on himself as a kid and saw the pathos in some of the things he resorted to. When he was in the fifth grade and knew how to use a hammer and nails, he'd go to where they sold Christmas trees, gather up fallen branches, and take them home and nail them to a wooden broomstick, making his own "tree" and standing it up by putting the end of it into a toy bucket full of rocks. He'd make paper decorations and color them, or pick broken ones out of the garbage and hang them on the branches. Then he'd spread a white cloth underneath and place his toy cars and stuff on it. It was his way of having his very own tree without any fights over it. As a kid, he wasn't aware of how sad and pathetic it all was, but later, as an adult, he came to realize it.

Through it all, he loved his parents in spite of their faults and in spite of the misery they had caused to him and to each other. He was terrified of losing them, by accident or by their own hand. He could never have wished them dead and certainly could not have done anything to harm them. But it seemed, even though he couldn't prove it, that something of that nature might have occurred in the Lopez household.

Families had always and forever been besieged by terrible problems and insidious evils, all the way to the beginning of time. The Plague of the Living Dead was only the latest horrible manifestation.

Because of his tormented childhood, Bill Curtis had always

hungered for a normal and loving family. He remained committed to that goal and hoped he would always keep striving toward
it, in spite of his wife's deep-seated anxieties and his daughter's
trials and tribulations. All of it weighed heavily upon his psyche.
But he was not only a staunch former soldier and a dedicated lawman, but also a person who would not give up in the face of the
many challenges that life could throw at him. He was determined
to love his wife, stand by his daughter, and save his marriage.

CHAPTER 37

Lauren was tense and jumpy but making a great effort to calm herself while she listened to Dr. Miller on her cell phone.

"Believe me, I totally understand your concerns, Mrs. Curtis. I've seen the same symptoms before, and I've dealt with them successfully. Jodie will come out of this just fine."

"Her temperature is a hundred and two, and even dim light hurts her eyes. She's all upset, acting strange."

"Strange in what way?"

"She snaps at me, even uses curse words. That's totally not like her."

"People sometimes get irrationally angry when they're in pain. I don't think she has to go to the emergency room. But pull the shades. Let her stay in a darkened bedroom. I'll phone a prescription to your pharmacist."

"Can you possibly come here? Please, can you do a house call?"

"I'm still working late, seeing patients. Don't panic. I've had other cases like this, and they've all gotten well. I'm not at liberty to tell you who, but some of her teenage friends have gone through the same symptoms. We don't know the exact cause, but we're able to treat them and at least help them manage the pain.

It seems to be a temporary anti-immune system response, probably due to the hormonal changes of puberty."

"Well, thank you for taking my call," Lauren said. "I'll pick up the prescription."

She killed her cell phone and stood in one spot, fidgeting, nervously rubbing her hands on her apron. She had been in the kitchen basting a chicken when Jodie had let out a shriek from her bedroom. She had gone up there to see what was the matter, had spoken to Jodie and tried to soothe her, and had taken her temperature. Then she had phoned Dr. Miller.

She listened again now, and wasn't hearing any more shrieks or sobs. So she tiptoed up the stairs. She stood for a long moment in the hall outside Jodie's room. Hearing nothing, she slowly opened the door.

The room was dark, so much so that she could barely make out Jodie lying on her bed.

She automatically reached out and flicked on the light switch, and Jodie immediately yelled at her, "Shut that damned light *out!*"

But Lauren froze at the sight of what had happened to her fifteen-year-old daughter in just the past fifteen minutes. Jodie's skin had turned an ugly pasty-white, and there were hideous purple blisters on her scarred arm and around her lips.

"Shut the fucking thing *off*, Mom!"

"Don't swear at me like that! I'll tell your father!"

"Big fucking deal!"

"Sometimes I could just smack you!" Lauren said. She angrily flipped the switch and the room was plunged into murkiness. Then she hesitated for a minute or so and didn't get cursed at again. So she crept into the bedroom and hovered at Jodie's bedside like the caring mother that she was. But Jodie turned her head away.

Lauren said, "Sweetheart, I can brew some tea with honey and lemon, to help you sweat out your fever."

"I don't want anything," Jodie said sullenly. "I'm sorry I swore at you, Mom."

"Dr. Miller said not to worry, he's seen cases like yours before. I'll be able to get a prescription."

"I'm so ugly!" Jodie wailed. "That salve didn't help at all! I look worse than before!"

Lauren risked getting cursed at again and reached out and held her daughter's hand. It felt amazingly hot to the touch. She said, "Honey, you're not ugly. And you're going to get well. Dr. Miller said the prescription will be sure to help."

"In how long?"

"Maybe no longer than a week."

"Great! I won't be able to go out of the house! I might as well be dead!"

"Well, I'll leave you alone for now. Try and get some rest. Are you sure you don't want to come down and eat? I'm roasting a chicken."

Jodie shook her head no, and Lauren bent over her and kissed her feverish forehead, then backed out of the room and softly closed the door.

As she came down the stairs, Bill came in the front door. Immediately he asked, "How's Jodie? What'd the doctor say?"

She gave Bill a hug and a kiss, then said, "She doesn't appear to be deathly ill, but she looks far worse than when she first came home from school. Her temperature is up pretty high, but not at the emergency level. Dr. Miller says temporary hormonal imbalances during puberty can produce strange symptoms. But nothing like that ever happened to me."

She followed her husband into the dining room where he performed the standard ritual of taking off his suit jacket, removing his shoulder holster, and locking his gun in the cabinet.

Suddenly they heard a loud scream from upstairs.

Jodie was yelling hysterically.

But the screaming stopped before Bill and Lauren could get up there.

The light was on in the bathroom, and they saw Jodie lying on the floor. Her eyes were staring glassily upward.

Lauren yelled, "Oh my God! Bill! Shut that light off! I don't know why—"

Bill didn't immediately shut the light off. Instead he knelt over his daughter. He saw her blisters. And now they were oozing a purplish pus.

"She's still breathing," he said. "Help me carry her into bed."

"*Look*, Bill!" Lauren shrieked.

She was pointing at the water in the commode bowl. It was as purple as the blisters on Jodie's arm and lips.

CHAPTER 38

Steve Kallen was applying beautifying touches to the corpse of a silver-haired woman already wearing the frilly blue dressing gown she would be wearing in one of the viewing rooms. For now, she was still in the embalming room, and Kallen's daughter, Brenda, was at his side, observing and listening.

As he began cleaning the cadaver's nails with a nail file, he said, "I used a half-and-half mixture of embalming fluid on Mrs. Filbert here. If you get a body that's already partially decayed, you have to make your mixture much more potent. But bear in mind, honey, that if your mixture is too strong you might get fluid burns—the skin will turn splotchy red and the tissues will get like hard rubber. However, a too weak mixture will cause discoloration and odor. And you don't want that when the family comes to see their loved one."

She said, "I still don't understand why people want corpses to be prettied up like this. It seems bizarre to me, a weird way for us to make money."

"Maybe I agree with you, but I wouldn't say it out loud," Kallen admitted.

He laid the nail file down. Already knowing what he'd be doing next, Brenda showed off her knowledge by handing her father a fine-bristled brush and jar of dusting powder.

"Now we've got to make her look healthy," he said, "even though her long bout with cancer wasted her away, emaciated her. But her family doesn't want to see her that way. So we use Sun Tone flesh-dusting powder."

"I already know that, Daddy."

He began brushing the powder artfully on the cadaver's face as he instructed, "You've got to take your time . . . study her . . . make her look tanned and robust. Then use a touch of ruby lip gloss."

"She still looks ghastly to me!" said Brenda.

"But her loved ones are getting exactly what they're paying for," said Kallen. "Believe me, they're going to be happy campers."

As he reached for the lip gloss, the night bell rang. He went to the steel door and looked through the peephole. He was surprised when he saw it was Dr. Miller. He let him in, and the doctor, normally a dapper-looking professional, was sweaty and disheveled. He wasn't wearing his suit jacket or his necktie, and his shirt was rumpled and had a brownish stain on it. The top two shirt buttons were unfastened, and he had whisky on his breath.

"Made a house call," he said, blinking and shaking his head. "Wish I didn't. No wonder I seldom do it. The Curtis girl . . . I saw her tonight . . . same as the others . . . only worse."

When he suddenly focused on Kallen's daughter, standing by the corpse of Mrs. Filbert, he clammed up and said, "Oh, hi, Brenda," with an attempt at nonchalance.

Kallen said, "She's learning the family business, Doc. I see you remember her."

"Sure . . . sure I do. I remember all my patients . . . all the kids I make healthy." He stared at Brenda for a long moment, then said, "Can we talk alone, Steve? It's important."

Brenda said rather coyly, "Nice to see you again, Doctor." Then she pivoted and left the basement.

Steve Kallen returned to the cadaver and started applying lip gloss.

Following him over there, Dr. Miller blurted, "They all exhibit signs of porphyria! Then they get better, like a miracle!"

Continuing to paint the cadaver's lips, Kallen said, "I'm afraid I don't have the slightest idea what you're talking about, Doc."

"Don't you, Steve? Are you sure Brenda is everything you think she is?"

"I've never seen you drunk like this, Doc. You should go home and sober up. I don't know what the heck you're babbling about."

"Was Brenda ever in a fight with the Hornsby boy when they were in kindergarten? Did he ever bite her that you know about?"

"No, nothing like that ever happened," Kallen said. "At least not to my knowledge. These days they're buddies. They pal around together."

"Did her skin ever break out in purplish blisters?"

Kallen stopped the tube of lip gloss in midair. "Not that I ever saw, no. But she's been going to summer camp. If it happened there, at the church camp—"

"*Whose* church camp?" Dr. Miller pounced.

"Reverend Carnes's. She joined his youth group."

"Damn! Maybe he treated her with something, some crazy method of his, without my finding out about it. I wish Brenda had told me. Maybe she had the disease last summer, or the summer before, while she was at that camp. Or maybe she never got it at all. Maybe she's immune to it."

"Immune to *what?* You're scaring me, Doc!"

"Porphyria! It's what the Curtis girl has. They get it when they reach puberty. A blood disease—a metabolic disturbance. It's like shingles, it lies dormant, but when it comes out, it makes their skin blister and bleed. Even their urine changes color, it turns purple. They can't go out in the sun. Back in the Middle Ages they were called vampires, and in a way that's what they were—the disease caused them to lose so many nutrients that drinking blood seemed to help them, or at least they believed so.

When they were caught, stakes were driven into their hearts. Don't you get it, Steve? It was the origin of the vampire myth! We don't have any idea what these kids are going to turn into!"

"Even if my daughter had it and I didn't know about it," Kallen said desperately, "she must have gotten over it, and maybe she'll remain healthy from now on. She never gets sick anymore. That's a very good sign, isn't it, Doc?"

"I'd like to believe that, because it used to be that most por-phyria sufferers, once they got the disease, would have it for the rest of their lives. They'd have to stay on tranquilizers and corti-sone creams and injections. If they drank any alcohol, used drugs, got pregnant, or even stayed in the sun too long, they'd get those severe blisters and develop all kinds of mental aberrations, in-cluding psychosis."

"But the Foster Project kids all get completely better. Isn't that what you've been saying? You and Dr. Traeger," Kallen said. "You're supposed to be the experts! I totally *believed* you! I thought that if Brenda ever had any of those kind of symptoms, she surely would've told me."

"The Foster Project kids don't exhibit the outward signs of it. It could be because their abnormality was passed on to them while they were bathed in amniotic fluid. It's the ones who are infected by *those* children who develop the outwardly manifested symptoms. I think it's possible that the condition can be trans-mitted not just by biting but by the transfer of saliva by kissing or even sharing candy or soft drinks. Heaven help us! Some of them could've gotten it by licking each other's ice cream cones!"

"What does Dr. Traeger say? Does she know all this?"

"We discussed it in her office earlier today. We compared notes and were able to put two and two together. She intimately knows her research, of course, and I know more about what's been going on out in the community. When the facts are merged, it leads to the conclusions I revealed to you. Dr. Traeger wants to keep all of it top secret. But I felt like I should warn you about your daughter."

"Is there any chance she's really okay?" Kallen asked desperately.

"I don't know," said Dr. Miller. "She's first generation, so maybe. The others who are infected by them exhibit these ungodly symptoms, and then they appear to become perfectly normal, as if someone passed a magic wand over them. But beneath the surface they might be anything *but* normal."

CHAPTER 39

Pete Danko used his secure Skype system to report to Colonel Spence at the Pentagon.

"We've got another loose cannon in our midst, besides Bill Curtis," he told Spence as soon as the colonel's image appeared on the computer screen.

"Who is it?" the colonel asked.

"Dr. Miller. The pediatrician we put in business here in Chapel Grove. Apparently, he's had some kind of mental lapse. He showed up at the funeral parlor unannounced late last night, apparently had too much to drink, and babbled about things that Steve Kallen wasn't authorized to know. Kallen had the good sense to tell me about it right away."

"What was the gist of it?"

Danko related the details of what Steve Kallen had told him, including the speculation about porphyria, which up till now hadn't even been on anybody's radar and was a stunning new development.

"Porphyria," Colonel Spence mused. "Are we sure that such a thing actually *exists?*"

"It does. And it seems that Dr. Traeger was the first one to start thinking in that direction. She ran it by Dr. Miller, then

Miller blabbed to Kallen about it, out of a misguided intention to warn him about his own daughter."

"Does Dr. Traeger know about the leak?" Colonel Spence asked.

"Yes, I discussed it with her. She's quite upset about it, as she would be about anything that threatens to expose her work. But she's also jumping at the chance to get the Foster Project reinstated and funded again. She said it never should have been discontinued so abruptly."

"Maybe she's right. In the meantime, what do you suggest?"

"Dr. Miller should be replaced."

"Of course. I'll summon him to Washington. But I think something should happen to him at the airport."

"The departure airport or the arrival airport?" Danko asked.

"Departure."

"Good," said Danko, "because then I can handle the matter myself. No one else needs to be involved."

"You have my authorization," said Colonel Spence.

After terminating the Skype meeting, Pete Danko began thinking of how he would ensure a clean departure for Dr. Miller, not just from Chapel Grove but from his loose-lipped life.

CHAPTER 40

Thinking back to his courtship of Lauren, Bill Curtis recalled how, quite a while after they began dating, he took a chance and revealed to her that he was an agnostic. She was so appalled that she almost broke up with him right then and there. She was raised so strictly in her religion and within her family that she harbored the two usual complexes: guilt and inferiority. But in the process of falling in love and getting to know each other intimately, Bill felt that he was opening up her mind by communicating some of the history of religion and its origins that he had gotten to know through his reading and his conversations with other doubters. By the time of their wedding, neither he nor Lauren was any longer willing to accept religious doctrine on faith alone, but not wanting to break it to her parents and shatter Howard and Mildred's doctrinaire, nailed-down little world, they faked their way through mandatory marriage instructions from a priest and got married in church.

But Lauren was becoming religious again, of late. And worse, she was consulting with Reverend James Carnes. This was a regression, in Bill's opinion, a backslide brought on by fear over their daughter's enigmatic illness. Lauren was running scared and giving up too much of the intellectual maturity that he had helped awaken in her, and which he thought had germinated and blossomed.

It was his hope that no matter what kind of severe pressure he might be under, he would not give in and start praying to a god who probably wasn't there. But regrettably, Lauren wasn't strong enough. She was caving, out of desperation, and Reverend Carnes was aiding and abetting her motherly fears, filling her head with what Bill considered nonsense. Carnes had come to the house when Bill wasn't there and told her, "I treated Brenda Kallen when she got sick at my church camp. Prayer saved her body and her soul."

Lauren had told Bill about the reverend's visit when he got home from work yesterday.

"Please, why don't we at least try it?" she pleaded.

"Carnes is pushing nothing but Iron Age superstitions," Bill said. "I'm sure he believes in what he's saying, but you and I should be above all that. If Brenda Kallen got well, she was going to, anyway, in spite of Carnes and his mumbo-jumbo. It's like the savages who stick pins in voodoo dolls, then if the person happens to die, they think *they* caused it."

"Maybe there really *are* miracles sometimes," Lauren persisted.

"Ignorant, vulnerable people want to believe that," Bill told her. "But I can't afford to lose my objectivity. If I did that, I'd be no good as a detective, right?"

It saddened him to think that he and Lauren weren't on the same page anymore. But she surely knew that he would do almost anything to heal his daughter or preserve her from harm. If it came down to it, he would give his own life. But he wasn't cowardly enough to cling to the false hope offered by charms and potions, and he thought that in essence it was all that Reverend Carnes was offering.

He also still believed that somehow Carnes and some of his followers were behind the theft of the three bodies of the Ron Haley family from Kallen's Funeral Home. Totally frustrated, he had even asked Pete Danko for advice on how to move forward on the case, much as he hated to come to his autocratic boss with an admission of failure. But Pete wasn't at all helpful; in fact he seemed to like hearing that Bill was stymied because to him it was further proof that he was superior to his underling.

"What if we could get hold of Carnes's cell phone and see where it was pinging that night?" Bill pressed.

"We don't have enough probable cause," Pete said. "You should know that without even asking."

"I do know it," Bill defended. "I was hoping you could pull some strings."

"I'm not God," said Pete. "There's a good chance the Haleys' remains have been burned or buried in some remote place where we'll never find them."

"I can't help hoping otherwise," said Bill.

As he left Pete's office, he despaired of the plague's ongoing legacy of fear and despair, which made people give in to the raw primitive aspects of human nature, instead of clinging to the higher level of enlightenment that had been so hard-won down through the ages.

CHAPTER 41

In her office at the Chapel Grove Medical Research Institute, Dr. Traeger was hastily composing a report for Colonel Spence at the Homeland Security Department. It disgusted her that Dr. Miller, whom she had previously thought entirely trustworthy, had chosen to betray that trust. But at the same time she felt vindicated. She had advocated for a continuation of the Foster Project but had been denied, and now the stupidity of that denial was threatening to come home to roost. Therefore she hoped that she would quickly be able to gain approval for the renewed funding that she was urgently requesting.

In her cover letter, she admitted to Colonel Spence that she had harbored nagging suspicions about the children of the Foster Project, but had not suspected that they might be carriers of a disease as rare and exotic as porphyria. Deflecting blame from herself, she pointed out that it only manifested in children who were *infected* by the adoptees, not the adoptees themselves, and when those children were young their symptoms were too far too mild to accurately diagnose. She put the blame on Dr. Miller for not alerting her to what she now realized fully, that the more alarming symptoms only started appearing when certain of the children reached puberty. Up until then, they had always tested normal in every respect, and on that basis funding for the project had been discontinued. However, now that so much more was known, it was imperative to ascertain how many other children may have been infected by the Foster Project adoptees, and to zero in on which ones and subject them to intensive tests. That was why substantial additional funding was needed.

Thinking back over key events connected with the adoptees, Dr. Traeger recalled that Darius Hornsby had bitten Jodie Curtis, the detective's daughter, when Jodie and Darius were both six years old. Over time, the event had faded in Dr. Traeger's memory because it seemed for the succeeding years nothing much had come of it. Till now. She knew more now, and she searched her conscience for any trace of self-blame that she ought to accept, but she didn't see how she could've drawn any different conclusions based on what she knew back then.

She pulled Darius's file and reread it, in case there was something that she should not have missed. Something that should have alarmed her more, in other words. Darius's biological father was Hal Rotini, the drummer of the rock band the Hateful Dead, druggies whose use of the infected needles had caused that terrible outbreak sixteen years ago. The mother, bitten by Rotini and turned into one of the undead, had given birth to Darius in Chapel Grove Hospital; then she had been dispatched, and her corpse had been cremated. The baby was subsequently adopted by a conservative, straitlaced CPA, Cyrus Hornsby, and his wife, Lila, a first-grade teacher. Darius had grown up with a fondness for music and at least a smidgen of talent, likely inherited from his low-life father.

Dr. Traeger did not see anything in the folder that pointed to culpability or willful error on her own part, so she put the folder back in her file cabinet and resumed writing her report. In her summation, she refrained from pointing out that she had argued that the Foster Project should not have been terminated in the first place. She hoped that Colonel Spence and the other bigwigs at HSD would realize that fact without having their noses rubbed in it, and would give her credit for her prescience.

She contemplated the evil tendencies that she had come to

tentatively suspect in her adopted daughter and her closest friends. For the time being, she decided to hold back on voicing those suspicions, for her daughter's sake, not wanting to prematurely place a stigma upon her. But she knew that withholding vital information, even conjecture, from the watchdogs of Homeland Security could cost her her freedom or even her life.

She elected to end her report on a bright, hopeful note. She reiterated that not only the children of the Foster Project, but also the others known to have recovered from bouts of porphyria, needed to be studied further. She stated that, since these others had recovered and afterward appeared every bit as normal as the ones who had likely infected *them*, the cure for porphyria, as well as for the plague itself, might be unveiled by more exhaustive, more sharply focused studies. She concluded by pointing out that much needed to be learned before the proper steps should be taken concerning the infected children, whatever those steps might ultimately turn out to be.

After she put her imprimatur on the report and handed it over to an armed courier, which was the prescribed procedure since e-mails were not trusted, she let herself into the lockdown wing where Kelly Ann Garfield was kept. She just wanted to talk with her for a while, without having to take notes. She had found, to her surprise, that with Kelly Ann she shared the closest thing to an intellectual rapport that had come her way ever since her husband's accidental death. That is, if it actually had *been* an accident. It was obvious that Bill Curtis had suspicions, but they were squelched by the institute's watchdog, Pete Danko, before they could amount to anything. On the day of her husband's death, Dr. Traeger had been thankful that her daughter was let off the hook. But more and more, upon further reflection, she became increasingly uneasy about Kathy's potential involvement. Daniel was so frail and crippled that perhaps an angry child could have pushed him down the stairs. Those disturbing kinds of thoughts kept Dr. Traeger awake at night, tossing and turning.

Kelly Ann was poorly educated, but she had good instincts, a sound intellect, and an offbeat sense of humor. Conversation with her was actually a delight. It seemed clear that with the proper advantages, like the ones Kathy was ignoring or even blatantly mocking, Kelly Ann could have had a long, meaningful life. A daughter like that would have made Dr. Traeger proud. Sometimes, in her more wistful dreams, she would treat Kelly Ann as her daughter, instead of Kathy, as if a transformation had occurred—but then she would suddenly wake up with tears running down her face, as disappointed as a little girl who had dreamed of having a pony only to have it vanish when the dream ended.

Kelly Ann was lying down watching a TV news channel when Dr. Traeger entered her room. She constantly had either the news or a documentary of some sort playing in front of her, as she tried to educate herself about what was currently going on in the world, since she had hopes of soon entering a new life of freedom. She also watched quite a few evangelical religious programs, but far from excluding all else. Dr. Traeger viewed this as a testament to her innate intellectual curiosity, and for now she wanted to nurture it, even though it was bound to lead to a dead end. She hung her lab coat on a hook behind the door, sat on the chair next to the bed, and said, "Let's just chat informally. I'd like to know whatever you choose to tell me about yourself, without regard to any diagnostic issues."

"I'd like to learn more about you, too," Kelly Ann said. "You're sort of my only friend. In prison I had only myself and my eight-foot cell."

"We don't need the TV, do we?" Dr. Traeger said. "I think its constant presence can insulate us from our thoughts."

Kelly Ann picked up the remote and made the screen go blank. "I wish I could go to church," she said after a long, thoughtful pause.

"You'll be able to do that by and by," Dr. Traeger lied.

"But when?"

"Soon. I promise you. In the meantime, nothing stops you from praying, right here in your room."

"Most hospitals have a chapel. So do most prisons. Or at least visits from a chaplain. Why can't I see a Baptist preacher, like that Reverend Carnes I've seen on television."

"He's a charlatan. Don't you think so?"

"I don't know what to think. He's trying to do his best, as God gives him to see the light, and that's all any of us can aspire to. I think his heart is in the right place. I wish I could talk with him about his beliefs."

"I'll make it a point to allow you to meet him, as soon as you're released."

"Oh, good! I can hardly wait!"

"Do you give any credence to his preaching about the dead and how they must be spiked or burned?"

"I don't know. I was almost glad I was safe in my cell when some of the epidemics broke out. But after my execution date became ironclad, I would have given anything to be let out, even if I had to battle a horde of zombies."

"You wouldn't want to *become* one of them, would you? They can't easily be put to death." Dr. Traeger chuckled to show she was making a macabre joke.

"Well, I ended up cheating death without becoming a flesh-eating zombie," Kelly Ann said. "I'd rather die of a lethal injection than become one of *them!*"

Dr. Traeger resolved to keep this sentiment in mind when she decided her patient's ultimate fate. She wished fervently that the decision would be taken out of her hands, but she couldn't foresee any way that was possible. If she wanted her experiments to continue, she'd have to maintain her position as director of the institute, and she'd have to accept all the responsibilities, even the ugly ones. If she wavered, her own fate would surely be decided unfavorably by her superiors at the HSD. She lived all the days of her life in unmitigated dread of them and their bureaucracy. And this all-encompassing dread was amplified by her stark memory of Jamie Dugan in the room in the basement, his blood and brains splattered against the padded wall.

Pete Danko was a misogynist, a hater of women, and a skilled, enthusiastic torturer. Dr. Traeger had no doubt he would enjoy having her at his mercy. There was only one way to come out on top, where he was concerned. She dreamed of finding her long-sought-after cure for the plague, after which she was certain to receive a bonus of at least a million dollars, and then flying off to some quiet, enchanted place with Kelly Ann to live the rest of their lives together, as mother-and-daughter soul mates, in peace and seclusion.

But she knew it was pure fantasy.

Even if a cure for the plague came into being, and experimental subjects were no longer needed, any that remained would have to be destroyed. And if that happened there would be no way for her to save Kelly Ann.

CHAPTER 42

Kathy Traeger knew how pretty and innocent she looked in her long blue dress, pink blouse, and emerald beads, sitting all by herself in the sunlit cemetery. Most girls of sixteen would be scared to be alone here even though it was such a lovely and peaceful day. But Kathy wasn't the least bit nervous. She was calm and watchful. She had positioned herself here as bait because she and her friends needed a special kind of sustenance and today they were going to get it from someone who richly deserved to become a donor.

Kathy had with her a butterfly collection that had actually belonged to her mother. She had no real interest in butterflies. They were a prop, for today only. She pretended to write on their labels, acting far too absorbed in her task to take much notice of what was going on around her.

But she knew she was being stalked. Brenda and Tricia had told her about the fellow who lurked in the cemetery. He had raped three of their classmates who had been too scared to report him. His name was Roger Dalton, and his wealthy parents were avid supporters and enablers, who always bailed him out of trouble. He never got any serious punishment for the hideous things he did, going back as far as grade school and junior high school.

His mother and father paid for high-priced lawyers when they needed to, and even paid off his victims when they could.

Two years ago, he had been arrested by Bill Curtis, Jodie's father, and was scheduled to go on trial until the thirteen-year-old girl he beat up and raped was pressured by *her* distraught and loving parents not to testify in court, for fear that she'd be ripped apart by Roger Dalton's defense attorneys. Brenda and Tricia had asked Jodie if she remembered anything about that case, and Jodie told them that she had overheard her dad complaining to her mother that the girl's parents had suddenly bought a new home about three months after the case was thrown out. He said that he felt like taking the law into his own hands sometimes, and this was one of those times. He said he didn't blame the girl's parents for at least extracting some money from the rapist. He warned Jodie to stay away from Roger Dalton, who was known to lurk in quiet, relatively unpopulated places, trolling for young girls to victimize. He didn't usually stoop to hanging out in cemeteries, but Kathy and her friends had made a game of following him from time to time and found out that he often came here.

Now he was going to pay in blood for his life of rape and cruelty to women. How fitting and proper that this should be his fate!

Kathy risked a sneaky glance in his direction, and spotted the lecherous gleam in his eyes as he pretended to fuss with an ornament on a nearby grave. He was a bland-looking boy, only nineteen, dressed in sharply creased tan trousers and a green polo shirt. His outward appearance definitely did not inspire fear. The infamous serial killer Ted Bundy was the same way. Bundy had a harmless look about him, especially when he approached young women with a fake cast on his arm and asked them to help him wheel his bike or something.

Without even turning around, Kathy could feel Roger Dalton edging toward her, like a sixth sense or something, but she pretended to be unaware. She faked tinkering with the dead butterflies and resolved to burn them in the fireplace when she got home.

She whirled around just as Roger was lunging at her. She dropped the case of insects and grabbed his wrists. Surprisingly strong, she bent his wrists back till he moaned in pain as she stared fixedly at him, her flashing green eyes only inches from his face.

He gasped and trembled. His mouth gaped open and his eyes bulged.

Her incisors had become fangs!

She laughed at him, a weird, demonic, ululating sound that was bolstered by laughter from additional voices, louder and shriller, eerily amplified.

"C'mon, join the party!" Kathy called out.

Brenda and Tricia appeared from among the tombstones. Baring their fangs, they closed in on the would-be rapist. Kathy placed her fingers tenderly on Roger Dalton's right shoulder, pushing him down slowly and effortlessly to the ground. He began to babble, saying that he never harmed anybody, and begging to go free.

The teenage girls converged upon him with their sharp, glistening fangs. He screamed when they began to bite into his flesh.

Kathy smiled at him as sweetly as she could, very much enjoying his terror. Then she bit into his jugular vein where the rich, salty blood flowed most easily. Soon he would become one of the undead. He would not have the honor of becoming a blood seeker, and he did not deserve to. Anyone bitten by fully transformed blood seekers after they had passed through puberty could not become *like* them. They could only become slaves. Flesh-eaters. Once living. Now living dead.

CHAPTER 43

Margaret Stein, Attorney Bennett Stein's wife, parked her SUV in front of Mildred Hornsby's house. To her disgust, she noticed Darius Hornsby's garish van parked in the driveway. Bottling up her anger, she headed for the front door, but changed direction when she heard loud music coming from the backyard. She stopped short when she saw Tricia, Kathy, and Darius lounging on the patio in swimsuits, all three of them smoking cigars and swilling vodka straight from the bottle.

Darius eyed Margaret coolly. Her mouth dropped open, and she was suddenly fearful of him even though she was an adult and he was a juvenile.

He said sneeringly, "Well, hello, Mrs. Stein. Care for a slug of vodka? A fine Cuban cigar?"

"You better watch your mouth!" she scolded.

The kids laughed at her.

"Don't laugh at me!' she screeched at them. "I've had enough of your insolence! You all played hooky from youth group—rest assured I'm going to tell your parents!"

"My parents don't give a shit," said Darius.

"My dad didn't give a shit either," said Kathy. "All he cared about was his research."

Mockingly, Tricia asked, "Are you sure you won't have a cigar,

Mrs. Stein? They were my father's, straight from Havana, on the black market."

The kids giggled and took big drags.

Appalled at the snotty looks on their faces, Margaret fumed at them. "I *see* why you three didn't come to church! This is a disgrace! You ought to be ashamed of yourselves! Playing hooky is like giving God and Reverend Carnes a slap in the face!"

Kathy and Tricia giggled uproariously, passing the vodka bottle back and forth and swigging from it.

Darius said, "Hold on, Mrs. Stein. I'll be at the weenie roast tomorrow night, and I have a strong hunch you'll be there too."

Margaret snapped, "I most certainly will *not!* The campfire cookout is for the boys *only*. I supervise the girls."

Darius leered at her. He said, "Still, I happen to know that you *will* be there, even though you're not planning on it. I'm looking forward to seeing you. It'll be a delightful evening."

"Nonsense! You're drunk and disgusting! Where's your mother, Tricia? I want to speak with her!"

The kids snickered.

"She's . . . uh . . . indisposed," Tricia fabricated. "You can't see her now. But when you do see her you're going to have a lot in common. Soul mates, that's what you'll be. You're even going to enjoy meals together. My mother used to prefer Spanish cuisine, remember? But now you're both going to like the same *kind* of food! And I'm not telling what kind that is! Can you guess, Margaret?"

Again the kids snickered.

Margaret took her cell phone from her purse. "All right, Miss Smart Mouth, if you won't let me see your mother, I'm not playing games with you—I'm going to call the police. I'll have you arrested. There are laws against underage drinking, and as a good citizen and the wife of an attorney, I'm compelled to report you."

Punching in 9-1-1 on her phone, she pivoted sharply and started to head out of the yard.

But Darius jumped in front of her and blocked the gate.

"You insolent little punk!" she yelled. "Get out of my way! Let me pass!"

Arms folded, Darius eyed her smugly, not budging an inch.

Now Margaret was even more scared than before. Her eyes darted from one kid to another, and she backed away from them.

She suddenly believed, with absolute conviction in the tenets of her religion, that they were indeed children of Satan.

She recoiled when Tricia called out to her.

"Mrs. Stein . . . look at me. Look at me, Mrs. Stein."

She turned and gasped. Tricia was staring fixedly at her. And the young girl's incisors were now fangs.

Kathy bared her fangs, too, and they were glistening with saliva.

Darius came up on Margaret from behind, and when she turned to run, she bumped right into him and found herself locked in his tight embrace. He bit into her neck as Kathy and Tricia emitted demonic laughter. Then the girls closed in too, and Margaret sank to the earth still in Darius's powerful predatory embrace. The girls bit into Margaret's arms and legs as Darius continued to suck blood from her neck.

When Darius had drunk his fill, he pulled out his smartphone and shot video of the girls satiating themselves on Margaret's blood. He got an erotic thrill out of watching them do their thing on the tiny screen. He was glad that now they were ready to wholeheartedly satisfy their craving, which had to wait until puberty to become fully manifested. Long before that, he had made his followers join Reverend Carnes's youth group because he knew that Carnes and his congregation would actively seek dead bodies to be spiked or burned. And he believed that he might be able to take some of those bodies for his own purposes, instead of spiking them. He needed as many dead ones as he could get, so he could make them into zombies with a mindless craving for human flesh. By sowing terror and disruption, and by building an army of undead slaves, he and his kind, with their more delicate craving for blood instead of raw flesh, would more easily take over the town, the nation, and ultimately, the entire world.

CHAPTER 44

A large group of boys was gathered around a campfire, being led in a religious song by Margaret's husband, Attorney Bennett Stein. Darius and his fellow band members didn't bother to sing, and Mr. Stein grimaced at them, but they didn't care. They merely stared at him insolently and moved away from the campfire. By moonlight they worked their way deeper into the woods.

As they got farther from the campfire, they observed ghostly figures who appeared to be staring at them from the dark foliage. Unperturbed, they watched these strange beings but did not remark upon them or pay them any special attention.

Hank said, "Are we almost there, Darius?"

"Shut up and keep moving."

Doug said, "Right on. Darius knows where the goodies are."

They kept going on a weed-grown path, and when they came to a pile of brush at the foot of a large gnarled tree, they grinned at one another, looking pleased and excited. "Uncover it," Darius said, and the three other boys pulled aside some of the leaves and branches. Margaret Stein's corpse stared up at them, her skin ghastly white, her body caked with dried blood from the punctures of many fangs.

Hank said, "That's so cool, Darius! Is she ready to join the others?"

As if in answer to Hank's question, Margaret began to stir. Her arms and legs twitched a little, and she made her first efforts to sit up.

"The morphine is wearing off now," Darius said. "She's already undead, and she's going to get really, really hungry."

"What a trip!" Ben said.

Hank and Doug could not stifle an outburst of laughter.

"Let's get outta here," Darius said. "Let the fun and games begin!"

He led his three followers back toward the campfire, leaving the corpse lying there, writhing around in her first struggles to come back to life. As the boys trudged along the path, eyeing the glow of the fire in the distance, Bennett Stein barged out at them and yelled, "You four boys! What do you mean by sneaking off like this?"

Darius and his friends snickered and stared defiantly at Stein.

Stein stomped toward them and indignantly grabbed Doug and Hank, spinning them around till they were facing him, and barking at Darius, "This is all *your* fault! You used to be a role model for the younger boys, but now you're just a bad influence!"

Darius laughed, and his laugh was frighteningly sinister.

The ghoulish figures, who previously were staring at the boys from back in the foliage as they headed toward Margaret's corpse, now came forward openly, as if Darius's evil laugh had summoned them.

Doug yelled, "Turn us loose, fat man!"

And Hank jeered, "You don't know who you're messin' with!"

Ben suddenly punched Stein in his soft belly, and he sank to his knees, groaning, with the wind knocked out of him. Then, out of the shadows, his dead wife stepped toward him, and he recoiled in absolute terror. She was undead now, and so were her ghoulish companions. In varying stages of decay, and with various wounds and deformities having to do with their deaths, they rasped and drooled hungrily as they encircled Bennett Stein, letting his dead wife take the lead.

Stein cowered, mumbling, "Margaret? Oh, no . . . oh God! It's happening . . . it's actually happening . . . the way the reverend said . . ."

Darius, Ben, and Hank returned to the campfire without Doug, who had been given a special assignment by Darius, and joined the other boys in singing a traditional hymn, "The Church in the Wildwood," as if nothing untoward was going on. They raised their voices and sang as loudly as they could to cover the sounds of Bennett Stein being ripped apart.

After they sang the final notes of the song, Darius announced to the rest of the kids that Mr. Stein had gotten a late call from his legal secretary and had left for his law office to fill out papers for a client of his who needed to be bailed out of jail. The kids whispered and giggled and bought the story. In the meantime, on Darius's instructions Doug was driving Mr. Stein's Cadillac to the Steins' home so he could park it in their driveway.

CHAPTER 45

Watching anxiously from behind a heavy curtain pulled aside slightly, Lauren Curtis saw Reverend Carnes pulling up and parking, then getting out of a rusty black Chevy pickup with the windows wound down. It was a stifling hot day, and Lauren realized the truck probably didn't have air-conditioning, or else the system wasn't functioning. She knew from the recent sermons she had heard him preach that he considered self-deprivation a virtue and a form of self-imposed punishment for his sins. She hoped against hope that he could do what he had to do before Bill came home from work and caught them at it. She also hoped that somehow Jodie wouldn't tell on her. And at the same time, she thought that if Jodie got well, it would all be worth it, even at the risk of alienating Bill.

She came out onto the front porch to greet Carnes so she could have a few words with him before he came into the house, where Jodie could easily overhear. She knew she looked a mess, and it embarrassed her. She was wearing faded jeans, a green sweater, and brown leather sandals with no socks. No makeup on her face either. The red paint on her fingernails was chipped and the nails needed trimmed. When her daughter's well-being was at issue, she tended to let herself go. She was sweaty from hurry-up housework, and hadn't dared take the time to shower for fear that

Jodie would have some sort of crisis, call out to her, and with the water running she wouldn't be able to hear. She thought that Carnes, who always had four o'clock shadow, even in the morning, was better groomed right now than she was, though he was wearing the same worn-out black suit and yellowed Roman collar that he always wore, and his black shoes were dull and scuffed.

Confronting him on the porch steps, Lauren said, "I'm sorry you came all the way over here, Reverend Carnes. I'm not sure I should be going through with this."

"That's what you said on the phone. I came prepared anyway. I have a crucifix and a bottle of holy water in my truck."

"Again, I'm sorry to put you through so much trouble. I may back out."

While Lauren and Carnes conversed on the front porch, Kathy Traeger got out of the red Mustang convertible that her mother had bought her for her sixteenth birthday. She had followed Reverend Carnes to the Curtises' home and had parked a short distance down the street. At first she had no special reason for doing this; she was simply out for mischief. But now she realized what the reverend must be up to. He must have suspected that Jodie was in the clutches of something evil, and he had the nerve to think he could thwart it. Fat chance! Smiling at the joke she was about to play on him, Kathy sneaked over to his truck, reached in, and grabbed his little bottle of holy water. She didn't believe it was in any way special or holy. It was just distilled water mixed with a couple drops of olive oil. No way could it stop the inner forces that were taking over the body and mind of Jodie Curtis. Nevertheless, Kathy decided to have some fun with it. She knew that Jodie's blisters were going to clear up on their own, because that was how the process worked, but it would be a kick to let the reverend think that his prayers were the thing that did the trick. The gullible old fool!

Kathy looked all around, and when she noticed a birdbath in the front lawn next door, she went over to it, uncapped the little bottle, poured the so-called holy water onto the ground, and re-filled the bottle with water from the birdbath. Then she put the bottle back on the passenger seat of the reverend's truck, got into her Mustang, and drove away.

On the porch of the Curtis home, Reverend Carnes was still trying to convince Lauren to go ahead with what in essence would be an exorcism. "If you back out now, Satan will be mightily pleased. You'll be playing right into the devil's hands."

"I thought I was ready for this, but now I'm having second thoughts," Lauren said, highly worried. "If my daughter tells my husband, he'll flip out. I'm not sure Jodie will help me keep it secret, no matter how it turns out. She's a daddy's girl, and she knows full well that her dad doesn't believe in prayers and miracles."

"But unbelievers can be your downfall. It's time for you to think about what *you* want. Don't you want Jodie's soul to be washed clean?"

"Bill would scoff at that. He'd call me a superstitious fool."

"He's a good man," said Carnes, "but he'll burn in hell if he doesn't change his ways. If it makes you feel better, I can assure you that your daughter will emerge with little or no memory of how she was cleansed."

"If that's true, it'd be a comfort," said Lauren. "I wouldn't have to tell Bill about my part in this, and even if he found out he'd be thrilled that Jodie is healed."

"Healed not only physically but spiritually," Carnes promised adamantly.

"She's going to fight me tooth and nail," Lauren said. "We might not even be able to hold her down."

"Did you give her the codeine?"

"Yes, a heavy dose of cough syrup. Plus I crushed two Xanax and mixed the powder into her orange juice."

"She'll likely be sound asleep by now," said Carnes. "If she's awake, we don't have to go forward if you don't want to."

Lauren bit her lip and said, "All right, come on in."

"I'll get the holy water and the crucifix," said Carnes. "It healed Brenda Kallen when she got sick at my church camp. Holy water and prayer. It will save *your* daughter too, Mrs. Curtis. You won't regret this."

Kathy Traeger was on her phone with Tricia Lopez as she motored along Main Street in her red Mustang with the top down, loving the feel of the breeze in her long dark hair. "So I filled the bottle with water from the birdbath!" she boasted with a mischievous laugh.

"Love it, babe!" Tricia said.

They both erupted in giggles.

"Maybe Carnes will drive a stake in Jodie's heart," Kathy said giddily.

"Or her head," Tricia chirped, going along with the joke.

"I hope not," Kathy said soberly. "I like her. So does Darius."

"I know. He has the screaming hots for her."

"She's soon going to be ready to lose her virginity."

"Thanks to us," said Tricia.

"We have more fun than anybody!" Kathy said.

"Right on! Everybody in the world should be like us!"

"Maybe more people soon will be," said Kathy, and she hit the gas harder as she turned onto the highway that would take her home.

The living room was lit with candles, and Jodie's limp body was lying in the middle of the carpet as Reverend Carnes and Lauren knelt over her. Now that the exorcism was in progress, she couldn't believe it was actually happening. She was profoundly wavering, and she hoped the reverend couldn't tell, because if he knew, he would mock her backslide, her lapse of faith.

All the crises she and Bill had been through with Jodie—from her near-strangulation with the umbilical cord to her near-death experiences with life-threatening allergies, then the plummet into PTSD—tumbled through Lauren's mind, producing a bitter anger over the unfairness of her life and the many losses she had suffered. She wished she could accept it all as God's will, and that was what was beckoning her back to religion, but she was still failing to get herself permanently in that frame of mind. In other words, in Carnes's judgment, she was refusing to give herself fully to Jesus. She was still a doubting Thomas, no matter how hard she tried to surrender to a Greater Power.

The reverend began whispering a prayer, and Lauren knew he was whispering because he didn't want to take the chance of waking Jodie out of her drug-induced sleep. The whispering seemed less impressive than the booming voices of the evangelical preachers on TV, who always spoke at the top of their lungs, as if God's people and God Himself were hard of hearing.

"Oh, unclean spirit," Carnes said, "I command you to leave the body of this innocent child! Return to the fiery bowels of hell! Go back into the arms of Satan, your unholy master!"

Lauren knew that if Bill walked through the door right now and caught her at this, it might end their marriage. He was kind, he was considerate, he was loving. But he couldn't abide what he thought of as ignorance. Ignorant groveling before God and demons. He had nothing but contempt for it. But she, more than he, was willing to try anything.

Reverend Carnes soaked his white handkerchief with water from his little bottle and began to gently swab Jodie's purplish blisters. Then he handed the bottle and cloth to Lauren, wordlessly urging her to continue swabbing.

"By the power of the Holy Spirit," he whispered, "I ask that this child be made pure! Let sanctifying grace purify and protect her immortal soul!"

When Lauren wiped Jodie's blistered lips, she moaned feverishly, as if the touch of wetness might wake her up. Then suddenly she began writhing in obvious agony. She let out a horrible scream.

But to Lauren's amazement, the reverend kept on praying, seemingly unperturbed.

"Our Father who art in heaven, hallowed be Thy Name . . ."

Lauren joined him in the Lord's Prayer.

"Thy kingdom come, Thy will be done, on earth as it is in heaven. Give us this day our daily bread, and forgive us our trespasses, as we forgive those who trespass against us. And lead us not into temptation, but deliver us from evil . . ."

Lauren was surprised how easily the words came back to her, now that she hadn't really belonged to any church for a long time. It was Bill who had gotten her away from her Catholic religion. And the Catholic clergy taught that giving in to the beliefs of any other kind of church was heresy—one of the worst sins anyone could ever commit.

Lauren was being torn in so many directions that she didn't know who or what to believe anymore. She only hoped that somehow she was doing the right thing for her daughter, even if her marriage did not survive.

CHAPTER 46

On a bright Saturday morning in mid-June, Jodie Curtis was jubilant! Her ugly blisters were gone, and she was going mall hopping with her BFFs! She couldn't stop looking at her glowing complexion in the bathroom mirror, and as a result she wasn't quite ready when Kathy honked the horn. She peered out of her parents' front bedroom window and saw the red Mustang with its top down, dashed back into her own bedroom, hurried up and fastened her bra and put on a Metallica T-shirt, then kissed her mother's cheek, ran out the door, and piled into the back seat, between Brenda and Tricia.

Immediately she blurted, "Look at me! My blisters are gone!"

"We told you so," Kathy said, smiling back at her from behind the wheel.

"I wanna hit the Gap," Tricia said. "They're having a summer sale."

"I wanna hit a *lot* of stores!" Brenda chimed in.

"Cool!" said Jodie. "My blisters are gone! My blisters are gone! My blisters are *gone!*"

"So good for you," said Kathy, peeling out.

"So shaddup about it already!" said Brenda.

Jodie clammed up, but she wished her friends would be happier for her than they sounded. They were so incredibly blasé, in her opinion.

Later, at Banana Republic, as the four girls gleefully browsed among dresses, skirts, blouses, and sweaters, Tricia eyed Jodie over one of the racks of jeans on plastic hangers and said, "Didn't we tell you those blisters would go away, Jodie? You were acting like such a dweeb over it! Such a scaredy-cat! And there was never really anything to worry about."

Jodie said, "My mother told me that Reverend Carnes came and cured me with prayers and holy water, but I don't remember a thing about it. She made me promise not to tell my dad. But she's making me go to church now. She didn't used to care much about religion, but now it's like she's trying to be some kind of saint or something."

"Bullshit!" said Tricia. "Carnes the Bible thumper had nothing to do with it! You were going to get better anyway. Aren't you glad? Now you're like us."

Brenda came to Jodie's side in time to hear Tricia's last statement, and she partially disagreed with it, saying, "Well . . . almost."

Her feelings hurt, Jodie said, "What do you mean, Brenda? I've always been a lot like both of you. Kathy, too. We like the same kind of music and stuff, and we can tell each other just about anything—heck!—that's why we're best friends."

Kathy looked up from a counter where she was busy spraying different kinds of perfume on her wrist and then sniffing it. With a rather sly look on her face, she said, "Well, now we're going to be even better friends, Jodie. You're not a kid anymore, you're a young woman. Now you're ready to have a boyfriend."

This was something Jodie had dreamed of, but didn't dare think it could really happen to her. When she was going through her bouts of PTSD and life-threatening allergies, and then breakouts of pus-filled purple blisters on top of everything else, she didn't think that any boy would ever want her. But now maybe there was a glimmer of hope. Still, aspects of it were frightening, and she said, "I don't want to have sex till I'm older."

Kathy, came up to them with a pile of jeans over her arm and said, "Jodie, you don't have to have sex till you're good and ready. But you *will* be ready for it sooner rather than later, believe me."

Flashing a mischievous wink, Brenda said, "As good as sex is for ordinary people, like our mothers and fathers, or even other kids our age, it's a lot better for *us*, honey. So don't be scared of it, just let it happen."

"You act like you do it all the time!" Jodie blurted.

Almost in perfect unison, Brenda and Tricia said, "Well, we *do!*"

They burst out laughing, and Jodie half-heartedly laughed with them, thinking they were just kidding. But were they? It didn't seem like they were, and she was stunned. But also a bit jealous. Her BFFs were so far ahead of her in life experience that she despaired of ever catching up. And she wasn't totally certain that she wanted to.

Still standing there with a pile of jeans over her arm, Kathy said, "I'm taking these and trying them on one after another while we're here. I don't want to take them home and then have to bring back the ones that don't fit. Sometimes *none* of them end up looking good on me, and it really pisses me off."

She disappeared into a changing room.

Tricia watched her go, then in a hushed but singsong voice, she said, "Somebody likes you, Jodie."

"Yeah," said Brenda, "you have a secret admirer."

"Get out! Who?" Jodie said disbelievingly.

Coyly, Benda said, "If we tell you, do you promise to come and meet him?"

"I don't believe you! It's nobody! You're making it up!"

But she secretly wished it were true.

"Then take us up on it," Brenda challenged.

Jodie thought it over, and her desire to be liked by a boy got the best of her. "I still think you're bullshitting me, but for now I'll play along. So come on and tell me—who?"

Slyly, Tricia said, "Well, if we're bullshitting, I guess I'll let the cat out of the bag. You really want to know who? It's Darius, that's who."

"*Nuh-uh!*" Jodie gasped.

"Yeah, Darius. We're not shitting you," Brenda said.

"Ugh!" Jodie blurted. "He's the one who bit me! I can't stand to look at him! The creep! Why would he want me when he can have any majorette or cheerleader he wants?"

Brenda said, "But he happens to want *you*, Jodie. He's sorry for what he did and he knows how you must feel. He outgrew that sort of thing. He's older now, more mature, and he doesn't bite anybody anymore."

"Listen to *us!* Of *course* he doesn't!" Tricia said.

"We're being just too damned silly!" Brenda agreed.

They laughed at the absurdity of it, and Jodie laughed along with them.

"Darius wants us to come to his band rehearsal today," Tricia said. "And he wants you to be there, Jodie."

It was an amazing turn of events. Almost like a date. And she had to admit she was now intrigued. She craved romance, but had to stifle the craving when she suffered from life-threatening allergies. She used to wonder, in utter despair, how she could ever let any boy kiss her, because she'd have to ask him to wash his mouth out first, if he had been eating nuts. She had read about a man who killed his fiancée by French kissing her and spitting a lump of peanut butter down her throat. This was an extreme case, for sure, but there were plenty of more "ordinary" cases, like quite recently when a fifteen-year-old boy died after eating a pancake with milk in it. He had forgotten his EpiPen and had been told by the restaurant staff that there was no milk in their pancakes.

But now Jodie's allergies seemed to be magically gone, and perhaps a longed-for world of romantic love was opening up to her at last.

She knew that Darius was what parents called a *bad boy*, almost a modern-day equivalent of an aspiring outlaw, a gunslinger. But maybe she should give him a chance. Maybe he wasn't all bad.

Maybe he kept his finer qualities hidden from everyone, and she would be the one to draw him out. If he truly liked her. But if he didn't and her BFFs were just running a game on her, she'd be mortified and would never live it down. Her classmates would pillory her on Facebook and everywhere else.

CHAPTER 47

Darius Hornsby's band, Darius & the Demons, was rehearsing in a garage at his parents' ranch-style home on a pleasant treelined avenue in one of the best parts of Chapel Grove. The big double doors of the garage were wide open. Jodie could hear the blaring of drums and guitars even before she and her BFFs got out of the Mustang. The top was still down and there were no wound-up windows to mute the music. They had to park in the street because the driveway was blocked by Darius's van, plus two SUVs and two motorcycles.

Jodie tentatively entered the front of the garage, following behind Kathy, Brenda, and Tricia. She had never been to a band rehearsal before, and the brand-new experience awed her and made her feel sort of special, even though they weren't in a huge auditorium but were spread out and hanging back in the murky semidarkness of a garage.

Darius was the lead singer and lead guitarist—and he was so amazingly, undeniably *good!* Jodie was enthralled, in spite of all the negative feelings she had nurtured about him throughout her young life. His tenor voice was clear as a bell, and yet he was belting out his lyrics in an angry, sinister way that was simultaneously soft and sexy, a combination of qualities that didn't fit but somehow magically *did.* Lost in his passion for his music, he was extremely alluring, a rock star in the making perhaps, and much more than that in Jodie's eyes—to her it seemed as though he had already arrived! He had a wild, energetic charisma that cast a spell over her that was palpable and real. She glanced at Brenda, Kathy, and Tricia and saw that they were as blown away as she was.

The song ended in a thunderous climax, and all the girls yelled, whistled, and applauded. Darius was flushed with excitement and bathed in sweat, his long blond hair lank and wet, hanging down over his forehead. The other band members were breathing hard but beamingly elated. Drummer Ben Kerr whipped his dreadlocks like a cat-o'-nine-tails as he flailed his sticks, while Hank Lawson wiped sweat from his brow and ran his hand through the tight curls of his huge Afro. The third guitarist, a lank and bony white boy, wielded his guitar like a weapon, and the veins on his arms stood out between the tattoos of skulls, dragons, and bloody knives inked into his pale, pasty skin. None of the boys were in any of Jodie's classes, so she thought maybe they were dropouts. They ended their song with a cacophony of loud, vicious drum and cymbal crashes and guitar riffs, and Darius wiped perspiration from his shiny face and said, "Now we're gonna do an original, written by me, of course, and it's called, 'The Devil Made Me.'" He focused on Jodie, and his violet eyes bored into her as he sang.

> *I wrapped my arms tight around you*
> *Kissed you deep while I killed you*
> *My demon looked down from my shelf*
> *No way could I control myself*
> *'Cause the devil made me*
> *The devil made me*
> *The devil made me do it to ya!*
>
> *We went to the graveyard at midnight*
> *Held our Black Mass in the moonlight*
> *We sucked each other's blood*
> *You dropped dead with a thud*

'Cause the devil made me
The devil made me
The devil made me do it to ya!

The song got louder, wilder, and crazier, and Darius kept on staring straight at Jodie while he was singing and playing. During the instrumental bridge, Hank handed Darius a canteen and he took a sip of whatever was in it. Then he passed it back, and the other boys took turns sipping. That's when Jodie noticed that the boys, other than Darius, all had numerous scars on their arms, as if they had been sliced a number of times with knives or razors and then the wounds had healed.

She shuddered because it made her remember her own scar, from the bite Darius had given her in the sandbox, when she was only six years old. There was no sign of that scar now, which had magically disappeared only two days ago.

Darius motioned for Jodie to come closer, and he handed the canteen to her. Somehow she couldn't refuse it, even though it scared her. But she didn't want to displease Darius. So she drank, and to her surprise she liked it very much. Turning toward the other girls, she exclaimed, "This is *good!*" She licked the red stuff from her lips, whatever it was.

"We knew you'd love it!" Tricia said.

As Jodie went to take another sip, Brenda said, "Don't hog it, now—let *us* have some."

They kept passing the canteen around and taking sips as Darius & the Demons pounded to the conclusion of "The Devil Made Me."

Darius laid down his guitar and came toward Jodie. The other three boys joined up with Tricia, Kathy, and Brenda, closing around them tightly as they introduced themselves to Jodie as Ben, Hank, and Doug—first names only. Ben wore dreads with silver death's heads tied into them and Hank wore his hair in an Afro.

Darius took Jodie's face between the palms of his hands and kissed her lips tenderly, as if he had been doing it his whole life and had a perfect right. A thrill coursed through her, and her legs went weak, and the feeling was so intensely pleasurable that she wanted more of it, in spite of herself. He said, "Stick around, huh, babe? I wanna get to know you."

She flashed her friends an unsure look and murmured, "Brenda? Tricia?"

Kathy said, "Oh, don't worry about us, hon. We're gonna cruise. If we don't hook up again, Darius will drive you home."

Jodie's three gal pals departed, and with trepidation she watched them go, feeling almost as if she were being ditched. And scared. Was she really about to be alone with a boy, for the first time?

As if he had read her thoughts, Darius said, "Don't worry, babe, it'll be cool."

CHAPTER 48

Reverend Carnes knocked on the door to Pete Danko's office and was in a dither from the moment the police chief let him in. "Bennett and Margaret Stein are missing! No one's heard from them for two days! Neither one of them showed up at his law office this morning."

"All right," Pete said. "Have a seat and try to calm down. They're both sensible adults, and there might be a good reason for this."

Pete sat behind his desk, and the reverend sat opposite him, still fidgety. "I was supposed to meet Bennett at ten a.m. to discuss church business. He's always there promptly at nine, if not sooner. He and Margaret normally come in together—she's his head paralegal. But they're not there, and neither one of them called in. His private secretary is extremely worried. This is so unlike them!"

"Did you check your phone for messages?"

"Of course! There are none, except from a couple of my other parishioners. He's never missed an appointment with me—never! He's an extremely successful attorney, but the church means even more to him than his law practice."

"Well, something must've come up that was very important to both of them," Pete said. "It will probably turn out to be something outside of their normal routine, but nothing to be alarmed about. Have you talked with any of their family members?"

"I tried unsuccessfully to reach their daughter, Marilyn. She lives here in Chapel Grove with her husband and their son, a three-year-old. They all belong to my congregation."

"Did you go to their house?"

"No, I tried their landline and both of their cell phones, and they all went to message. I left messages, but no one has called back."

"This looks like some kind of family emergency might've cropped up," Pete said. "Maybe an illness or an accident."

"If so, I should have heard from them," said Carnes. "I'm their pastor, and I'm the first person they lean on."

"Come to think of it, there haven't been any accident reports," said Pete. "Not in the past couple of days. We'll have to check with the hospital to see if Bennett or Margaret Stein might be listed as patients. Maybe one of them fell ill all of a sudden."

"Anything that serious, they would've called me already," Reverend Carnes said quite adamantly.

"Well, try to relax. We'll get on it," Pete told him.

"I never relax. I stay vigilant," said Carnes. "These are perilous times, and both God and the devil work in strange ways."

CHAPTER 49

Bill and Lauren were watching TV, a true-crime story on ID Discovery, which was one of Bill's favorite channels, but not Lauren's, when a horn honked in front of the house. Bill got up, peeled back a curtain, and got upset when he saw Darius Hornsby out there in his van, parked by the curb in front of the house. Jodie, in ass-tight jeans and a stretchy white halter, came running down the stairs trying to run out the door before her father could yell at her and make her put on something he considered more dignified.

Bill spun from the window and said, "Whoa, young lady! Where are you going?"

"To a movie. With my date."

"What date?" Lauren said, startled.

"Darius Hornsby. Bye, Mom. Bye, Dad!"

Totally surprised by this new information, which went against every opinion his daughter had previously uttered against Darius, Bill said, "Not so fast, Jodie! You're not going anywhere till he knocks on the door and shakes hands with me so we can have a man-to-man talk. And while we're doing that, you're going to go up to your room and change into something decent. Those jeans you're wearing would've fit you when you were thirteen, but now they look like you were poured into them."

"Awww, Dad . . ."

"Go out there and tell him what I said. Or else you're grounded."

"Why do you always have to act like a policeman?"

"I'm acting like a father. If he really cares about you, he'll treat you like a lady, especially if you dress like one. And he'll pay proper respect to me and your mom."

Shrugging, sighing, and shaking her head, Jodie stomped out the door. When she returned, she led her "date" into the living room and said, as if the words hurt her tongue, "Dad, this is Darius. Darius, this is my mom and dad." She bit her lip, looking embarrassed, and hastily added, "It's a little cooler outside than I thought, Darius. I'm going to take a minute to put on something warmer."

As Jodie scampered back upstairs, Bill reached out to shake Darius's hand, but Darius turned it into a fist-bump, and Bill gave in to it, awkwardly, then said, "Nice to meet you."

Darius said, "How ya shakin', dude."

Bill immediately took the heat. "Listen to me, young man. I'm Mr. Curtis to you, and you better keep it that way if you expect to date my daughter. And you will address my wife as 'Mrs. Curtis' at all times. Is that fine with you, or not."

"A-okay . . . er . . . sir."

There was no mistaking the taint of sarcasm on the word "sir"—but Bill decided, rightly or wrongly, to let it slide for now and come down harder on the boy in the near future. He said, "It's no secret, Darius, that you have a bad reputation, not just in the community but with the police force. I hope your bad behavior is behind you. But if I find out, or even suspect, that it isn't, then you won't be taking my daughter anywhere. Understand me?"

"Yes, sir," Darius slurred, and punctuated it with a thumbs-up. And Bill didn't like it one bit.

"I'll have Jodie home by twelve," Darius said, which at least was some acknowledgment of parental authority.

"That's what I like to hear," said Bill.

Jodie came back from upstairs, dressed more suitably in a not-too-tight skirt, and shrugged at Darius as if to say, *I can't help it, my dad made me change clothes.*

Lauren, who had remained silent till now, said, "Have a good time, dear." And after the young couple went out the door, she turned toward Bill and said, "You were too hard on them."

"You're kidding."

"No, I'm not. Jodie doesn't have many close friends, let alone a boyfriend, and if this one dumped her she'd be utterly devastated. Nothing hurts worse when a girl is at her age. They're so vulnerable. Some of them even commit suicide when puppy love doesn't survive."

"*Who's* being overly dramatic?" Bill said.

"I'm just glad our daughter is finally doing some things that all normal teenagers do," said Lauren.

Bill flipped the porch light on for his daughter for when she came home, then reclined in his La-Z-Boy while Lauren plumped up a pillow and stretched out on the sofa. They resumed watching the ID channel, a rerun of a program called *Homicide Hunter* about brutal murders in the career of a detective named Joe Kenda, who had retired from the Colorado Springs Police Force after solving nearly four hundred cases. Lauren wasn't keen on this kind of stuff, far from it, but Bill was addicted to it, partly because he sometimes picked up professional tips, but mostly because he derived satisfaction out of seeing the guilty bastards get caught and punished. Right now, he wasn't working in a place that had one-hundredth the murder rate of Colorado Springs, at least not murders of the ordinary kind. But like every town in America, Chapel Grove was under the constant dark shadow of the plague. One outbreak had already occurred, sixteen years ago, and another one could be lurking, for all anybody knew. So Bill felt he was as battle-hardened as any cop in America, when it came right down to it.

At least, thankfully, the case he was working on right now wasn't a homicide. Not to trivialize it, but it was a simple, probably eventually explainable disappearance. For now, it was an intriguing puzzle, and not necessarily a crime. Bennett and Margaret Stein were missing. There was no reason to think they were dead. Probably because they had both been on television with Reverend Carnes, and were thus high-profile by Chapel Grove standards, Captain Pete Danko had taken charge of the investigation, with Bill forced into the role of sidekick. Sidekick and gofer, which was even more demeaning. Pete had assigned Bill the routine job of filling out paperwork and canvassing the Steins' neighbors while he, Pete, talked with the people he deemed "more important."

So far nothing much had turned up. Neither the daughter nor her husband knew anything, and were understandably terribly upset. So was Reverend Carnes, who had initially reported it.

Bill and Pete had started by going to the Steins' home, where their daughter let them in with her key. Nothing seemed out of place, and both of their vehicles were in the garage. Neither had left any notes, and neither had told anyone where they were going, so far as was known at this point from questioning neighbors, friends, and associates. Chapel Grove Hospital had no record of any admissions under the name Stein. Margaret's last known destination was the Lopezes' house, and Tricia said that she never arrived there. Apparently, the last time Bennett Stein was seen was at a youth group campfire meeting for boys only. According to the kids, he had gotten a phone call from his secretary and had left the campfire thing early to arrange bail for a client. That detail was strange, and highly questionable, because the secretary said there was no such phone call made by her, and moreover no such reason for any. It was an anomaly. But most cases had these types of anomalies. And maybe this one would iron itself out. Maybe tomorrow.

Bill wondered if, years from now, he would embody the hardened but still empathetic demeanor of Detective Joe Kenda. Was he seeing a glimmer of his own future? Since he had seen this particular program once before, his mind easily wandered. He glanced at Lauren and saw that she had picked up a book but now her eyes were shut and the book had fallen aside. What a nice picture they made of domestic suburban bliss. And he even thought that maybe they were actually getting closer to achieving it. In the fifteen years that Jodie had been with them, the family had gone through one crisis after another, and the poor kid had suffered the most. She had almost died in the womb, before the even got a chance to live. Then the life-threatening allergies had struck on Christmas Day when she was only five. Then the descent into PTSD. But now, thankfully, it was all behind her, almost miraculously, and Bill dared to hope that the miracle might last.

He knew that even if it did last, that did not mean that all his parental fears would end. They probably never would. As most parents would say, they are still your children, even after they are adults. But Jodie hadn't gotten that far yet. The latest pitfall was this snotty, bratty kid, Darius Hornsby, who in Bill's opinion was jeopardy personified. Of all the boys her age, did it have to be *this* one? What if he took her virginity? What if he had done so already? And how much of that kind of thing was really a father's business, at the tender age of fifteen, or at any other age? He'd have to just get used to the fact that his daughter had a life, and a sex life, that was her very own, and very private, as it should be. She and that boy had been seeing each other for a week and a half already, as nearly as Bill could figure out, and tonight was the first time he had shown up at the house. Plenty of time for the worst to already have happened. And Jodie was more sheltered, more naïve, than most girls her age. What if she got pregnant?

Oh, stop it already, Bill told himself. *Just get off it. Take things one step at a time, like you do on the job. Most people's worst imaginings never happen. Step back and let your daughter live her life. Be happy that she's doing a lot better now. Give her a chance, and try to trust her. You raised her right, and she'll do the right thing.*

Yet at the same time, Bill made up his mind to dig up more information on Darius Hornsby and to try to keep tabs on him as much as he could, under the guise of doing due diligence as a detective.

At fifteen minutes past midnight when *The Late Show* was almost over, Lauren kissed Bill good night and said she was going to bed. Jodie still wasn't home. Bill said, "She's late, damn it! That boy was supposed to have her here by now."

"So they're a little late," said Lauren. "Kids will be kids. They're enjoying each other's company and they get carried away. You and I weren't any different at their age."

"You used to be the one who'd be driven nuts by this."

"Believe me, my guts are grinding, but I'm working hard to rein myself in. Jodie seems so much happier now, I don't want to spoil it. Good night. Try not to have a heart attack."

He knew she was joking, but he didn't smile. He took her place on the couch and stretched out. Usually the TV would've put him to sleep, but it didn't happen. At three a.m. he was still awake, but groggy, and Jodie still wasn't home. Stalling, he went into the kitchen and drank a glass of cold milk. Then he finally went upstairs and brushed his teeth, then climbed into bed, only to toss and turn. At some point he must've conked out.

When he came to, after what must've been only an hour or two worth of sleep, or even less, it was because he got woken by an argument between Jodie and Lauren. He realized the ruckus was coming from Jodie's bedroom. Lauren was yelling, "Look what I found in the hamper! These are *your* panties!"

"Oh my God, Mom! Now you're inspecting my underwear? I can't believe it!"

"I know what these stains are! You're having sex with that boy!"

"So what, everybody does it."

"You're going to get pregnant! If you do, you can kiss college good-bye."

"I don't care if I don't go to college. Big deal. Anyhow, I know how to protect myself. I'm on the pill."

"*What!* Who gave them to you?"

"Dr. Miller—who do you think?"

This was too much for Bill. He got out of bed and pulled on his pants, then hustled into his daughter's room. "What's going on here?" he demanded, as if he hadn't already overheard.

"Nothing," Jodie said, and clammed up.

"Don't tell me 'nothing,'" Bill said angrily. "I heard every word!"

"So what're you gonna do about it?" Jodie sassed.

This threw him for a loop. He didn't really know what he would, or even could, do. With a sudden hurtful impact, it hit him that parents could be essentially helpless in the face of an adolescent who got too big or too wiseass to be controlled. "I'll make you stop seeing that boy," he said, giving in to threatening her, because for the moment he couldn't think of anything else.

"You can't stop me!" she said. "I'll run away!"

"I'll have him arrested."

"You can't! We're not doing anything wrong! We're in love and I'll never leave him! No matter what you do!"

Lauren took Bill's arm and said, "Let's just leave her be. Give her time to cool off."

He allowed himself to be led out of Jodie's bedroom, and he felt more helpless than he had felt even as a child, when his father was wreaking havoc and his mother was threatening to hang herself and he, as a terrified six-year-old, was running down the cellar stairs after her, trying to pull the clothesline out of her hands.

He knew he had to find a way to get through to Jodie, before she ruined her life. He loved her too much to let her make a potentially devastating mistake. And, to his mind, there could not be a worse walking mistake than Darius Hornsby.

CHAPTER 50

Kathy Traeger had left her iPhone on the dining room table so it wouldn't get wet while she was outside washing her Mustang. Giving in to curiosity, Dr. Traeger picked it up, figuring that if her daughter caught her fooling with it, she'd say she thought it was hers. They both had the same kind of phone, so she knew how to use the video app. She wanted to see what Kathy might be up to when she was out gallivanting and probably keeping secrets. She told herself she wasn't really snooping, she was just being a good, protective mom, exercising her deep concern about her daughter's welfare.

What she saw on the little screen knocked her for a loop. At first she thought Kathy and her friends must be making their own horror movie, wearing plastic fangs and drinking blood from a fake corpse. But then the shot panned onto the corpse's face, and Dr. Traeger broke into a cold sweat. The dead face wasn't a fake—it was all too real! It was the wife of that blustery attorney, Bennett Stein, who represented that religious nut, Reverend Carnes. Dr. Traeger had seen them on TV together, blathering to crowds of people on the steps of the courthouse.

Fear and confusion swept over her as she realized that Kathy and her friends had killed Mrs. Stein. Pretending to be vampires, they had filmed themselves desecrating her corpse. They weren't just making a horror move, they were making a *snuff* movie! Reeling from the shock of it, Dr. Traeger tried to pull herself together as her nagging worries about the children of the Foster Project transformed into abject fear.

For God's sake, what was going to happen to Kathy? She still loved her, no matter what she had done. What was going to happen to *all* of those kids? And to Dr. Traeger's research, her life's work?

Whom should she tell? Should she tell Pete Danko? Should she tell Colonel Spence? Should she tell nobody? Her mind was in a spin. She felt like her entire world was crumbling all around her.

She thought of deleting the video and putting her daughter's phone back on the table. But before she could do that, Kathy came into the living room and saw her with it in her hand, and she was still standing right by the purse. Worse, her own phone was in the breast pocket of her blouse and she had forgotten it was there.

"What're you doing with my phone?" Kathy snapped. "You have your own."

"My battery is low on bars. Is it okay if I use yours?"

"Who do you want to call?" Kathy asked suspiciously.

"Uh . . . Captain Danko. Something has come up."

"Captain Danko?" Kathy said, even more suspiciously.

Damn! Dr. Traeger thought belatedly. She shouldn't have mentioned Danko's name. Now Kathy might wonder if she could've seen something on that cursed phone that made her think of the police chief. Or could she really be that prescient?

"I'd rather you didn't use my phone," Kathy said flatly.

Dr. Traeger decided to let the matter drop, and she walked away, pulling her own phone out of her breast pocket as if she were going to use it.

"Mother, I wish you wouldn't lie to me," Kathy warned. And her face was twisted into a hard scowl that looked absolutely threatening. Then she pivoted and left the room.

In despair, Dr. Traeger realized that the game was up, in more ways than one. Her daughter probably knew what she had discovered, or at the very least she must suspect it. If she didn't tell on Kathy and her friends, she'd be complicit in the murder of Margaret Stein and a cover-up after the fact. If she did tell on them, the children of the Foster Project were done for. If they were biologically inclined to be killers, whatever made them that way should be rooted out. They should be quarantined, imprisoned, and studied. But Pete Danko would probably say they should be killed. And Colonel Spence would likely go along with that.

If her daughter was a murderess, which the images on her phone seemed to prove, what did that imply about the death of Dr. Traeger's husband, Daniel, so long ago, when Kathy was only seven? Had she actually had a hand in her father's death? If so, what else was she capable of? Who else might she have killed?

Dr. Traeger didn't know whom to turn to. She had no true allies, not even her own daughter. In fact Kathy seemed to hate her. But she clearly wasn't scared of her. She acted as if she would do whatever she wanted to do, and nobody would stop her.

Dr. Traeger could foresee nothing but total calamity. The situation called for intensive damage control—but even extreme measures might not prove adequate.

She came to a reluctant conclusion that she must tell everything she knew or suspected to Captain Danko. He was damage control personified, the Homeland Security Department's man on the ground. *Let him take control,* Dr. Traeger thought. *Give full disclosure so your superiors will not come down on you with full force. No matter what happens, save your own skin. The plague is still the main enemy and everyone's prime concern. And without you and your experiments they will never find a cure. Therefore they will not dare to get rid of you.*

She pulled her phone out again and punched in Pete Danko's secure number. The police chief answered immediately, and Dr. Traeger held her breath, trying not to slur her words. "I have to talk with you. I think there's been a homicide."

"You mean a suspicious death? Or something you witnessed?"

"My daughter . . . I know she's evil. They *all* are . . . I know

now . . . the video is on her phone. They killed Margaret Stein. Who knows what else they've done. . . ."

Danko said, "Are you drunk? You're not making total sense. Calm yourself, woman!"

"The children are more contaminated than we thought. Kathy . . . she just keeps wearing that innocent smile of hers . . . but she hates me. We have to stop her . . . stop them all . . . or everything will be ruined."

"Where are you?" Danko demanded.

"At my house."

"Stay where you are. I'm coming out there."

Dr. Traeger broke the connection. Then she heard her daughter's sinister-sounding voice.

"Who were you talking to, *Mommy?*"

She whirled around and was stunned by the demonically angry look on her daughter's face.

"Did you like our little movie, Mommy? Now you know one of my secrets," Kathy said. "So you might as well know the rest of them."

"I don't *want* to know! I'll get you an attorney. We'll get through this somehow."

"Too late, much too late, *Mommy!* I know you don't like me the way I am. You don't even *understand* the way I am. You never did, even though you'd like to believe that you're one of the world's greatest scientists. But you're not as smart as *we* are—me and my friends. You can't control *us* anymore. We're ready to take over."

"What do you mean? You're still a child!"

"Not anymore," Kathy said smugly. "I used to be a very precocious child. I pushed Daddy down the stairs, and I got away with it. And my friend Tricia smothered her baby brother and shot her father. He didn't die right away, but she corrected that little mistake in the hospital. You see, Mommy, we're much more clever than our parents are, or ever were. We've outsmarted our mothers and fathers, the police, the doctors, and all the other adults here in Chapel Grove."

Stunned, Dr. Traeger stood rooted in her tracks for a long moment while Kathy snickered at her. Then her anger overwhelmed her, and she slapped Kathy's face.

Kathy snarled—and her fangs involuntarily hinged forward and revealed themselves behind her pulled-back lips. She clawed at her mother, knocked her down, pinned her arms down underneath her, and bit savagely into her throat.

Kathy took a long, deep drink of her own mother's blood.

Then she got up, leaving Dr. Traeger lying there in pain and misery as she ran out the door, slamming it hard.

Dr. Traeger stumbled to a living room window and saw her daughter jump into the little red Mustang that she had bought for her birthday in an attempt to get gratitude, if not love, from her. But now it was clear that being born of a ghoul-bitten mother had caused her to turn into some kind of demon. The realization crashed in on her that the children of the Foster Project were probably about to run hog wild in some unfathomable way, unleashing a havoc that no one could hide from—a possible cataclysm that would consume her and her most cherished ambitions.

As Kathy peeled out in her Mustang, Dr. Traeger staggered into the kitchen, soaked a washcloth in water from a spigot, and pressed it to her bloody throat.

Then she thought of Kelly Ann Garfield. What to do about her—now that things were falling apart? She had delayed any final "disposition" of her while she toyed with the idea that Kelly Ann was worthier of parental love than her own daughter. But now she was under the gun, and the main thing was self-preservation. Her illusions were quickly eroding in a flood of urgency to protect herself and her research. She feared that the whole truth about the Medical Research Institute might come out. If so, she would be caught and swept under. She could no longer put aside a decision to deal with Kelly Ann in a humane way.

She phoned Captain Danko again and said, "If you didn't leave yet, stay there and I'll come to your office. First I have to take care of an urgent matter at the institute."

"More urgent than the homicide you want to tell me about?" Danko prodded.

"Well, at least *as* urgent. I'll fill you in."

"You sound drunk."

"No, just upset. I'll see you at your office."

She pulled the wet washcloth aside and saw that the bleeding had slowed considerably and the puncture marks felt actually small. She blotted the blood dry and went to the medicine cabinet in the bathroom and covered the wound with a bandage.

She got into her Toyota Camry and drove fast even though she realized she wasn't in full control of her faculties. But she had to do what she had to do. Before she had to tell Pete Danko anything that might cause things to unravel even faster, she needed to prepare a lethal dose for Kelly Ann. She intended to use succinylcholine. It was a drug used to anesthetize patients in the operating room, so it was painless, not like cyanide, for example, which produced an agonizing death. She still cared enough about Kelly Ann to treat her in the most comforting way possible. She had given her the gift of a few more months of life and excellent institutional care that she otherwise would not have had, and now she must protect her own interests, for the good of humanity. All was not lost yet, if only she could bail herself out of this disaster by convincing Homeland Security to deal with the children in a proper way and hold her harmless from blame. How could she have known what was going on behind her back? She was a dedicated scientist, a true genius. But she didn't have a crystal ball.

Driving fast and somewhat woozily, she made it into the parking lot of the institute, pulled crookedly into a slot but did not back up and straighten the car out, then hurried onto an elevator that took her to the wing on the third floor where Kelly Ann was kept. She used her key to the steel cabinet where the drugs were kept and filled a syringe with succinylcholine. Then she went down the hall to Kelly Ann's room. She took a deep breath and eased the door open, hoping she'd find her asleep so the task at hand would go easier.

She entered and did not see Kelly Ann on the bed. Maybe in the bathroom, she thought—then she got pounced on from behind the open door. Taken by surprise, she couldn't fight back, and she was knocked to the floor with Kelly Ann on top of her. They wrestled for the syringe, and Kelly Ann got it and plunged it into her shoulder. She rolled over, feeling herself quickly going groggy.

"I never trusted you," Kelly Ann said as she stood up. "You and your scientific gobbledygook!"

Dr. Traeger's vision was going blurry. She was already losing consciousness as Kelly Ann hurried out of the room and down the hall, where there was a keypad with a combination of numbers that allowed the doors to the lockdown facility to come open. Dr. Traeger imagined, somewhere in the dimming recesses of her drugged mind, that Kelly Ann was going to run away, out into the plague-ridden world.

Dr. Traeger roused herself from near-unconsciousness, realizing she must not have gotten a full injection, the needle wasn't plunged all the way in. Half-delirious from the anesthetic, she staggered to the elevator, took it down to the lobby, then made it to her car. She started the engine, flicked the headlights on, then jammed the Camry into gear and headed toward town.

Her vision was still blurry, and she blinked repeatedly, trying to maneuver the car successfully around the curves.

Suddenly she saw Kathy standing in the middle of the road. She blinked again, and the image wavered, then became insubstantial, ghostlike. But around a sharp bend the ghostly presence became stronger, almost *real*. She angrily hit the gas, figuring she'd prove that Kathy wasn't actually there by running her down. But now she found herself heading for a collision with a huge truck. She swerved and skidded—her tires screamed—and she narrowly avoided the truck as it roared by with its horn blaring.

Just as she breathed a sigh of relief, she started to go into convulsions, and she knew it was from the hypodermic that Kelly Ann had plunged into her. Her body jerked with painful spasms and her hands flew off the wheel and went to her aching head. She let loose a long, agonizing scream as her car burst through a guardrail and crashed into a utility pole.

CHAPTER 51

Dr. Traeger's corpse was lying on a steel table where it would be embalmed and then worked on by Steve Kallen and his daughter, Brenda, who was learning how to reconstruct and "pretty up" parts of dead, mutilated bodies—a task that she very much liked. Staring at the corpse after they had given it a good washing and cleaning, Brenda said, "As long as she's going to have a closed-casket funeral, why will we have to embalm her, Dad?"

"Because when people come to the service, and they kneel to pray over her coffin, they don't want to have to picture her rapidly decomposing, honey. It's just how people are, even if they're not particularly religious. They hate to think they're going to decay someday. Besides, it's a state law—all bodies not cremated must be embalmed, for sanitary purposes. And you'd be surprised—if we didn't do it this way, the odor of a body only a couple days old would soon get our attention, even with the lid closed."

He glanced at his watch, then put his arm around his daughter.

She said, "You're tired, Dad."

"Trying to get rid of me?"

"I think I can handle the embalming on my own this time. Why don't you let me?"

"Okay. I think I'll take your advice and turn in."

He kissed her on her cheek, then went upstairs. He wasn't really all that tired. It was only ten o'clock, and he figured he could watch something on TV. He wanted his daughter to feel that he trusted her to work on her own, without her dad needing to always be looking over her shoulder.

Brenda was glad he went upstairs without much prodding, because a few minutes later, as she had expected, the night bell rang. She opened up for Darius, Kathy, and Tricia and saw that Darius's van was parked in the near side of the lot a few feet from the door. She let them in, and they bemusedly eyed the corpse.

"Poor Dr. Traeger," Darius said, shaking his head exaggeratedly. "Now *we* get to examine *her.*"

"Well, not exactly *examine* her," Kathy said, grinning slyly. "I told you we fought and I bit her throat. I thought she'd already become one of our undead pets."

"It doesn't always happen so quickly," said Darius. "We all know that. It depends on their immune systems."

"Well, she *loves* the undead," said Tricia. "So now she gets to find out what it's like to *be* one."

They laughed.

"Not so loud," Brenda said. "My dad is upstairs."

Just then Steve Kallen called out, "Brenda? Are you still up, honey?"

He crept quietly halfway down the stairs. He was in his pajamas, and he had a gun.

Before he got to the landing he called out again. "Who's there? Brenda? Do you have company?"

For an instant he was relieved when he saw that it was only Brenda and her friends. But, strangely, they were formed into a little group around Dr. Traeger's body, with their backs toward him.

Darius said, "Why, hello, Mr. Kallen."

Steve said, "Why won't you look at me? What's going on here?"

Now each kid turned slowly, in unison. And at the same time Dr. Traeger's naked corpse sat up from the table.

The kids sprouted glistening fangs, their countenances markedly demonic, their eyes staring, their expressions fiendish.

Scared out of his wits, Kallen fired his pistol at them, but the shot went wild, thudding into Dr. Traeger's left breast.

The corpse fell back onto the table, groaning and hissing.

Kallen fired again, and his second bullet hit Tricia Lopez. She sagged and fell dead—and now he knew they could be killed, which gave him a modicum of hope. But by then his own daughter was clawing at him, seizing his gun hand and pushing him down. As he fell to the floor, he squeezed off another round that went wild.

Dr. Traeger's corpse sat up again, even with the gaping hole in her chest. Kallen tried to aim his gun at the corpse's head, but dropped the weapon when Darius kicked him in the groin and Kathy kicked him in the side of his head. Then the revived corpse of Dr. Traeger came at him, rasping and drooling. Kallen tried to crawl away, but he was too weak by now and in too much pain. Kathy and Darius rolled him onto his back and his eyes were wide with horror as his own daughter sank her fangs into his neck.

Minutes later, a 9-1-1 operator took a frantic call from a clerk in a dollar store across the street from Kallen's Funeral Home. She reported hearing gunshots, and the report was relayed to the desk sergeant at the Chapel Grove police station. Most of the cops on the small force were out on patrol, so Pete Danko took Bill Curtis with him to respond to the incident. While Pete drove the short distance down Main Street to the funeral home, Bill radioed for backup. As they swung over to the curb, they spotted Darius Hornsby's satanically decorated silver van peeling out of the back lot.

"Get a BOLO out on that van!" Pete told Bill. "All our guys know it, they should be able to chase it down. But make sure at least a couple of squad cars don't split off. We need them to get here."

"The van came from in back," Bill said. "Maybe that's the way we'll need to get in."

They ran back there and found the steel door half ajar. Drawing their weapons, they went in cautiously, covering each other. The first thing they saw was Steve Kallen's mutilated body, his brown skin turned a shade of ghastly whitish tan, drained of blood. Fang marks were all over his limbs and face. There was also a bullet hole in his head. And his torso was eviscerated, as if the abdomen was clawed open to grant access to the soft internal organs.

The fang marks were something new to Bill, but his past experiences told him that the ripping open of the abdomen had to be the work of the undead. "Oh, shit!" he said to Pete. "It's happening all over again!"

A short distance away from Kallen's body, Tricia Lopez was lying dead from a gunshot to her head, and a .38 revolver was lying near her.

Pete said, "Dr. Traeger's body is missing. She was badly torn up in that head-on collision, and Steve told me he would need to do a lot of cosmetic reconstruction on her."

"Maybe she's already upstairs in a coffin," Bill suggested. "Does her daughter know that she was killed?"

"I don't think so. The medical examiner tried to reach her, but couldn't. I tried too. No one seems to know where Kathy is."

"I could make a pretty good guess," Bill said. "She's probably in that van. Brenda Kallen, too, Pete."

"You think those three kids did all this?"

"Doesn't it look that way to you?"

"Yeah, it does," Pete said. "I'll wait down here for backup. Go upstairs and see if you find a closed casket in one of the viewing rooms. Dr. Traeger might be in it."

"I doubt it," Bill said. "This is right in line with the disappearance of Ron Haley and his wife and daughter."

Pete wondered just how bad things were going to get. He hoped that no matter what happened, he'd be able to do damage control. He vowed to do his best, no matter whom he might have to kill.

CHAPTER 52

As he always did each night before he went to bed, Reverend James Carnes was kneeling in the church cemetery, at the foot of a large, ornate, poured-concrete cross, reciting his Prayer for the Dead, hoping to keep them from arising again before Judgment Day.

> *May these souls rest in peace*
> *May their bodies return to dust*
> *May they never rise again*
> *May they remain in Purgatory*
> *Or with the Lord till Judgment Day*
> *May they enjoy Perpetual Light*
> *Amen.*

About to get up and dust off the dirt from his knees, the reverend thought he heard a noise from behind him. He stood and looked all around, trying to peer between the moonlit gravestones and monuments. Was someone sneaking up on him? He was well aware that he had enemies in Chapel Grove, people who thought he was fixated or half-deranged, even some who wanted to stop him before he got a chance to spike their loved ones. When he was all alone like this in the church cemetery, he was vulnerable and he knew it, though he tried to believe that the Lord would protect him. He could be mugged or bludgeoned to death by anyone who coveted the little bit of money he carried, or who wanted to vandalize the church or steal its few valuable artifacts.

He was relieved when his close friend and attorney, Bennett Stein, appeared from behind a maple tree at the far edge of the burial ground. He hadn't seen or heard from Bennett for several days and had been worried about him. Darius and some of the other kids had said that the youth group leader had left the campfire meeting early because of an emergency. But that explanation never sat well with Carnes.

He started to call out a cheerful greeting to Bennett, just as Margaret Stein also stepped out from behind the maple tree. They both came forward, seeming to move awkwardly, perhaps even painfully, as if they both had been hurt in an accident or something.

But then they got close enough for a better look at them, in the moonlight—and a shock of sudden fear rippled through the reverend. He could now see that their clothing was ripped and blood-spattered, and there were puncture marks all over them.

He grabbed a gold cross from around his neck and thrust it toward them, saying, "By the power of the Holy Spirit, I condemn you to eternal death and damnation! Be gone from me, unclean beings!"

But the two undead creatures kept on coming.

Carnes stood his ground. He lowered his little gold cross and let it dangle on its chain.

The zombies got closer, and Margaret was in the lead.

Carnes pulled out an old long-barreled revolver that he always tucked under his belt when he went out to pray in the cemetery at night. "May she rest in peace," he said. Then he shot Margaret in the head. She let out a tiny hiss of breath as she staggered and fell.

The reverend's hand shook with the emotion of vanquishing someone whose friendship he had known and treasured, but now the other undead being was almost upon him and he had to steady his aim.

BLAM! The Bennett Stein effigy reeled backward and fell heavily to the ground.

Carnes stared at it, his hand shaking worse.

"May your soul rest in peace," he murmured.

Then he looked skyward and begged the Lord to forgive him for what he had done.

CHAPTER 53

Ben, Doug, and Hank, the three sidemen of Darius & the Demons, were in a rented U-Haul, driving the streets and neighborhoods of Chapel Grove, dropping off what Darius had referred to as "special gifts for the community."

The special gifts were the zombies they had created.

Some of them had already been "planted" around the stores, bars, and restaurants on Main Street. Darius's intention was that they would start attacking the citizens of the town, creating havoc. He and his blood-seeking companions were endowed with an impish sense of humor as point-counterpoint to their more bizarre qualities. They loved playing macabre and often deadly pranks on the adults of the town, especially the authorities and even more especially their own parents. Hopped-up Bob Dylan lyrics that Darius's biological father, Hal Rotini, used to sing in a blaring heavy-metal rendition on an old Hateful Dead CD often came into his mind.

Darius knew that he and his kind would soon be taking over the world. The seeds of destruction were planted here in Chapel Grove, an innocent little town that became the womb of the New Order. It might take a decade or more, but archaic humanity was finished, they just didn't know it yet. A stronger, more ruthless breed was taking over. And Darius was one of its leaders. Sometimes he allowed himself to believe that he would even be the Grand Leader someday. And Jodie, his beloved, would be his consort, basking in power and always by his side.

When they fed on the blood of primitive humans, those victims became archaic husks of humanity, like the dry husks of dead insects in a spider's web. They were dumb, flesh-hungry slaves, useful for creating havoc, spreading terror, and paving the way for Darius and his cohorts to rise to power. He knew that in the future, when the bulk of humanity would be kept in pens as a source of blood, like farm animals were now kept as a source of meat, the poor dumb zombies would no longer be needed, and would be put to death, like the prisoners in concentration camps who were too sick to work anymore.

Jodie didn't know all this quite yet. He was slowly indoctrinating her, teaching her to accept her new, superior persona and to relish her destiny, which was to rule alongside him.

CHAPTER 54

At Kallen's Funeral Home, Bill Curtis and Pete Danko were waiting for the CSI team to get there. Pete was sitting on a gray steel folding chair, and Bill couldn't stop pacing, hoping they'd soon get a call from a patrol car saying that Darius's van had been pulled over and the occupants were in custody.

Pete said, "Let's step outside for some air, till they get here."

"Neither one of us still smoke or that's what we'd probably do," Bill said.

They went out through the steel door—and Pete pulled out his Glock and aimed it at Bill's back just as Bill turned around and saw him do it.

"What the hell!" Bill blurted.

"Sorry, partner," Pete said with a sly chuckle. "You've been a pain in the ass long enough. The shit is going to hit the fan, and I can't have you around for the party. You know too much already, and you won't stop pushing."

"You sonofabitch!" Bill shouted. "You kept me from doing my job! I *knew* there was some ulterior motive going on!"

"Well, you're going to die not knowing any more than that," Pete said. "This ain't the part where I get stalled blabbing everything, while somebody comes and rescues you in the nick of time. So don't get your hopes up."

"Ballistics will trace the bullet to your gun. Where's your drop weapon?"

"Fuck you, I don't need one. I'll say you were a fuckin' hero, shot in the line of duty by persons unknown."

But just as Pete was going to pull the trigger, he was pounced on by undead Hilda Lopez!

She had crept around the side of the building to leap on him from behind.

She sunk her teeth into Pete's soft throat, severing the jugular, making blood spurt like a fountain, before Bill could draw his Glock. Yanking it from its holster, he stepped close enough to give Hilda a head shot. BLAM! She sagged to the asphalt as Pete bled and died, emitting a final trickle of blood.

Two more zombies came at Bill, and he whirled and fired at them, hitting one and missing the other. Then another one appeared, from around the corner of the building. He fired two more times in rapid succession and both shots hit home this time, splattering the zombies' blood and brains.

But three more were coming at him. He killed one, but then he was out of ammo. No time to ram in another clip. He clubbed the nearest zombie over the head—a big fellow in bibbed coveralls—who did not go down but instead clawed the gun out of Bill's hand.

Desperately, Bill ran for Pete's car and jumped in. But he didn't have the keys, Pete did.

Frantically he locked all the doors. But the big zombie in the bibbed coveralls picked up the fallen gun and used it like a hammer to shatter the driver's-side window. Two others joined him, pounding and pounding at the other windows, trying to get in. With a shudder, Bill recognized one of them as the rapist, Roger Dalton, whom he had tried to sock away in prison, but had failed. His body was ghastly white, drained of blood and covered with bite marks. He looked as if he had been attacked by a pack of wild animals.

Bill thought he was going to die, ripped apart and devoured. To him, it was a worse fate than being killed in combat. He didn't think he was this terrified even when he was fighting in the Middle East. Or were those older fears now muted by time and distance?

Right now he didn't think he would ever see his wife and daughter again.

But as he was thinking he was done for, Reverend Carnes's pickup truck screeched into the lot. Carnes plowed into two zombies, running them over. Then he jumped out of the truck with a revolver in his hand. He shot two of the zombies who were pounding and clawing at all the windows of Pete's car, trying to get at Bill. Then he shot another one who was munching on Pete Danko's arm.

Lastly, he shot Pete in the head to stop him from arising.

"May he rest in peace," the reverend said. "The rotten bastard!"

CHAPTER 55

Lauren was in bed, sleeping fitfully, when an eerie, childlike voice began calling to her.

"Mommy . . . Mommy . . . wake up . . . come on out . . . come on out, Mommy . . ."

It was Jodie's voice, but it sounded distorted, metallic, unusually high-pitched, calling out in a strange singsong rhythm.

"Mommy . . . wake up . . . come on out . . ."

Lauren came fully awake, went to the bedroom window, and looked out. She was shocked when she saw her own daughter outside in the middle of the night, in the open yard surrounded by woods. She flung open the window and cried, "Jodie! My God! What are you doing down there?"

Jodie didn't answer. Didn't even look at her. She just kept calling, "Mommy . . . come out . . ." She looked like Jodie, wearing the same jeans and blouse she had worn to go out on a date with Darius, and yet she didn't look like herself, and it was unnerving. She appeared to be stoned, zonked out, removed from reality in some strange way.

Again Lauren cried, "Oh my God!"

She slammed the window shut and ran out of the bedroom, down the stairs, and out onto the porch steps. She peered into the moonlight.

"What are you doing?" Lauren said. "Are you sleepwalking?"

Jodie slowly turned around and started walking away from her, toward the surrounding woods. Lauren came down off the porch steps. Jodie kept going, getting even closer to the woods. Then she stopped and turned around, near the first line of trees. She faced her mother, smiling weirdly.

Lauren called out more desperately. *"Jodie!"*

Then Darius stepped out of the woods. He silently came to Jodie's side and took her hand in his. They smiled lovingly, and yet demonically, at each other.

Lauren gasped. She wondered vaguely if she were dreaming. And she desperately hoped it were so.

Darius and Jodie both laughed at her.

Then a pack of zombies stepped out of the woods—seven of them—looking utterly hideous in the moonlight.

Lauren stepped back in utter fear.

She recognized one of the zombies as the Dr. Traeger she had once known, not as a close friend, but as one of the important people in Chapel Grove. Now this formerly solid citizen was standing in front of her naked, her body bruised and battered, her face gruesome-looking. She took a step toward Lauren, and Lauren backed away.

Still holding hands, Darius and Jodie backed into the woods and completely disappeared in the foliage, leaving Lauren to face the pack of flesh-hungry zombies who were coming at her, rasping and groaning.

She was frozen for an instant, and the zombies were reaching for her, and she knew she would be torn apart. Too late, she started to run, and was tripped up by an undead woman, beefy and rawboned, at least 250 pounds of her.

But then, when Lauren thought she was doomed, a shot rang out, and the undead woman reeled back, struck in the chest. But at first she did not fall.

Bill Curtis had fired the bullet. He jumped down from the passenger side of a truck driven by Reverend Carnes, leaving the doors wide open. He aimed and fired once more, dispatching the woman he had shot in the chest with a bullet to the left side of her head.

Reverend Carnes jumped out of his pickup and fired off balance, missing an attempted head shot at one of the zombies but getting him with a well-placed second round.

Still firing as he ran, Bill got to Lauren and shielded her with his body as he and Reverend Carnes kept firing at the rest of the zombies in the yard.

Bill took careful aim at undead Dr. Traeger, squeezed his trigger and—BLAM!—she, or *it*, crumpled to the earth.

Then Bill, Lauren, and the reverend heard helicopter sounds! The chopper circled a few times over their heads, as if scoping out the situation. Then it moved on.

"They don't think we need help!" Bill yelled. "They're looking for other people who do!"

"But there may be more of the undead creatures back in the woods," the reverend said.

"Let's get into the house and lock the doors," Bill said.

Lauren cried out, "But our daughter is out there somewhere, and they might kill her, Bill!"

"Was she *here?*" Bill blurted out.

"Yes! With Darius! He's got some kind of weird control over her."

He put his arm around her and said, "I think she may be one of *them* now, honey. If so, I don't think there's anything we can do."

"But she didn't *look* like one of them," Lauren told him. "Not completely, anyway. I think she can be saved."

Shaking his head sadly, Reverend Carnes said, "I tried, but I couldn't save her soul."

"I won't give up on her!" Lauren said adamantly.

They could hear gunfire in the distance, all around town, and knew that the battle against the undead was still going on.

CHAPTER 56

The chopper hovered and strafed. Cops and posse men deployed in squads, firing their weapons.

Ghouls were exterminated outside a church, near a school, at a playground.

A group of armed men burst into a house just in time to save some of the family members, while others had been partially devoured. Outside in the street they shot an undead mailman about to bite into a dead woman's arm. They watched until the dead woman opened her eyes and started to come back to life. Then they shot her in the head.

There weren't near as many of the flesh-hungry creatures as in the first outbreak, sixteen years ago.

This time the cleanup was easier, and by morning it was done.

Some of the ungodly creatures may have gotten away, but nobody knew for sure.

CHAPTER 57

Reverend Carnes parked his pickup in Bill and Lauren's driveway and went up onto the front porch and rang the bell. Bill invited him into the living room, and they sat down and eyed each other solemnly.

Lauren, with an anxious, forlorn look in her eyes, came in carrying a tray and set it on the coffee table, then sat next to Bill on the couch. The tray was laden with a plate of cookies, hot coffee, and fixings. But nobody reached for anything.

Finally Carnes opened up and said, "I just came from the mayor's news conference. None of the missing children can be accounted for. None of them apparently were killed, except for the one Steve Kallen shot, at his funeral home."

"That's what we think right now," Bill said, "Ballistics will almost certainly confirm that the bullet came from his gun."

"Quite a few Chapel Grove children are still missing," Carnes said. "Among them are Darius Hornsby, Kathy Traeger, Brenda Kallen, and of course, your daughter."

"Those are just about all of Jodie's closest friends," Lauren said. "We're supposed to believe they're just plain *missing?* Maybe Homeland Security knows more than they're telling us. Maybe somebody has them in custody somewhere, and they just aren't admitting it. I wouldn't put it past them."

She pulled a balled-up tissue from her apron pocket and tried to wipe away tears even though the tissue was soggy. She had been crying off and on all through the morning and afternoon.

Bill said, "I don't think we were ever told the complete truth about much of anything connected to the plague. I think we were fed a pack of lies, going all the way back to our first outbreak."

"What about Tricia Lopez?" Lauren asked Reverend Carnes. "You didn't mention her."

He gave her an odd, hesitant look, then looked over at Bill as if wondering how much he should say.

She picked up on it and said, "Don't tell me she's—"

Bill put his arm around her. He said, "I wasn't going to tell you right away. I'm sorry, honey."

"But what about the others?" Lauren asked through her tears. "Maybe they didn't survive either."

"Their bodies weren't found anywhere," Bill said. "So there's still hope for our daughter, and I prefer to believe that."

Reverend Carnes said, "My gut feeling tells me that they'll be very hard to track down, and they must have some secret destination and some purpose of their own. I think they got clean away."

"To where?" Lauren asked anxiously.

"God only knows," said Carnes. "But they're carriers. They can start the plague again anywhere."

Bill said, "I'm going to find Jodie, and I won't rest until I do."

"But you don't know what she's become!" the reverend exclaimed.

"Nothing's wrong with her," Lauren told him. "I *saw* her! She seemed to be drugged or something. Brainwashed. If we can get her away from *that boy*, she'll be all right. I'm sure of it."

"I hate to say it, but you're in denial," Carnes said. "You both are. She's your daughter and you don't want to believe the worst of her. But she's given in to Satan."

Lauren started weeping again. Bill certainly couldn't blame her, in light of all she had been through. Last night in the wee hours he had shed some tears in private, after Lauren had gone up to bed, because he didn't want to show weakness in front of her.

"The strangest thing," Reverend Carnes said, "is that the SWAT team found the body of that notorious pickax murderer from Texas, Kelly Ann Garfield. The news reports say there's no doubt that it's really her. Hard to believe, isn't it?"

"I heard about it down at the station," Bill said. "It's her all right. DNA doesn't lie. Nor fingerprints."

"But she was executed," Carnes persisted. "I watched it on television. I don't believe in the death penalty. And she had become a true Christian."

"Well, she was ghoul-bitten," Bill said. "And the SWAT guys had to gun her down."

"She must've come back from the dead after she was executed," Carnes speculated.

Bill said, "I wouldn't begin to know. I don't know what to believe anymore."

Lauren told him, "You should start going to church. After all that's happened to us, you need to believe in *something*, Bill."

"That's exactly my point," he countered. "When people are scared and uncertain, they need to believe in something. But I believe in myself. And I'm going to find Jodie, come hell or high water. Maybe she's been brainwashed or something. But I'll never stop loving her, and I think she must know that."

CHAPTER 58

After checking their luggage, Darius Hornsby and Jodie Curtis took an escalator down toward the security gate at Pittsburgh International Airport. They had bright angelic smiles on their youthful faces. He smiled his handsome, dimpled smile at her and put his arm around her. He was wearing gray trousers and a nicely tailored dark blue sport jacket with an open-necked white shirt. She was wearing an organdy dress.

She smiled back at him and said, "Darius, will we ever see our friends again?"

"Someday we will, love. We'll gather for a reunion."

"I'm going to miss them a lot. Where did you send them?"

"All to different cities, in groups of two, like us. To the bigger cities mostly . . . New York, Philadelphia, Cleveland, Los Angeles, Rome . . ."

"Rome!" she exclaimed. "Who got to go there?"

"You don't know them. They wanted badly to see Italy. You and I get to live in New York, so cheer up, honey. If we all work hard and do the right thing, soon there will be many more like us. And still more of the undead ones, to do our bidding until the day when they're not needed anymore."

"What are we trying to do?" Jodie asked. "What are we trying to achieve, Darius?"

"The survival of our kind," he told her confidently. "We will eventually become the only free and noble human species inhabiting the earth. Just as Neanderthals took over from their less capable precursors, and then intellectually superior Cro-Magnons exterminated the Neanderthals, we shall supersede the races that came before us. It's survival of the fittest, Jodie. We were taught that in biology class."

"But why do we deserve to live and others to die?" Jodie asked.

"Because we *can!*" Darius responded smugly. "We're smarter than the adults who spawned us. We're more intelligent and more ruthless. And we will have an army of our own creation to help us. The undead creatures that we make when we sink our fangs into them are good for little except to become our slaves."

"But . . . what about extremely brave and smart people, like my father?"

"I actually like him in a way, but he's not one of us," Darius explained. "You'll get over the loss. Together we'll have the kind of life he can't even dream about."

"Yes, I'm sure you're right, honey," Jodie brightly agreed, then fell silent as she and her young lover entered the security checkpoint and got in line behind a slew of people.

CHAPTER 59

Bill Curtis peeled back a living room curtain to see who was pulling into his driveway. To his surprise, it was a black stretch limo, and two army corporals got out, then held doors open for a major and a full-bird colonel. Bill came out onto the porch and watched them approach. The sun had been up for two hours now, and the dew was still on the grass, sparkling like diamonds, as if nothing was wrong in his plague-ridden world.

As they mounted the steps, the colonel said, "Good morning, Detective Curtis. I'm Colonel William Spence, and this is Major Steven Thurston. We're both from Homeland Security. May we come in?"

"Have a seat, gentlemen. We can talk right here. I don't want to disturb my wife."

They all sat on white wicker chairs with flower-patterned cushions.

"We've examined your personnel records," Colonel Spence said. "You did two tours, Iraq and Afghanistan. You have a Purple Heart and a Bronze Star. You were a good soldier. And a brave policeman, we know that for a fact."

"Thanks. But what brings you here?" Bill said warily.

"First of all, we have some good news for you," Major Thurston said.

"Good news with a caveat," Colonel Spence added.

"Good news and bad news," Bill said wearily. "I hope it has a good punch line."

Colonel Spence chuckled. Major Thurston didn't.

"The good news is that we have your daughter in custody," Major Spence said. "The bad news is that her boyfriend got away."

"Is Jodie okay?" Bill blurted, completely stunned and wanting to see his daughter as soon as he could. "I have to let my wife know, one way or another."

Major Spence said, "They were halted at the Pittsburgh airport, trying to get through security. We had a BOLO out on them, and an Interpol bulletin. Your daughter bit one of the officers before she was taken down. Darius Hornsby punched and kicked two passengers in the X-ray line and fled onto an escalator, shoving people aside and leaping up two and three steps at a time. Eyewitnesses said they never saw anybody move so fast or leap that high. At this time, we don't know where he can be hiding. He must've made it out of the airport, so he could be anywhere right now."

"We'll get him though. I know we will," said Major Thurston.

Bill had his doubts. He asked, "Where are you keeping Jodie? Is she under arrest?"

"You'll be glad to know she's not far from you," Major Thurston said. "We're holding her at the Chapel Grove Medical Research Institute. We think she has a DNA mutation."

"You *think?*" Bill shot back at him.

"Well, we think that in time we may be able to cure her and the other children who fell prey to Dr. Marissa Traeger and her illegal experiments. She and your boss, Captain Peter Danko, were coconspirators. They were working under Homeland Security supervision, but they went rogue on us. We were unaware of the things they were doing behind our backs. Their experiments went awry, and we now know that they were responsible not only for the first outbreak of the plague here in Chapel Grove, but also the strain of the disease that developed in the

children they co-opted. Your daughter was one of the unfortunate ones."

"When can I see her?" Bill asked. He wanted badly to get into
his car right now and fly to the institute.

"Give us a few days to stabilize her," Major Thurston said.
"Right now she's too tough to handle. Frankly, we had to restrain
her. You won't like to hear this, but she's in a straitjacket. We hate
to have to do that, but it's absolutely necessary."

"You realize by now that she has a strange disease?" said
Colonel Spence.

"Yes, it's called porphyria. I read up on it after news of it was
leaked from Dr. Traeger's e-mails and lab notes. I know what the
symptoms are."

"At the institute they're trying to find dietary substitutes for
the blood craving," Major Thurston said. "We want you to have a
conference with her doctors before you're allowed to see her.
Being near her is too dangerous. Seeing her the way she is now is
going to be hard on your wife, and she may not be able to easily
assimilate it. She may want to believe that your daughter is normal, because she looks that way, but she is not."

"Why should I trust the doctors at the institute?" Bill asked.
"That's where you admit that things went terribly wrong in the
first place."

"Dr. Traeger is no longer there. She's dead. You killed her.
She's been replaced by a new director. He's been thoroughly vet-
ted, and we're keeping extremely close tabs on him."

"Listen, Bill," Colonel Spence said. "We'd like you to remain
on the Chapel Grove police force and take Danko's place as captain. You're honest, and you have excellent leadership qualities.
Frankly, we'd like you to become a Homeland Security agent.
We need people like you who have proven themselves to be pa-
triotic Americans."

"Maybe we can eventually talk about that," Bill said. "I'm too
badly shaken right now. There's entirely too much to digest. I'm
tired of my life being turned upside down."

"Once we can be sure you're one of us," Major Thurston said, "you'll have special input when it comes to the way your daughter is handled. Also enhanced visitation privileges. If she recovers quickly enough, you may be able to have her released from custody sooner rather than later."

"What if she doesn't recover at all?" Bill said. "I hate to ask that, but I have to."

"I admit it's a possibility," said the major. "But we must be hopeful, mustn't we, Bill?"

"We don't even know what causes the plague or anything related to it," Bill said. "It's hard to have faith in the future."

"But you love your daughter and you have to stick with her," said Major Thurston.

"How soon might I be able to visit her?" Bill asked.

"We'll just have to wait and see," said Colonel Spence.